SHADOWBOXING

Tyner Gillies

Also by Tyner Gillies

The Watch
Dark Resolution
The Black Door (Forthcoming)

Shadowboxing

SHADOWBOXING

Tyner Gillies

Dark Dragon Publishing
Toronto, Ontario, Canada

Shadowboxing

Dark Dragon Publishing
88 Charleswood Drive
Toronto, Ontario
M3H 1X6
CANADA
www.darkdragonpublishing.com

Printed in the United States of America.

For more information on Tyner Gillies

www.tynergillies.com

To Sayeh
For loving me even when it was hard.

.

Acknowledgements

To Kathy Chung and Jennifer Browne; you spoke up for me when you didn't have to, and I will not forget it.

To Ellen Michelle, for being my biggest fan and trying endlessly to convince other people to be my fans, too.

To Karen Dales, my editor, and the other good folks at Dark Dragon Publishing. We've come a long way in the last decade. Thanks for believing in me and my stories.

CHAPTER ONE

He couldn't remember how he got there, but the canvas felt cool and smooth against his face, and Jake Ross was happy to lie on it. The only thing ruining the moment was the man in the blue shirt and black bow-tie standing above, pointing at him and shouting numbers.

"… Three… Four… " Bow-tie yelled.

Jake blinked, and frowned. He knew he should be doing something, but couldn't see through the fog in his head to remember what. Another man stood behind Bow-tie, wearing shiny blue trunks and looking at Jake with a smug expression on his face.

"… Five… Six… " Bow-tie shouted, each shout punctuated with a jab of his white-gloved finger.

Jake blinked and the world came back into focus. He remembered where he was and what he was supposed to be doing, and cursed around the mouth-piece clenched in his teeth.

"… Seven… Eight…" Bow-tie counted, as Jake got his gloved hands beneath his shoulders and heaved himself up. He found his feet and stood on lax and watery legs. He tried to bounce and show the referee he was all right and could continue, but the bounce had gone out of him and all he could come up with was an enthusiastic stagger.

Bow-tie, a pudgy referee named Neil, grabbed Jake's gloves and wiped them on his already-damp shirt. "You wanna keep going, Ross?"

Jake glanced around the community hall, at the half-bored audience sprinkled under the dim lighting. He didn't want to lose to this kid, even if no one paid attention. He nodded and glanced over Neil's shoulder to the man in the blue trunks whose knees did not appear at all watery.

"Okay, kid." The referee shrugged. "You must like getting punched in the face." He stepped back and chopped his hand through the air. "Box!"

Jake stepped forward, blowing out two bloody gobs from his oft-broken nose, trying get enough air to clear his head and get his feet to work properly. There seemed to be a disconnect somewhere, because he knew his brain told his legs to move, but they didn't seem particularly interested in cooperating. He flexed his jaw, the skin of his face pulpy and tender from all the punches he'd taken, and suddenly felt far too old to be standing in a boxing ring.

His opponent stepped in and threw a crisp jab. Jake managed to dip his head and slap it away. His old man would have said he looked like a cub-bear playing with his prick, but he didn't get knocked down again.

Blue-trunks, a sharp kid Jake thought might be named Kennedy, continued to pursue him around the ring, sharp, cutting little punches popping off Kennedy's shoulder. Jake kept backing up, letting the fog clear and the molasses drain from his legs. Kennedy feinted before lunging in a combination: jab to the head, straight right hand, left hook to the body.

Jake blocked the jab, ate most of the right hand, and felt the hook sink in under his ribs. The hook knocked away most of the wind Jake had left, but the kid grew cocky, thinking the fight was his, and he failed to bring his left hand back up to protect his face.

Where Kennedy had youth and speed, Jake had experience and timing. Making full use of both, he drove his right foot into the ground and twisted his body, slamming his right hand into

2

his opponent's exposed chin. The kid's head snapped sideways and he dropped to the canvas like someone had sucked all the bones out of his body.

The referee looked down at the unconscious youth for the space of a breath, then shook his head and waved his arms. "Fight's over." He peered into the darkness beside the ring. "Where's the fucking doctor?"

A bell sounded and a skinny, balding man slipped through the ropes and knelt down beside Kennedy to gently lift his eyelids and shine a pen light into them.

Jake tried to raise a hand in victory, but the movement sent a jolt of pain through his ribs and he sagged against the ropes, sucking in great shuddering breaths.

Shaking his head, Neil slapped Jake on the shoulder. "Jesus, Ross. Most days you don't fight for shit anymore, but you still got a punch."

Jake wasn't sure whether he wanted to thank him, or use his punch on Neil's alcohol-reddened face, so he just nodded and swung his leg between the ropes and stepped down to the concrete floor of the dingy community hall.

The corner-man he'd hired for the fight threw a silk robe over Jake's shoulders and slapped him on the back. "Thanks for the job, Ross. I'd like to stay, but I got a date. Remember me for next time." The guy turned and gave a little salute over his shoulder, as he walked between the rows of folding chairs and made for the door. Jake shook his head and regretted the forty dollars he'd had to pay the man for the six-round fight. He blew a breath out through his nose, clearing more half-coagulated blood, and picked at the laces of his gloves with his teeth as he stalked towards the dressing room he shared for the night with a dozen other fighters.

He stopped once he'd made it past the rows of chairs and disinterested fans, and looked back at the ring. Kennedy now sat on a stool in his corner, talking to the doctor, and appeared to be okay. Jake nodded, glad the kid was all right, and turned back towards the dressing room.

Beside the door a slim man with a grey crew cut stood with his hands in the pockets of his denim coat. The man watched Jake intently, his steady gaze on the boxer's face. There was either a question or a comment in the look that quickly turned into a creepy stare. Jake met the man's gaze, jaw clenched. He didn't much care to be stared at.

Jake tucked his loosened glove under his arm and yanked his hand out, then pulled out his mouth guard. "There something I can do for you?"

The man smiled, the lines around his eyes bunching, and shook his head. "I just came to see your upcoming fight."

"What do you mean, 'upcoming'?" Jake asked, turning to face the man. "I just got out of the ring, in case you didn't notice."

The man continued to smile and shrugged, then gave his attention to the ring where Kennedy, now on his feet, stepped between the ropes.

Jake stood for another moment, waiting for the man in the jean jacket to say something else, but he didn't. He just continued to grin study the ring.

"Asshole," Jake said, loud enough to be sure the man heard it, and pushed through the door.

Several other fighters crowded the dressing room, which was really more like a big storage closet. Several wooden benches were bolted to the concrete floor and the wall had several hooks for guys to hang their ragged coats. Jake grabbed his gym bag off one of the hooks, sat down heavily on the end of a bench and dropped the bag between his feet. He put his elbows on his knees and leaned forward, letting his head hang. His face felt ragged and swollen. As he pressed gingerly at his bruises, he thought getting punched in the melon wasn't near as much fun as ten years ago.

"Not bad tonight, Ross."

Jake lifted his gaze to see Warren Boyd, the chubby promoter who put on these local shows, standing in front of him. He had a small black notebook in his thick hands and dug about in his ear enthusiastically with a short pencil.

"Thanks," Jake said, as he tugged off his other boxing glove and started to peel the tape and gauze off his hands. "That mean you're gonna put me on one of the big casino cards?"

Warren hissed through his teeth and took the pencil out of his ear to jot something down in the notebook. "Let's not get ahead of ourselves. You been out of the game a long time, and it's been even longer since anyone wanted to see you. You were lucky to get this spot. You win a couple more fights and we'll see about getting you on a big card with a decent pay day. Until then, here's your purse for tonight." Warren reached into the pocket of his baggy slacks and held out a few folded bills. Jake took them.

"Two hundred bucks, Warren?" Jake growled, spreading the bills in his fingers. "Are you kidding me? I won, for fuck's sakes."

Warren tucked his notebook in the pocket of his old coat and ran a hand over his thin, slicked-back hair. "You have a look out there and tell me how many people you see, Ross. Boxing ain't what it used to be. Kids nowadays wanna see that ultimate fighting shit, not old men like you getting beat up. The gate was small and that's your piece of it. Shut up and take it, or shut up and fuck off."

Jake sighed wearily and stuffed the money into a pocket of his gym bag. "Okay. When can you get me in here again?"

Warren shrugged. "Come see me at the gym next week, and we'll talk about it. I got another show in Bridgeview in two weeks. I might be able to put you on the card."

Jake nodded, but Warren turned to step out of the room and didn't see the nod – or maybe saw it and didn't care. Jake sighed again and went back to unwrapping his hands. This grand come-back to professional boxing wasn't turning out exactly as planned. He'd won his last two fights, his first in years, but his opponents were novice fighters—little more than kids—and he'd hardly impressed himself let alone anyone who'd mattered. Perhaps Warren was right. No one wanted to see a forty-year-old has-been get beat up. It didn't matter that his fight poster had "Former Canadian Heavyweight Champion" under his picture. People didn't give a shit.

There was no shower in the smelly closet, so Jake stripped off his trunks and wiped himself down with a towel from his bag, resigning himself to walk home in his own stink. He pulled off his boxing boots, yanked on his worn jeans, a t-shirt and battered brown leather jacket. He stuffed his feet into his steel-toed work boots, the only footwear he owned besides the boxing boots, slung his bag over his shoulder and walked out the back door of the closet into the nearly empty parking lot.

The crisp autumn night air carried a stink on it. The venue for the fights, the run-down community hall that was only ever seemed to be used for Warren's little boxing cards, punk-rock concerts, and 'professional' wrestling matches, was only a block away from Surrey's Whalley strip. The strip, a reeking stretch of concrete and asphalt, was the ugliest place Jake had ever seen, where sex, drugs and desperation were all for sale in equal measure. It was also within pissing distance of several high-rise condo developments, where yuppies drove expensive European cars into underground parking lots guarded by men in stupid-looking yellow coats, and did their best to ignore their impoverished neighbours. Jake breathed in deep through his nose. Despite the stink, he'd grown to love this place with all its filth and beauty, and called it home.

He'd only taken a dozen steps across the parking lot when he heard the scuff of a shoe behind him and turned, his legs flexing automatically, his big hands balling into fists. This was a shitty neighbourhood and the idea he might get robbed on his way home was not outside the realm of possibility. He relaxed slightly when he saw the man in the denim coat, leaning against the brick wall on the other side of the door, where Jake hadn't see him. The man had his arms folded as he looked off into the murky night, then turned his head towards Jake and gave him a smile.

"Good luck tonight, Jake," he said, still leaning against the wall.

Jake grunted. "Good luck? Don't you mean congratulations?"

The man stood silent for a handful of heartbeats, then shrugged. "Sure. Something like that."

Studying the man, Jake wondered if perhaps the loony bastard would benefit from a good beating, just to knock a bit of the crazy out of him.

"Okay, freak show," Jake said, deciding against the beating. The man in the denim coat nodded cordially and continued to smile.

Jake snorted, hitched the strap of his bag higher on his

shoulder and turned to continue on across the parking lot.

Home, or the one bedroom apartment that bore the name, was only a dozen blocks from the community hall, and Jake didn't have a car, so he started walking. His route took him past the Surrey bus-loop. He eyed it for a moment, fingering the change in his jeans, but shook his head. It was only a half hour walk and his legs weren't so rubbery that he needed to spend money on bus fare.

He strode with his head down, hands jammed into his coat pockets and the fight running through his mind. It seemed that winning it rough didn't buy him enough credit to get another fight, so he'd have to try and win pretty. Maybe cut a few pounds, go down a weight class, get lighter on his feet and move more.

He was bobbing and weaving in his head, eyes on the ground, when a sound in front of him made him glance up.

A blonde girl, in knee-high, pointy-toed boots, stepped out of a side street in front of him, her heels click-clacking on the sidewalk. She turned her head quickly side to side, causing her blonde hair to fly around her face like blown silk. Her gaze fell on Jake and her eyes widened, startled. She took him in, crown to boots, and Jake returned her scrutiny. She was a stunner, no question, but nearly young enough to be Jake's kid, and out of his league even if she wasn't. She studied him a moment more, then turned, her hair flipping again, and hurried down the side-walk. Jake took a moment to admire the fine view of her retreat, slowed a little so she was far enough ahead she wouldn't think he was following her, then ignored her and continued bobbing and weaving in his mind.

The girl in the boots quickened her pace and made distance on him. She kept checking over her shoulder and into every al-ley she passed. It occurred to Jake, perhaps, she was looking for someone. Or looking out for them.

She passed the entrance to a huge, multi-level parkade and veered into it, still looking over her shoulder. The clicking of her boots made sharp echoes in the enclosed space, and Jake slowed his pace a little as he passed the entrance. As he watched her disappear into the gloom of the parkade, a deeply unfamiliar feeling of concern creeped over him. Something pulled at him, something he could not place, and he cleared his voice to crack the feeling.

He shook his head and turned his gaze to the sidewalk. He didn't know the chick and didn't have any reasonable business worrying about her, stunner or not, and had no idea why it had occurred to him to care. Even if he asked if she needed help she'd probably take another look at him and start screaming for the cops, and that would just about make his night perfect. He kept his eyes on the ground in front of him and quickened his pace, shaking his head again to clear the thoughts of the blonde girl from his mind.

For a second time, the sound of footsteps in front of him made him look up. This time, it wasn't the click of pretty boots, but the thud of a heavy tread, emanating from equally heavy bodies. Coming diagonally across the empty street in front of Jake were two young men, both with the tight haircuts and expensive brand name sweatshirts of wanna-be gangsters. They glanced at Jake, then ignored him, their attention on the entrance to the parkade.

"That was her, wasn't it?" Jake heard the bigger of the two ask his companion, as they reached the entrance.

"Had to be," said the other. "He said she'd come this way. C'mon." The shorter of the two quickened his pace, but the other slowed, looking hesitant. The smaller wanna-be noticed and cursed at his companion. "Hurry the fuck up, man. No time to bitch-out now."

The bigger man nodded, his resolve hardening, and followed.

Jake slackened his pace and watched over his shoulder as the two thugs disappeared into the parkade. He slowed, and finally stopped, turning to face the building. His common sense warred with an unfamiliar idea. He knew, without a doubt, the two wanna-be's had bad intentions towards the blonde girl in the pointy boots. He also knew if they caught up to her, she was going to be in a world of shit. What he didn't know was what he wanted to do about it.

Not particularly altruistic by nature, Jake had gotten through life by keeping his chin tucked down so no one could drive a fist into it and minding his own business. But, strangely enough, he had the urge to run after the girl and keep those two douche-bags away from her. He couldn't seem to shake the feeling, despite the fact it was none of his concern.

A sharp yelp, a cry of fear, or perhaps pain, echoed from the mouth of the parkade, as though the structure itself called out. Indecision flew from Jake's mind and he ran towards the building's entrance, throwing his bag behind a bank of shrubs that lined the sidewalk in front of the building. He sprinted into the parkade and skidded to a stop, as he saw there were several directions the girl could have gone. There were ramps going both up and down, and narrow lanes between the concrete pillars led from the lit entrance into the gloom. He didn't hear anything. Balanced on the balls of his feet, flexing his hands, Jake tried to figure where he should run.

Trying to decide on a direction, his eyes landed on a familiar figure leaning against one of the pillars. The man in the denim coat looked up from picking at his fingernails and gave Jake a smile.

Jake stared, the incredulity of seeing the man giving way to an idea.

"Hey," he said, jerking his chin at the man in the denim coat. "Call 9-1-1."

The man shrugged. "What for?"

"I think that girl needs help."

The man's smile grew, the lines in his face spreading and shifting. "Then you better go help her."

Once again, the feeling that the man would benefit from a good beating, and the desire to dish it out, flooded Jake, but he tamped it down. "Are you gonna do it, or not?"

The man shrugged again and patted the pockets of his coat. "Ain't got no phone, Jake. Looks like you're it."

Frustrated, Jake helplessly searched the level he was on. There was no one else around, no cars, no pay phones, no sign of any help. Another scream, more panicked this time, echoed down the ramp leading to the upper levels. He glanced up, then back at the man, who now examined him with what appeared to be polite interest.

"Fuck, man," Jake said, as he ran towards a set of stairs leading up. "Find a fucking pay phone. Just get some help."

The man smiled and nodded agreeably. "Sure thing, Jake."

Jake had no idea if the man would go for help or not, but he made a mental note to kill the prick if he ever saw him again. Jake reached the stairs and started up, taking them two at a time, the rubber in his legs forgotten.

On the third level, he saw them. The two wanna-be's had the blonde girl forced up against a cement balustrade, while the smaller of the two gripped her pony-tail with one hand and pressed a knife against her slender neck with the other.

"You were already told once, slut," the shorter thug shouted into the girl's face, as he leaned over top of her. She screamed again, tears streaming down her face, as the thug jerked her hair. "But you're too fucking stupid to do as you're told, aren't you? Now we're here, wasting our time dealing with you. How much do I have to carve out of you to get your attention?" Shorty pressed the knife harder against her tanned skin and she let out another cry.

"Hey!" Jake shouted, his voice bouncing off the walls.

The two men jerked their heads up, startled.

"Let her go," the boxer yelled, walking towards them.

"Who the fuck are you?" the smaller guy asked, pointing the knife at Jake. His face took on a distasteful twist while he looked Jake up and down, as though he were regarding a turd someone had dropped in front of him.

"Never mind who I am, you piece of shit. Let that girl go."

"Piece of shit? Do you have any fucking idea who I am?"

"Yeah, you're the knob picking on a girl half your size."

Shorty's eyes narrowed. He was obviously not someone who liked being criticized. He pulled the girl away from the railing by her hair held her between himself and Jake. He jerked his chin towards his larger companion. "Deal with this idiot."

The bigger guy looked at Jake, then to his demanding companion, then back at Jake, before swallowing dramatically. He didn't appear to have the same relish for this job as his friend.

"Come on man," Shorty said. "Get busy."

Reluctantly, the bigger man nodded.

Jake walked to meet him, like an opponent in the centre of the ring.

Jake, who himself was a head taller than the smaller guy, had to look up at the big man when they got close. Jake's opponent appeared unsure of himself, and Jake took careful measure of his reluctance.

"Get out of here and mind your own business, man," the big guy said and held his hand out in a halting gesture. "Before you get hurt."

When Jake didn't stop, the hand turned into a pointing finger, and his volume increased. "You better get the fuck out of here, right now. Are you listening to me?"

Jake had been in enough street fights to know when you should stop yapping and just get on with it, and that time had come.

As the boxer got close, the big thug made to grab his coat. Jake slipped underneath the grasping hand and slammed his fist into the bigger man's armpit. The thug let out a grunt of pain, sucked his elbow down to his body and hunched forward, leaving his face exposed and even closer to Jake. The boxer twisted his hips for a left hook and bashed his fist into the side of the man's head. The bigger man made a funny squawking noise and fell to the floor.

"Oh, you're in trouble now, bitch," Shorty said. He yanked back violently on the girl's hair, eliciting another cry, and threw her hard to ground before advancing towards Jake, weaving the knife through the air in front of him. "I'm gonna fuck you up. I'm gonna carve you a new asshole."

The kid had obviously seen too many movies because he couldn't use the knife for shit. As he got closer, still doing the stupid weaving thing, Jake slapped the knife hand down and shot over top of it with the same over-hand right he'd already used to knock a man out tonight. His fist collided with the thug's mouth and Jake felt several teeth give way. The smaller man fell to the ground, yelling in surprise and pain. His hand flew to his mouth, trying to hold in blood and teeth, while his knife clattered away.

Stepping quickly, Jake circled around the downed man and pulled the blonde girl to her feet. She looked up at him, eyes red rimmed with tears and awash in running make-up.

"Get up," said Jake. "And get out of here."

She nodded and wiped a hand across her nose, looking up into Jake's face for a moment. She was a looker, no doubt; absolutely stunning, even with tears and snot running down her face.

She turned towards the stairs and pulled on his hand. Jake looked past her at the bigger of the two idiots, who was back on his feet, holding the side of his head and glaring at the two of them. Jake pulled his hand from the girl's grip and gave her a gentle shove towards the stairs, even as he was thinking he must be nuts. I should be running like my ass is on fire, he thought, instead of playing at being a hero.

"Go," he said, making eye contact with the girl again. "I'll be right behind you."

The girl nodded, turned and trotted towards the stairs.

"Neither of you is going anywhere," the bigger of the two thugs growled.

Jake stepped between the thug and the stairway as the girl started descending, her boot heels tapping out her farewell.

"I'm gonna beat your ass, man," the thug said, as he advanced towards Jake. He came slowly this time, his hands up and clenched into fists. Jake adopted his normal boxer's stance, which worked just as well outside the ring as inside it.

The thug winged several punches at Jake; huge, whistling things that looked vaguely impressive, but took so long to reach the target you could sit down and eat a sandwich while you waited. Jake slipped under one of the haymakers and slammed his fist into the thug's liver. When the big man doubled over, Jake smashed a knee into his face. The man fell to his knees, clutching his newly broken nose and making a high, nasally cry. Jake thought about punching him again, just to make sure he'd had enough, but the man fell over on his side and made several small mewling sounds. Any fight that might have remained in the prone man had long since packed its bags and fucked off.

Jake turned towards the staircase, hoping he'd be able to catch up to the girl, maybe walk her home so he could be sure no one else grabbed her. He was about to break into a trot when he felt a tug on the collar of his coat, and a thud in his rib-cage. He spun to look down into the bloody, leering face of the smaller thug who, despite his missing teeth, glared triumphantly at Jake.

"I told you I was gonna fuck you up, didn't I? Don't you know who—"

Jake put an end to the man's prattling by head-butting him in the face. The smaller man's nose shattered to paste under Jake's forehead and he sprawled on the ground for the second time.

If there was one thing Jake hated it was cowards, and this asshole fit the bill perfectly. Not only would he threaten a girl with a knife, but he'd attack a man from behind. He needed to be taught a painful lesson so he didn't think on doing it again. Jake stood looking at the two assholes on the ground, who showed no sign of getting up in the near future, and lost all taste for the beating he knew they needed. He waved one hand at them, a gesture of dismissal.

"You two dick-heads aren't worth the energy." He looked at them again and snorted.

The smaller of the thugs looked up at Jake fearfully, his eyes running the aging boxer up and down from over top of the hands holding his face together. The sight was so comical that Jake chuckled.

As he laughed, something came up the back of his throat and spilled down his chin. He choked and gagged on warm stickiness. His legs suddenly got rubbery, far worse than when the kid in the blue trunks had rung his bell. Jake went down on one knee, his right hand on the ground to keep from falling on his face. His hand felt something wet on the cold concrete, and when he looked down he saw blood.

There was a deep throb in his side where the smaller man had punched him, and Jake reached back, his fingers finding the handle of the knife sticking out from his ribs. The thug hadn't punched him after all. Jake closed his fingers around the handle of the knife and gave a tug. The knife came smoothly away from his body, and he heard, rather than felt, a jet of blood spurt from the wound to splatter against the concrete floor. He knew, somewhere in his mind, that he was in deep shit.

The smaller thug climbed to his feet, pulling on the arm of his bigger, still moaning, companion. "Come on. We need to get out of here. I think I killed that guy."

Jake watched the two forms, his vision growing blurry, as

they fled. He wanted to shout at them, to call them cowards, to mock them as they ran, but all he could manage was a wheezing groan. He fell forward, his arm no longer able to bear his weight, and he lay with his face in his own sticky blood. It occurred to him that the parkade of a shopping mall was a fairly shitty place to die.

He tried to draw in a breath, but it felt like the air was as thick as pancake syrup. He felt horribly thirsty, hot and cold all at once, and keeping his eyes open grew more difficult. He gave up and let them close. As they flickered shut, he thought he caught the blurry sight of a figure in a denim coat crouching down in front of him.

"Well done, Jake. Good fight."

CHAPTER TWO

Jake's eyes snapped open, his whole body jerking, causing the springs of his old bed to creak. He'd kicked off all of his blankets in his sleep, and they were bunched up at the foot of his bed. The sheet beneath him felt wet and cold, soaked in his own sweat. He slowly sat up, his body a mass of bruises from his fight with the kid in the blue trunks, and swung his legs off the bed to settle his feet on the threadbare carpet.

He leaned forward, elbows on his knees, and tried to shake away the remnants of the horrible dream he'd just had. He'd dreamed he'd tried to help some girl and got stabbed for his trouble. He could still remember the feeling of hot blood coughed up and spattering his face, and would have sworn it actually happened. He shook his head, glad the dream was over, and stood up, running his fingers through his short, sand coloured hair. He reached down to scratch at his chest, which was strangely itchy. He frowned as he found something thick and crusty. He pulled away a chunk of the crusty material and held it up into the beam of a street light from outside. It was red glob of clotted blood.

He spun back to his bed, so fast he almost lost his balance and fell over. It wasn't only sweat making his bed wet, but large dark streaks as well. On the floor beside the bed he found a stack of clothing crusted with blood—the clothes he'd worn home from the boxing match. When he examined his leather coat, he found a broad stain and a puncture mark from the blade of a knife.

It hadn't been a dream.

He staggered down the narrow hallway to the bathroom and flicked the light switch on. As the bare bulbs above the sink flared to life, Jake studied himself in the mirror, turning his body one way then the other, searching for a stab wound. The left side of his body was covered in a rusty film of dried blood. It had dried in his short grey skivvies, turning them crusty and hard, and it was clotted in the hair of his broad chest. No matter how many different angles he checked, he didn't find a wound anywhere. His head spun, and he turned on the tap of the sink and splashed several handfuls of cold water onto his face. He leaned forward, his hands on the counter and his head hanging, as several fat drops, pink from the dried blood, fell from his nose to spatter against the white porcelain.

What the fuck happened to him? There was enough blood on his bed and his clothes for two people, but here he stood. Or maybe he wasn't. Maybe he was dead and hell was being stuck in this one bedroom shithole for the rest of eternity. He scrubbed at his face and hands until the water ran clear, then turned off the tap and wiped his face with the towel hanging beside the sink. He walked slowly down the short hallway from the bathroom to the rest of his shitty apartment, rubbing his face with one calloused hand, trying to get a grip on exactly what had happened.

There was a light on in his kitchen and the sounds of movement. His eyes snapped wide, his hands balling reflexively as he came around the corner to find a familiar garment reflecting the light of the open refrigerator.

The man in the denim coat turned and looked at him, his smile creasing his face. "Hi, Jake." He held a beer bottle and peered at it suspiciously. "Angry Sasquatch?" he read from the label. "You sure buy some shitty beer." He shrugged and twisted the top off, then took a long drink as he tossed the bottle cap onto the counter.

Jake was so amazed, for a moment, he couldn't speak. The clatter of the bottle cap on his counter top jerked him from his speechlessness, and he stepped forward to snatch the bottle from the intruder's hand.

"If you don't like my beer, don't drink it," Jake said, scowling. "And, what are you doing in my house? How'd you get in here?" He looked down at the bottle in his hand, glared at the man in the denim coat, then drank from the bottle himself, still scowling.

The man shrugged again. "Your keys were in your pocket, and your address was on the expired driver's license I found in your wallet. I'd figured I'd earned a beer dragging your heavy carcass up two flights of stairs."

Jake paused, the beer bottle halfway to his lips, as memories of what he'd thought was a dream came pounding back into his head; lying in a puddle of his own blood while looking up and seeing this asshole's grinning face as he died. It wasn't exactly the last sight he'd wanted.

He lowered the bottle, his mind reeling between comprehension and disbelief, unable to understand what was happening. He began with an obvious question, looking at the man in the denim coat. "Who are you?"

The man grinned again and paused in the act of opening the fridge to hold out his right hand. "Oliver MacKinnon is my name, but everyone calls me Mac. Pleased to meet you, Jake."

Jake looked down at the hand and back up into the lined face. Mac shrugged, and instead extended the hand into the fridge to grab another beer, twisting the cap off and tossing it on the counter with the other.

"Okay, Mac," Jake said, glaring first at the bottle cap on the counter, then onto the lined face and pale blue eyes. "What the fuck happened?"

Mac shrugged. "You got stabbed and died. You're a pretty good fighter, Jake, but you really should have seen that guy coming with the knife. Not to worry, though. We'll work with you a little and get you sorted out."

"Sorted out?" Jake said vaguely, his eyes moving from side to side as his hand ran over his foggy head. "What do you mean 'sorted out'? You just said I died, you fucking nut. If I died then this is certainly Hell, and you're the devil sent to torment me. I know I did some shitty things in my life, but I think this punishment is a little extreme."

Mac snorted as he took a swig of beer, then wiped his mouth with the back of his hand. "You're not in Hell, Jake."

"Then where in the Sam fuck am I?"

"You, my friend, are standing at the beginning of a second chance. A chance to do something important."

Jake looked at Mac, his head tilting sideways. "Okay, freak show. Just so I can understand what you're saying here, as you stand uninvited in my kitchen, drinking my beer; you're telling me that I got killed tonight, but I'm getting a second chance?"

"Ha!" Mac barked a laugh and slapped the counter top with the palm of his hand. "And people say boxers are all punch drunk and stupid. You're catching on quick. Now, do you have anything to ask or are you just going to stand there in your underpants stating the obvious all night?"

Jake looked down at himself, taking in his near nakedness, and thought for a moment about pants. He decided that clothing was the least of his concerns, leaned back against the counter and finished his beer in three long, sucking swallows. "This must be a nightmare. I can't be having this conversation with a man who is obviously trapped in the 60's and still wears a denim coat. I just can't."

"You can, and you are, my friend. I can't tell you precisely the how and why of it, but I can tell you you're not the first to receive such a gift, and probably won't be the last. It's up to you, now, to do something with it."

"Not the first?" Jake asked. "If I'm not the first, who else is there?"

Mac crossed his arms, beer bottle dangling from his right hand, and pursed his lips. "How old do I look to you, Jake?"

"If you're looking for flattery, you're looking in the wrong place," Jake said, crossing his own arms. "Let's say you look like a seventy year old raisin that's had too much hard living."

"In earnest, Jake, how old am I?"

"Fuck, man, I don't know. Forty-five? Fifty?"

Mac chuckled. "I was twenty when I was killed in Passchendaele, November 6th, nineteen hundred and seventeen."

Jake snorted. "Bullshit."

Mac uncrossed his arms and pulled up the checked work shirt that was tucked into his jeans. On his abdomen was a long, jagged scar from just above his navel to the bottom of his sternum. "A German bayonet," he said, tapping the scar. "We thought we'd taken the whole of the town, but there were a bunch of stubborn bastards hiding in a barn. I got it when I walked through the door."

"So you died in World War I, and now you're an immortal who breaks into people's shitty little apartments to steal their beer?"

"No, not immortal, Jake. I, like you, will die again one day. But for now we age slower than other people. And we're a little harder to kill."

Jake shook his head. "Don't use the word 'we'. There is no 'we'. There's me and my cheap beer, and some psycho who broke into my house and is feeding me a line of shit." He leaned forward. "In case you didn't know, the psycho is you."

The older man shrugged again and finished his beer, then set the empty bottle down on the counter with a hollow clink. "You'll come to understand in time. For now, I'll thank you for the drink and let you get some rest." He stepped past Jake and towards the door.

"Wait," Jake said, following him. "That's it? You're just going to break into my house, tell me I've got some kind of cosmic second chance at life after being stabbed in a parkade, and then leave?"

Mac grinned, the lines around his mouth bunching. "You'll be fine. I'll be by to see you very soon." He turned without another word, opened the door, stepped into the dim hallway and was gone.

Jake stood staring at the closed door for several long moments, itching at the dried blood on his chest, unsure of what he should do. Finally, he opened the fridge door and picked up the last beer bottle—sporting a smiling Sasquatch giving a jaunty thumbs up—and twisted the top off. He stood there in the shadows of the dark kitchen and held the bottle in his hand, not drinking from it, until long after the beer had gone warm.

*   *   *   *   *

After dumping the warm beer into the kitchen sink, Jake turned on the shower and got in. He stood under the water a long time, trying to slough off the dried blood and the bewildered amazement. Once cleaned up, he stood looking in the mirror, his left arm behind his head as he examined the place he'd been stabbed. He saw a faint, pink scar that looked like it had been healing for several weeks. He'd been stabbed before, an unfortunate incident in his wild youth. He'd spent a week in the hospital and another three months out of the gym. He frowned and continued to finger the new scar.

Once the examination lost its novelty, he went into his bedroom and stripped the bloody sheets off his bed. He sighed when he looked at the broad stains on his mattress, then stooped and flipped the mattress over. His mother would kill him if she could've seen him do that, but he didn't exactly have the means to get a new mattress. He snatched the sheets off the floor and cocked his arm to throw them into the laundry hamper, but changed his mind and instead took them to the kitchen and stuffed them into the garbage can.

After changing his sheets, he lay in his bed, convinced he wouldn't sleep as his mind replayed the events of the night, but it was only moments before he couldn't keep his eyes open.

When he opened them again, it was still dark, and he guessed that he'd only slept a few minutes before waking up. He checked his bedside clock and saw that it was shortly after nine pm. When the crazy old guy left it had been well after midnight. He'd slept the entire day.

He rubbed his hand over his head, trying to remember what day it was, and what he was supposed to be doing. He hadn't meant to sleep that long, but apparently getting killed and coming back to life took the piss right out of you. More likely the crazy guy, Mac, had drugged his beer. After several long moments of blurred thought, he remembered that his fight was on Wednesday, so it must be Thursday. Thursday was good. Thursday meant he wasn't supposed to be working and wouldn't get fired from his shitty job. He only worked a couple days a

20

week anyway. The warehouse had slashed their hours due to the drop in the economy, so getting fired wouldn't make that much of a difference in his dismal financial situation.

He went into the kitchen and opened the fridge, standing there, naked, looking at the sparse contents. His stomach rumbled and he sighed. Apparently the whole dying thing made you hungry as well. He closed the door, and rubbing his head again, tried to think on what to do, both about his newfound life change and his hunger.

He looked around his thinly furnished apartment and his eyes fell on his gym bag, which he'd thought forgotten behind the bushes near the parkade. He dug through the pockets and smiled when he found the folded bills given to him by Warren Boyd the night before.

"At least that fucking Mac guy didn't rob me when he stripped me down and tucked me into bed," he said to the folded bills. He showered again, thinking that sleeping for almost twenty-four hours would leave a bit of a stink, and rummaged around his beat up old dresser for clean clothing. He dressed in one of his remaining pairs of jeans that didn't have any extra holes and a white t-shirt. He picked up his battered coat—the only one he owned—and decided the blood stain was mostly on the interior lining and it wouldn't earn him too many ugly looks. He sniffed it once, grimaced, then threw it on and stepped out his front door with his fight winnings in the pocket of his jeans.

Standing on the sidewalk in front of his building, Jake took in a deep breath. For once, the air of Surrey didn't stink quite so badly. Apparently, dying made the air smell cleaner, too. Taking in another breath, he looked around him and, with no clear goal in mind, other than possibly filling his belly, he started away from the apartment block he lived on and towards the city centre.

This whole coming back to life thing, whether it had actually happened or was a carefully created hoax by the denim wearing freak, had really put a spring in his step, and he felt better than he had felt in recent memory. His joints didn't ache, his knuckles didn't feel swollen and arthritic, and the bruises from the night before appeared to have completely healed.

He walked briskly, his head up, taking in his surroundings;

the sights and sounds of the city coming to him, clear and welcome. After a short time, he found himself in front of the entrance to the parking garage he'd allegedly died in. There was no police tape or traffic cones blocking the place off, and none of the people driving in or out gave the slightest hint that anything might be wrong inside. Curiosity grabbed hold of him and Jake walked through the entrance, then trotted up the concrete steps to the floor where he'd fought the two assholes over the blonde girl.

There was a broad stain on the concrete that someone had made a half hearted attempt at washing away, but it was still obvious that a large pool of blood had recently been there. Jake shook his head, as he thought about so much blood going unnoticed and unreported to anyone that mattered. Life was cheap enough in the city that blood splatter on the ground was a regular occurrence and people had learned to ignore it.

Despite the state of the city's humanity, the stain gave credence to Jake's memories, proved they actually happened, and he wasn't suffering some kind of hallucination brought on by repeated blows to the head. It did not, however, explain exactly why, or how, this had happened. He was still scratching his head, lips pursed, as he turned away from the mark of his blood on the concrete and went back down the stairs.

He continued to walk the familiar streets, going where he happened to wander. He still had the idea of food in his mind, but it was bullied into the background by the collection of miserable questions that whined and bitched in all corners of his head. The questions were so vague he could barely make them out, let alone start to answer them. He allowed them to toss about as the desire to eat stood up and waved its hand, looking for his attention.

He was trying to chase down a thought, to lay hold of the slippery little bastard, when a sign caught his eye. 'Two dollar burgers,' it read. Jake would never actually refer to himself as cheap—well, okay, he was cheap as fuck and he damned well knew it, but he blamed it on a childhood spent below the poverty line, and several years of always being broke. The questions that refused to be pinned down were corralled and forgotten for a moment, as a fresh rumble from his stomach and the promise of cheap food shouldered their way to the front of his consciousness.

If he'd been a little more aware and just a little less cheap he might have read the sign and realised he wasn't walking into a restaurant. It was a building that was well away from his normal route back and forth to either work or his gym, and he'd never before been inside. As he stepped through the door, he was faced with an extremely large man, with the puffed up look of someone who did a lot of pharmaceutically enhanced weight lifting, wearing a comically tight, black t-shirt and dress pants.

"Arms out," the man said, flicking the power button of a metal detector with his thumb.

Puzzled as he was, Jake moved to obey, and the huge man waved the wand about his person. When the doorman was satisfied with the wand waving, he nodded—a ridiculously short movement as the muscles of his shoulders appeared to be trying their best to consume his head—and stood aside.

"Have a good time, man," the doorman said, giving Jake a knowing wink.

Jake nodded back, no idea what the muscle bound twit was talking about. Then, as Jake walked down the short hallway and around the corner, he realised his location in a fairly significant hurry.

The short hallway lead into a wide, dark room smelling of old beer, new aggression and constant desperation. On Jake's right, there was a round, raised stage, dim lights ringing the perimeter, and chairs pushed up against the bar built into it. A brass pole, covered in greasy fingerprints, protruded from the floor in the middle of the stage, and a mirror in the back wall doubled the scene—a strip bar.

The floor between the stage and the bar built into the wall on his left was covered in round tables and narrow chairs. Only a few of the tables were occupied, with a couple of guys sitting right up at the stage; what was commonly referred to as 'gynecology row'.

He sighed and wondered if he could get the hell out of there without looking like an idiot. It was not strippers he minded. In fact, he liked a naked woman as much as the next guy. It was the people that hung around in strip bars he wasn't overly keen on.

The stage was deserted and the other occupants of the room quietly talked, ignoring Jake. He might actually be able to get something to eat in relative peace. If he saw a show in the process, then all to the better.

He chose a table away from anyone else, or as far away as they could be, and sat with his back up against a wall. After a few minutes a bored looking waitress, who might have been pretty if she hadn't looked so miserable, approached his table in stiletto heels that lit up when she walked.

"What do you want?" she asked, as she carelessly tossed a cardboard coaster onto the table, glancing around the room instead of at Jake.

"Uh," he said. He followed her gaze to see what she was looking at, but quickly realised it was nothing. He settled back in his chair and jerked his thumb towards the door. "I saw a sign outside… "

She gave an exaggerated sigh and rolled her eyes, still not looking at him. "You have to buy a drink to get the burger." She continued to drift her gaze around the room, and blew out a weary breath, her lips flapping.

"Uh, okay," Jake said. "I'll get a beer and a burger, then."

"What kind of beer do you want?"

Jake shrugged. "Surprise me." She rolled her eyes and slouched away. Jake instantly regretted his answer, fearing she would bring him some kind of foreign swill that tasted like piss and cost twelve dollars a bottle.

In a few minutes, the waitress came back, her tray balanced on her shoulder, and deposited a dismal looking hamburger with a side of soggy French fries, in front of him. They were joined by a mug of flat, pale beer. "That's six dollars," she huffed, still looking around somewhat desperately, as though she was expecting something to happen and didn't want to miss it. Jake dug into his pocket, looking down carefully, and pulled out a ten dollar bill.

"Keep it," he said, as he held it out to her. It burned him, more than a little, to give such a big tip for such awful service, but her mood was rubbing off on him and he didn't want her to have to come back with change.

She brightened slightly, only a shade or two, and looked at

24

Jake for the first time. She was not, apparently, used to getting tips.

"Thanks," she said, tucking the bill into a little box perched on her tray. As she turned and headed back across the room, her slouch improved to a stalk.

Despite the poor quality of the food, Jake tucked into it with relish, consuming the burger with five big bites and eating the fries four at a time. Not bad for two dollars, he thought, as he lifted the mug of flat beer.

The mug was half empty when music started to blare out of the numerous speakers around the stage. A falsely deep, disembodied voice boomed into the room. "Gentlemen, please welcome to the stage, our favorite hometown girl: Chastity."

Jake chuckled into his beer. Strippers always seemed to have a penchant for choosing the most ridiculous names. It hadn't changed since he was a kid using a fake driver's license to sneak into similar establishments.

A girl, with her hair dyed fire engine red and fake breasts so large they looked like a practical joke, strutted on stage and began swinging around the pole.

"And," the DJ continued, "for you gentlemen who caught the last show, our house dancer, Miss Veronica Rain, will be offering private dances." The words 'private dances' was said in a low, rolling, conspiratorial tone that Jake inferred to mean that more than dancing was offered in private. He laughed again as he drank.

The laugh turned into a choke and a spray of bad beer, as Jake looked to the left of the stage and saw who he presumed was the house dancer, come out and start speaking to the guys at the other tables.

It was the girl from the parkade.

He wiped a rough hand across his mouth, then leaned forward and squinted to be sure his eyes weren't playing tricks on him. No mistake. It was her.

Jake sat, rapt and attentive, as she walked between the tables, smiling as she went. With every step she took towards him, Jake became more certain. She even wore the same boots from the night before. They clicked on the black tile floor, the sound carrying above the raucous dance music favored by the girl occupying the stage.

Every head in the bar turned towards her, the patrons watching her like a pack of starving wolves. She stopped and talked to a few people, apparently negotiating a price for the 'private dance'. Most seemed to find the price too steep and each head she leaned towards shook out a refusal, even though they continued to stare as she walked away. Eventually, she made her way across the room and stood in front of Jake's table.

"Hey, honey," she said, giving him a broad smile. "You interested in a private dance? Only forty dollars to…" Her words drifted off as she looked at his face, her eyes wide. "Oh my God." Her hand covered her mouth as she sucked in a hurried breath. "It's you."

Speechless, looking at her, Jake had no inclination what he should say. 'How's it going,' or 'anyone else try and cut your throat recently?' didn't really seem to fit, so he settled for a nod.

She sat down in the chair next to him and laid her slender hand on his. "Wow, are you all right? I didn't get a chance to say thank you, last night. I… I just ran."

She was close enough that he could smell her perfume, a clean, flowery scent, and it filled his head to the point of distraction. Her long, unbound hair was silk on the back of his wrist as she leaned towards him to be heard over the music.

"I'm sorry," she said, gripping the back of his hand. "I didn't even think to call for help for you. I just took off. I'm so sorry. Did you get hurt?"

Her blue eyes looked into his, her question repeated in them. Jake dumbly shook his head as he tried to speak. He didn't normally have so much trouble talking to women, but this girl made him feel like an adolescent teenager, and he broke into a tingling sweat.

"How did you find me?" she asked, leaning closer still.

"Well," Jake began and then stalled. How did he find her? Should he tell her that he had recently been stabbed, but seemed to be suffering no ill effects? That he stumbled upon this bar, as he was wandering around trying to figure out what the fuck had happened to him? Or perhaps he should let her know some freak had broken into his house, stolen his beer, and fed him a line about a second chance at life. Would that be plausible, or

26

would he sound as freakish as he felt?

He worked his mouth, trying to get something, a word of any kind, to tumble out, but all he could manage was another, "Well…"

The more he stuttered, the more her eyes narrowed, and she started to pull back from him. "Come to think of it, how did you find me?" She pulled her hand from his and stood up, her mouth turning down to match her eyebrows. "You're with them aren't you?"

"What?" he managed. "No. I… what? With who?"

"Those guys that won't leave me the fuck alone. You're one of them. Last night was all just a trick to get me to trust you wasn't it? I knew your fucking boss was persistent, but this is ridiculous. I told you 'no' before, and I mean 'no' now, so get the fuck out of here." By the time she'd finished, she was yelling and pointing towards the door. The few other patrons in the bar had turned in their seats and stared at Jake, eyes wide in blank faces.

Jake looked from the girl to the stares and back to the girl. "I don't know what you're talking about," he managed to spit. "My boss? What the fuck?"

When she saw he wasn't jumping to leave, the girl turned her head towards the door. "Danny!" she yelled. The door man appeared, arms spread out to make himself look bigger, and cocked his chin towards Veronica. "This fucker is causing a problem and won't leave."

Jake stood up, mildly insulted to be referred to as 'this fucker', and held his hands up, palm out. "I'm not causing a problem," he said, more puzzled than angry. "I don't have any idea what you're on about. I just saw you in trouble last night and tried to help you out."

"Sure," she spat at him. "Then you figured you'd come down here and get in good with me for your boss? Or maybe you just wanted a free blow job."

The bouncer came to stand behind the girl, glowering at Jake.

"Really," Jake said, standing still and not making any sudden movements, as though he faced a venomous snake instead of a blonde table dancer. "I don't know what you're talking about. I don't have a boss and no one sent me here to talk to you."

"Whatever," she said, crossing her arms. "Get the fuck out of here." She turned to look at the doorman. "Danny?"

The big man moved around her and stood in front of Jake's table, making a great show of flexing his muscles and glaring at him. "You heard the lady, douchebag. Your patronage is no longer welcome here."

Jake looked the man up and down. He was big, for sure, even bigger than the guy last night, but he was tight, probably slow, and was far too busy flexing to dodge the over-hand right Jake was considering for his out-thrust chin.

Instead, Jake stepped to the side, around the table and away from the girl, circling towards the hallway to the exit. He didn't really want to hit the guy. He didn't have a beef with him and didn't want to start one. He had no idea why this girl was so ridiculously furious at him, but if she wanted him to leave, he'd oblige.

"Okay," he said, holding up his hands a little higher and headed towards the exit. "You want me to go? I'm gone. Believe me when I say I don't know what you're talking about, and I didn't come here looking for you."

"Then why did you come?" she asked.

He paused, hands still up. "I was wondering that myself."

The bouncer took a step towards him. "Walk, douchebag. Or I'll walk you."

Jake put his arms down and turned for the door. "You've been watching too many bad movies, kid."

"Yeah? Have you seen the one called 'I'm about to get my ass kicked for being a mouthy prick?'"

Jake nodded and laughed. "I've seen that one, more than once. But it was shown to me by guys a lot bigger and a lot tougher than you."

Danny wasn't impressed and stood there continuing to glare, as Jake shook his head and walked towards the exit. The blonde girl, Veronica, was still behind the bouncer, arms crossed, also throwing him a reasonably good scowl.

Jake clenched his jaw, as he walked towards the door. He certainly made himself popular in new circles of friends. Based on the night before, he was lucky he didn't get driven over with a bus.

CHAPTER THREE

Jake stepped out of the dim bar and into the pale glare of the street lights, and was greeted by a familiar creased face and denim jacket. Oliver MacKinnon leaned, arms crossed, against a dilapidated Chevy pick-up truck, which must have been at least seventy-three different colours, rust primary among them.

"'The Crimson Curtain'", he read off the sign above Jake's head. Jake turned and looked up. The sign, spelled out in red neon lights, showed the shape of a female leg protruding from behind a wavy line. When he was younger, a 'crimson curtain' was a derogatory term for a part of the female anatomy, and he could only assume the proprietor of the strip bar had that particular part in mind when he'd picked the name.

"Couldn't you have picked a classier place?" Mac asked. "I feel dirty just standing out front."

Jake considered trying to explain about the two dollar burgers, but discounted the idea. He didn't have the patience to be laughed at by this wrinkled asshole. "What do you want?"

"I need your help," Mac said, opening the passenger door to the truck. "Get in."

"My help?" Jake asked. "You're kidding right? I'm not going

anywhere with you. Not 'til I get some answers."

"Answers come in the truck, and we haven't any time to waste."

"How did you know I was here?"

"I had a feeling." Mac walked around to the driver's side of the truck, opened the door, stood on the frame, and looked at Jake over the multi-coloured roof. "There, I answered a question. Now, will you get in, please? We'll talk as we drive."

Jake looked up and down the sidewalk. He saw the odd pedestrian, but it was getting late and not many people were out in this part of Surrey in the dark. If he got into the truck and disappeared off the face of the earth, no one would have the slightest clue where he'd gone. He couldn't think of anyone who would care, either.

He rubbed a hand over his short hair and looked at the door to the truck. It yawned at him, like the maw of an animal waiting to swallow him whole. Or, perhaps like a portal to a place unexplored. Whatever it was, he had a sneaking suspicion it wasn't something he'd easily be able to turn back from.

"Seriously, Jake," Mac said. "I need your help. And we're running short on time."

In two decades of professional fighting, Jake had learned to read opponents carefully. To know when they were hurt and putting on a straight face, to know when they planned to throw a punch at you, to know when they were full of shit. There was no shit in the look Mac gave him. Jake took a deep breath in through his nose, the kind he drew in when he was waiting for the bell before the first round, and got in the truck. He slammed the door with a squeal of protest from the rusted hinges, and Mac slipped into the seat beside him, giving him a nod.

"Thanks," Mac said, as he turned the key. The engine chugged to life with a rattling cough. He looked carefully over his shoulder and pulled away from the curb, onto the deserted street.

"So," Jake said, watching Mac as he drove the shuddering pickup.

"So?" Mac asked, his attention on the road.

"You mind telling me where we're going?"

"We've got a little job needs doing. A child needs our help."

"A child?" Jake began to regret his decision to climb in the truck. "What are we doing? Bringing him a sweater? Making him a sandwich? What?"

Mac shook his head. "He's being held. We're going to rescue him."

"Rescue… " Jake said, bewildered. "You really are nuts. Shouldn't we call the cops, or something?"

Again, Mac shook his head. "This isn't a matter for the police. It's a job for us, and if we don't hurry, there won't be any job at all."

"Who are you, man? I mean, really? Why's this a job for 'us'? What has any of this got to do with me? This is fucking crazy."

"Do you remember when I said you'd have a chance to do something important?" Mac asked and glanced at him.

"You mean when you broke into my house last night and started raving like a madman? Yeah, I have some recollection of the conversation."

"Well, that 'something' is things like this. Service to something other than yourself. Right now, a child needs our help before his light is extinguished. We're going to him now."

"Before his light is extinguished?" Jake repeated, letting the meaning of that statement settle in his mind as it rolled off his tongue.

Mac nodded up and down once, slowly.

"How do you know this?"

Mac shrugged, his hands tilting slightly on the steering wheel. "This second chance I spoke of, for most of us, it comes with gifts. My gift is that I get feelings sometimes. Like when I knew you were going to die last night, or where this child is right now."

Jake's frown turned into a glare, and he felt his heavy right hand ball into a fist. "You knew I was going to die and didn't think to give me a hint? What's the matter with you?" He unclenched his hand and rubbed it over his face. "No, man. I can't do it. This isn't happening. I did not die in a parkade to be reborn as a side-kick to the wrinkled avenger."

Mac laughed. "Wrinkled Avenger. I like it."

"No, man I'm serious. Pull this piece of shit over. I'm

getting out."

Flicking on the turn signal with one index finger, Mac slowed the truck with a shudder and pulled over to the side of the road, in front of a dark coffee shop. Jake reached for the door handle and had it half-way pulled when he felt Mac's hand on his arm. Jake paused, and glanced back at him.

Mac's expression was flat, his smile gone, and it filled Jake with a sense of gravity. "Make no mistake, my friend," Mac said. "Last night happened. If I had warned you, nothing in your life would have changed. You'd have avoided that parkade and the confrontation you found there, and carried on with whatever it is you once called a life. Nothing would have come of the chance you were offered. Now, everything is different."

"Yeah, I'm hanging out with crazy bastards who drive shitty trucks."

"No, Jake. You have been handed a gift that very few ever receive, and I am asking you, begging you, to come with me and use that gift to do something important."

"Are you serious?" Jake asked.

"As much as any man can be," Mac said. "If we do not act, a child will die."

Jake's foremost and burning desire was to get out of the truck and pretend he'd never met Oliver MacKinnon, pretend he'd never been stabbed through his only coat, and get on with his boring, stupid life. But there was something in Mac's face, something past the heavy lines and stupid grins that affected Jake. Something that made Jake believe him.

"Aw, fuck," Jake said, taking his hand off the door handle and thumping his elbow on the window sill.

Mac's grin returned and he once more pulled away from the curb.

Jake sat silent, his hand cradling the side of his face as he watched the road churn towards him and pass under the Chevy's bald tires. He still could not comprehend the incident from the previous night, or the part he played in Mac's lunacy. Jake didn't know if he should help the man or run like his ass was on fire. He knew he didn't understand what was happening, which is where all the bloody questions came from.

"So, if your gift is funny feelings," Jake said. He glanced

over at Mac and twirled his fingers in the air. "What's my gift supposed to be?"

"I don't know, Jake. You'll have to come to that one on your own."

Jake's lips pursed in thought. "Are there more people like you?" he asked, after several breaths.

"Yes, Jake, there are a few more like us." Mac emphasized his last word heavily, and Jake rolled his eyes. "And, if we survive this, you'll meet some of them."

"If we survive?"

Mac pulled the truck over to the side of the road, flicked off the lights, and killed the engine. Jake looked around and realised they were in an area of Surrey called 'The Flats'; built on the flood plain near the Fraser river, at the foot of the Patullo bridge ,where the residential suburbs of Surrey faded out and gave way to an industrial area. The houses here were falling apart; overpriced slums, never maintained by careless landlords. Jake passed over them on the sky-train when he was on his way to the warehouse that employed him.

Mac opened his door and got out of the truck. Jake hesitated a moment, peering through the truck's dirty windshield, then did the same. Once Jake was out, Mac hit a lever behind the seat back and pushed it forward to rummage around under a blanket. He produced a long object that glinted dully in the sparse light from the street lamps.

"Do you know how to use one of these?" Mac asked.

Jake's eyes widened. "Is that a fucking sword?"

"I'll take that as a 'no'." Mac dropped the sword onto his seat and reached under the blanket to rummage around some more. "Here, take this."

He handed Jake a heavy, long-handled hammer, with a broad, serrated striking surface and a wicked, curved spike off the back of the head. The handle was made of some kind of hardwood riveted to a tang attached to the head, and the grip was wrapped in leather that was shiny from use.

"Holy fuck, it's Satan's drywall hammer," Jake said as he held it up for examination. "That's an evil tool if I ever saw one."

Mac snorted. "It's not the tool that's evil, Jake, it's the one holding it. That there," he jerked his chin towards the hammer while he continued to dig around behind the seat, "has been put to good purpose before, and will be again tonight."

"Oh yeah? What purpose is that?"

Mac smiled, the lines around his eyes bunching. "You're about to find out, my friend. You're about to find out."

Mac stood up from his rummaging, a small black flashlight in his hand, which he slipped into the back pocket of his faded jeans. He eased the back of the seat into place, then plucked the sword off his seat. He pushed the driver's door closed quietly, not slamming it, but shoving it with the heel of his hand to produce a faint click from the latch. He turned and began walking up the road without another word.

Jake stood for a time, his gaze moving from the truck, to the long hammer in his hands, and to Mac's departing form. Reluctantly, mimicking Mac's process of softly closing the door, the boxer followed.

He trotted a few steps to catch up to Mac, who held the sword close behind his leg, as he scanned the fronts of the run-down houses. Jake had never actually seen a sword in real life—it was a little shorter than his arm and the blade was as wide as three of his fingers together. He thought, as he looked at it, that it belonged in the movie "Gladiator", but here it was in the grip of a wrinkly head-case as he crept along the edge of a dark street in a shitty neighbourhood.

Jake felt a deep tension in the air, like the moments before an electrical storm, and no sound broke the heavy silence.

"This is it." Mac slowed and stepped up to a tilting fence.

Following Mac's gaze, Jake saw a narrow, two-story house, with peeling paint on the outer walls and trash littered across the muddy yard. A strong smell of wet decay and human filth filtered into his nostrils. "What a shit hole," he said with a grimace. "Makes my place look like a palace."

Mac nodded. "And we're going inside."

Jake's hands wrung the haft of the hammer, the texture and weight of it foreign in his grip. "Are you sure about this? Shouldn't we call for someone?"

Mac turned to him, smile gone, replaced by a scowl that creased his face even further. "I told you already," his voice a growl. "We cannot wait. By the time we call the police, and they finish scratching their asses and fucking about, there won't be anything left for them to do. I tell you, Jake, there is a child in there that is going to die if we don't go in and get him. Now, stop playing the coward and find your courage."

The word 'coward' stung Jake like a slap. "All right, then. Lead the way."

Mac turned his face back towards the house. "We'll go in the back, around the right side." He pointed with his left hand to the side of the house where the muted glow of the street lamp didn't reach.

"Okay, what are we going to find in there?"

Mac shrugged. "Misery and pain would be my guess."

Jake continued to wring the hammer. "Any chance you could stop talking in riddles? I meant how many people, jackass."

"Not sure," Mac said, lips pursing. "Tough to say. Might be two, might be twenty. Why, you scared?"

"Fucking rights, I am."

Another snort. "Good. A little fear keeps you sharp. A lot will fill your pants with shit. Keep a handle on it."

Jake had a strong desire to get a handle around Mac's neck and shake him until his teeth rattled, but he resisted the temptation and focused instead on taking deep breaths and slowing his heart rate, like he did sitting in the dressing room before a fight.

Without warning, Mac crouched low, slipped around the fence, and crept across the driveway. Jake lurched forward and trotted a few steps to keep up to him. Mac moved around the right side of the house, as planned, his back hunched and his steps short and silent, like a soldier moving through a trench. If he was to be believed, Jake thought, then he'd probably learned to do it in the war, over one hundred years ago.

Mac stopped at the rear corner of the house and slowly leaned forward to peer down the back wall. Jake stopped behind him, both hands on the hammer, and glanced the way they'd come. There was no movement in the house and the windows remained dark. Jake hoped there wasn't actually anyone inside and Mac was just proving himself to be off his gourd.

Once again, without warning, Mac moved around the

corner, crept a few more paces, and stopped at a back door. He tried the handle with gentle pressure and it didn't budge. Jake checked the windows above them and still saw no movement. Mac pushed on the door with his shoulder, adding pressure slowly to see if it would move. It didn't, and he shook his head. He stuck the sword between the edge of the door and the jamb, right where the door knob was and pushed down with a quick twist of his wrist. A muted crack destroyed the silence, as the bolt gave way and the door swung open.

"Be ready," Mac said, looking forward into the dark opening.

Jake nodded and gripped the hammer, his heartbeat pounding in his ears.

Mac stepped into the doorway and Jake followed. The stench of human filth and rot punched him in the face. He stopped in the doorway, gagging, trying to keep his two-dollar burger down. Mac reached back and pulled him out of the door, his eyes scanning the darkness, giving no indication the smell bothered him. Jake had never experienced anything like it before. As a child, he'd once found a dead raccoon in the alley behind his house that had been rotting in the July sun for a week. That smell didn't even come close to this. He didn't want to be here in the first place, didn't now know why he was doing it, and the smell almost turned him around and sent him on his way. He took one hand from the hammer and put it up to his mouth, biting down on his knuckles hard enough to draw blood in an attempt to distract himself from the smell. It worked, sort of.

Mac tilted his head toward the hallway and started forward. Jake kept close to him, still struggling to keep a handle on his building nausea. There were small rooms, presumably bedrooms at one time, on either side of the hallway. They checked each one as they went, but found nothing other than piles of garbage and human waste. They reached the end of the hall and found it opened up into a large room that was partially illuminated by the street light filtering through the dirty windows.

Three men, their clothes dirty and their hair matted, huddled together in a corner, kneeling on a dirty mattress, as they passed around a lighter which they held up to the ends of narrow glass pipes.

One of them looked up when they entered the room. "What the fuck?" he said, as he saw them. "Who are you?"

Mac stepped forward, drawing himself up to his full height and holding the sword away from his body, where they were sure to see it. He looked at each one, staring into their eyes. They looked back, fear and sullen aggression fighting for purchase on their faces.

"Nothing," Mac said finally. Jake had no idea what he meant, or if Mac was addressing him, or the filthy men in the room. "Simple sentries failing at their duty." He glanced over his shoulder at Jake. "When you learn what to look for, you'll be able to spot the more powerful among our enemies. These are not such." He turned back to the men in the room and pointed towards the front door with the tip of the sword. "Get out of here, if you want to live."

None of them moved, but continued to stare, the whites of their eyes bright in their dirty faces.

"Now," Mac said, his voice deep with the ring of command. He took a step forward and raised the sword. The blade appeared startlingly bright in the dark room, reflecting jagged bands of light into the eyes of the men facing him.

Two of the filthy addicts immediately began rummaging around them for their belongings, stuffing pipes, lighters and very small plastic bags into the pockets of their tattered clothing. But one slowly stood and faced Mac.

"Can't go," the man muttered, a knife appearing in his hand. "Won't let us."

Mac didn't move, but met the crack-head's stare, sword still raised. The other two addicts shuffled towards the front door, their backs to the wall. Once they reached the door they threw it open, the handle crashing into the interior wall, and bolted into the night.

The banging of the front door was a starter pistol to the addict with the knife. He charged at Mac, a snarl twisting his face as he raised his weapon. Mac slid sideways, quick and smooth, a practiced motion, and simply thrust his sword forward. The addict couldn't stop his forward momentum and squealed as he impaled himself. Mac shifted again and yanked the sword from the filthy body and let it fall. Jake stared down at the dead man and felt his mouth hanging open.

"You fucking killed that guy!" he said, his voice thick and his stomach churning.

Mac nodded once. "Be alert. He wasn't the chief among them."

Jake stared at the body before glancing up at Mac. "What?"

"There will be one greater than the others. He will be near the child." Mac examined a set of stairs beside the entrance to the hallway.

Checking the shadows of the room carefully, Jake didn't see anyone else, and the open front door looked extremely inviting. The dirty Surrey air filtering in smelled pure as a mountainside compared to the stench he wallowed in.

"We're not done, Jake," Mac said, apparently able to read Jake's intention, as the boxer stared at the open door. "We've got to finish the job."

There was a set of stairs, leading up, adjacent to the front door. Mac started up them and didn't look back to see if Jake followed.

Jake glanced from the door, to Mac's back, and back at the door again. If asked later why, he wouldn't have been able to answer, but he followed Mac up the stairs.

The stairway was almost black, devoid of light, and Jake's steps faltered as he put one hand on the wall while feeling his way clumsily with his heavy boots. A sudden light filled the small space, as Mac clicked on the small flashlight he'd tucked into his pocket. The muted glow did little to push back the darkness, but it gave Jake enough light to navigate the stairs without breaking his neck.

The smell at the top of the stairs grew worse, and Jake wanted to retch. Even Mac, who had shown no sign of noticing the stink, began to look a little pale, as he held a hand over his nose.

Jake concentrated on breathing through his mouth as Mac tapped him on the arm and pointed down the hallway that led through the upper floor. Jake looked and saw a faint glow coming through the gap of a half closed door. Voices came from the room, low, joined in what sounded like a rhythmic chant, and a sound that made Jake's heart lurch; the sobbing of a child.

Mac clicked off the flashlight and started down the hallway, his sword held up in front of him as he took his short, silent steps, and checked the doorway to every room they passed. Jake followed, wincing as his boots crunched in the debris littering the floor.

When they reached the door with the glow, Mac moved to one side of it, and Jake, instinctively, moved to the other. The chanting grew more distinct, but Jake couldn't understand a word of the language, and the awful smell grew more pronounced.

Mac looked at Jake, their eyes meeting across the door, and nodded once. Jake returned the nod, and Mac crashed into the door with his shoulder.

The sight inside was one Jake could have never been prepared for, even had someone sat him down before hand, explained the scene in great detail, and drew him a little diagram.

Two men and a woman knelt in the centre of the room, facing each other. Each of them, stripped to the waist, had sweat standing out in beads on their upper bodies and running across strange symbols painted on their skin. On the floor between them was another strange symbol, all jagged loops and sharp edges. Atop the symbol, in the centre, lay a sobbing boy, perhaps five years old. Stretched out on his back and dressed in filthy clothes that were little more than rags, the boy's hands were clasped and bound in front of him with tattered rope. Fat tears rolled down his wet cheeks as he twisted and cried.

The man facing the door in the triangle looked up at Mac and Jake, a smile spreading his dirty tangle of a beard. "Oliver MacKinnon, I might have known you'd show up with that Sight of yours." The man turned his gaze to Jake. The boxer counted himself a hard man, but he felt almost wilted under the man's stare. "And you've brought a friend. I can smell the stink of your kind on him. You fools multiply like rats." The man stood easily, an effortless movement that caused the corded muscle in his chest and shoulders to ripple beneath his sweaty skin. His matted hair nearly touched the stained ceiling, and Jake took a step backwards in spite of himself.

"Hello, Taber," Mac said, his voice even, conversational. "I thought we'd agreed you were going to leave my city and commit your acts of fuckery elsewhere."

"Ha!" the giant, Taber, barked, the sound sharp and biting in the small room. "I agreed to nothing. You made demands. I ignored them. You should have killed me then, MacKinnon. You always were soft."

Mac shrugged before a creased smile crept across his face. "Yes, I should have. I think today is a good day to make amends."

"Hard to make amends when I'm wearing your skull as a hat." Taber slid a knife from the small of his back and tilted his head towards the two kneeling figures. He jerked his chin at Jake. "Kill the newcomer. The old man is mine."

The man and woman rose to their feet, producing knives from the folds of their rags. Jake instinctively backed up, the hammer held in front of him, as he tried to think of something to say, some way to negotiate. He was shitty at conversation to begin with, and these two freaks didn't look like they were interested in hearing it anyway. They bared their teeth in feral snarls, as they inched towards him. The man licked his lips and smiled.

The child on the floor let out a muffled wail and the woman lunged at Jake, her dirty knife held high above her shoulder, as a scream ripped from her throat. Jake quickly sidestepped, but his knees hit something and he sprawled backwards onto the floor. The woman leapt at Jake, over the wooden crate he'd tripped over. He desperately swung the hammer and the spike on the back of the head ripped into her knee. Her charge turned into a tumble as she screamed in pain and rage, crashing into the dirty wall. Jake scrambled to his feet, his boots skidding in the filth coating the bare wood floor, and faced his other opponent.

The man bounded over the fallen woman, who howled in pain, clutching her ruined leg. He slashed at Jake's gut with his knife. Jake gripped the hammer in both hands and swept it across his body, catching the man in the wrist, stopping his wild swing and sending the knife spinning from his hand. The man's momentum carried him into Jake, and they crashed backwards into the wall as the man grappled and scratched at Jake's face.

Jake gagged as the man closed with him, the stench of filth and unwashed excrement thick on the shirtless body. Choking his bile down, Jake shoved the man away, pushing against the haft of the hammer with all his considerable strength. The reeking man grabbed the hammer and tried to yank it from Jake's grip, his legs spread in a crouch as he pulled. A veteran of many street fights, Jake was not above fighting dirty and kicked the filthy man in the crotch, as soon as the opportunity presented itself. The man hissed in pain, his fetid breath hitting Jake in the face almost as hard as a punch, as he slumped onto his knees.

"I'm going to paint this room with your blood, MacKinnon."

Jake looked over top of his downed opponent to see the giant, Taber, slashing at Mac with his long knife. Mac raised his sword in time to deflect the blow, but the force of the impact almost knocked the sword from his grip.

"You're getting weak, old man," Taber shouted. "You grow soft in your world of light, while the dark makes me strong. This city isn't yours anymore."

Mac's grim face gave nothing away, but he continually backed up, always giving ground in the face of the vicious attack.

Jake tried to move to help him, but the prone man latched onto his leg and sunk his teeth into Jake's calf. Jake howled in pain and used his free foot to stomp on the man's head. There was sharp crunch as the man's jaw broke, but a good-sized chunk of Jake's calf came away with it. The searing pain made him want to pass out. He staggered away from the limp, unconscious man, and then crashed onto the floor, the hammer flying from his grip, as the woman scrabbled up and threw herself onto him.

He tried to push her away, but she clambered atop him, her dirty knife still in her hand, jabbing towards his face. He grabbed her knife hand in both of his own and twisted as hard as he could. There was a wet, cracking noise and the woman screeched, high and desperate like an animal. She continued to gouge and dig at Jake's face with her good hand while the other flopped uselessly in his grip. With a grunt, he heaved her off, rolled away from her and scrambled to his feet, limping badly on his injured leg. She got up as well, also limping, but still snarling and shambling towards him.

41

She had one hand out, claw-like fingers reaching, and Jake slipped to the side of it and slammed his fist into the space just below her nose. He hit as hard as he could manage, the impact snapping her head back, and she dropped to the floor, motionless.

A guttural scream, filled with rage and triumph, brought Jake's focus to the other side of the room. Mac was bent backwards against an overturned dresser, Taber on top of him, the tip of Taber's long knife pressed against Mac's cheek, drawing blood. Mac held the giant's wrists, trying to push the blade away, but the smaller man's arms trembled as he slowly lost ground.

Jake snatched his hammer off the floor, made a clumsy leap over the broken crate, and smashed his weapon down onto the giant's shoulder. Taber roared in pain as his collarbone shattered, dropping him to one knee. Mac wrested the knife from Taber's weakened grip and drove it into his neck.

Blood poured down the hilt and onto Mac's hands. Taber fell onto his side, propped up on his elbow while his useless arm tried vainly to pull the blade from the spurting wound. He glared at Mac, hatred still burning hot in his eyes, and tried to speak but blood choked off the words. His final breath rattled between bared teeth and Taber collapsed, a hateful snarl still locked on his face.

"You should have hit him in the head," Mac said, as he held his hand to his side where blood seeped through his denim jacket.

"You're welcome," Jake said, as he limped towards the bound child. He knelt awkwardly beside the boy, picked up another knife from the inside of the drawn symbol, and used it to slice through the ropes binding the boy's arms and legs. The boy reached up and pulled the dirty rag from his mouth, then threw his arms around Jake, not speaking, but burying his face into the boxer's neck, continuing to cry.

"Come on, Jake," Mac said, picking up his sword and Jake's hammer, shuffling towards the door. "We need to get him out of here."

Jake nodded and stood, one arm scooping under the boy's seat. Pain lanced through his leg and he gritted his teeth, as he followed Mac.

As he started down the hallway, Jake noticed a door to one of the rooms Mac had checked was now partway open. Something, a niggling itch in the back of his mind, made him stop and look into the room. He saw the edge of a filthy bathtub and realised the smell that permeated the house originated here.

"Jake," Mac said. Jake met his gaze and the creased man shook his head. "You don't need to look in there. Let's go."

Something in the way he said it made Jake believe him, but he had to see for himself just the same. The itch would not go un-scratched. Still cradling the child, he nudged the door open with the toe of his work-boot and looked inside. He instantly wished he'd taken Mac's advice.

In the tub lay a small body, well on its journey of decay, bloated and purple. Jake couldn't tell if it was a boy or a girl, but it had a long jagged wound in the chest, which would have been empty if not for the maggots crawling in it.

Jake spun away from the sight, and pressed the boy's face into his neck so he wouldn't have to see.

"We were too late for that one," Mac said, his eyes on the floor. "I didn't See her in time. I didn't know she was here. I didn't know Taber had taken her."

Jake nodded mutely, the image of the child in the bathtub burning on the backs of his eyelids, and he hobbled towards the stairs.

Once they were clear of the house and back in the truck, Mac drove a few blocks and pulled up to a gas station. The child, wrapped in the old blanket from behind the truck's seat, huddled between them, both his small arms gripping Jake as he trembled. Mac parked the truck and looked down at the child, the beginnings of a smile playing across his lined face. He reached out a steady hand towards the small head that was turned away from him, paused, and then pulled his hand back.

He got out, fished into his pockets to produce two quarters, and walked up to the pay phone. Twice he deposited the coins, dialed and spoke briefly. Then he got back into the truck.

"Who were you calling?" Jake asked.

"The police."

"The police? Why? You just killed two people, Mac."

Mac turned the key in the ignition and the truck sputtered to life. "I told them someone had just broken into that house. They'll go in, find the bodies of the things we just killed, the two unconscious servants, and the little girl." Mac looked over at Jake. "Her parents deserve to know where she's gone. They shouldn't have to hope for the rest of their lives their daughter is going to come home one day. They deserve to move on."

Jake couldn't find an argument. "Who else did you call?"

"Our leader," Mac said, as he shoved the gear shift into first.

"Our leader? Who the fuck is that?" He winced at his own language, and looked down at the boy. The child hadn't noticed. In the time it had taken Mac to make his calls, exhaustion and the warmth from the rattling heater had claimed him. He slept, oblivious, both arms still clinging to Jake.

"The head of our clan," Mac said. He checked carefully over his left shoulder, as he pulled away from the curb of the gas station. "I wanted to let him know the job was done and we'll be seeing the boy home."

"Okay," Jake said, unconsciously smoothing boy's sandy hair. "Then what?"

Mac wiped at the bloody spot on his cheek where Taber had cut him, then reached down to change gears. "We'll go and get patched up, and you'll meet the others."

"What others? The other's like you?"

"No Jake, not like me. Like us. You'll meet your clan."

"Clan?" Jake asked, one eyebrow climbing.

Mac said nothing, but looked at the road, his gaze occasionally turning to the rear view mirror.

"Clan," Jake said again, as he looked out the window at a city that was now vastly, and irrevocably, different.

CHAPTER FOUR

The boy lived in a spacious, modern two storey house in the southern part of Surrey, where the housing prices climbed and the crime rate dropped. Mac parked several blocks away and Jake carried the boy down the street. He laid him, still sleeping, on the front step of the house, rang the doorbell and ran into the bushes like a child playing a prank. He waited until he saw movement in the upstairs windows, then hobbled away as quickly as his damaged leg could take him. Behind him, he heard frantic cries of surprise and joy.

Once he reached the still-running truck parked half a block away, he climbed in and Mac looked over at him. "The boy is home?"

Jake nodded, pulling the squealing door closed. "I didn't even ask the kid his name." He shrugged. "Not that it matters, or that he'd have been able to talk anyway."

"The child's name is Rudy, after his father," Mac said, as he turned the key in the ignition and the truck started with a groaning cough. "He'll be fine once the memory of the last few days fades. He'll grow and have a family of his own. We've done well."

"How do you know this stuff? Are you making it up to piss

45

with me?"

Mac shrugged and twisted his mouth, appearing to think of his response. "Like I said, I just get feelings sometimes." He shoulder checked carefully, then pulled the truck away from the curb and rattled slowly down the street.

"Right." Jake, as he propped his elbow on the sill, looking out the window. "What did they want with the kid anyway? And the other one in the… the other one we found." He tried to swallow the memory of the body in the bath tub. "What were they doing with the chanting and the symbols and shit?"

Mac clicked the side of his mouth. "That, my friend, is a good question. There are many rituals, or rites, that most of mankind has forgotten about. Old acts, from the dark days of humanity. It looked like they'd taken the heart from the other child, and I can only assume it was for such a ceremony. What their purpose is, I'm not sure."

"That Taber guy. You knew him?"

Mac nodded, eyes still on the road. "We've met before. Several years ago, when he was younger and wasn't as you saw him today. I tried to give him a chance to turn from the path he was walking, but he obviously didn't take it."

"If he wasn't 'as I saw him today', what was he?"

"He was only a man, then, albeit a man filled with anger and bad intentions. With his turning completely to the dark he'd become powerful, much more so than the last time I faced him. I could feel it."

Jake twisted in his seat to face Mac. "Feel it? Feel what? What do you mean, 'turning completely to the dark?'"

"When someone walks constantly in shadow, you know it. I don't mean like those fools we met guarding the place, clutching their pipes and shitting their pants. They were there only from desperation and circumstance. I mean those who are truly bad, who purposely seek the dark and give themselves over to it. That kind of evil leaves a taint you can feel. Just as the light leaves its mark as well. You can't feel it now, but you will in time, when you know what to look for."

Jake turned back to the window. "I don't want to look for anything, and I don't want any light leaving a mark on me. Are you some kind of religion? Is this like when people are 'touched' by Jesus?"

Mac sighed. "We are the good guys, Jake. We walk in the light. We try and keep people safe. Those who oppose us and try to bring people to ruin, kidnap children and carve their hearts from their chests, they walk in the dark. Choices are made and sides are picked. We just do what we can."

Jake snorted. "I didn't choose this."

"You chose to get in the truck and come with me, didn't you?"

"You said you needed my help," Jake said, his voice rising in both pitch and volume.

"And you made a choice to help me. I didn't tie you up and throw you into the bed of my truck. You made a decision to come with me and try to help a child. That means you walk in the light. That makes you one of us."

"Yeah, so I've got a soft spot for kids. What the fuck? I didn't ask to get stabbed last night. I didn't ask for you to show up at my house and drink my beer. I didn't want to meet you, or have you feed me a line of mythical shit about second chances and walking in the light. I just wanted to be left alone."

"You made a choice to help another person—that girl, last night. If you hadn't, she'd be dead or worse, and you'd not have been chosen."

"Chosen," he muttered, looking out the window, rubbing at his stubbled jaw with a calloused hand. "Bullshit. I didn't want to be chosen for anything."

"Well," Mac said, "the Fates spin as they will, and now you are here. You've been given a second chance, and you've used it well tonight. How you carry on from here is up to you."

Jake had the distinct impression he was being tricked. He folded his arms and continued to stare out the window. Mac didn't press him.

They rode in silence and the truck made enough noise for both of them, chattering its way down the suburban streets.

Gradually the streets narrowed, and the spaces between the street lights increased. The new, densely packed houses of South Surrey gave way to bigger, older properties. Chain link fences were replaced with barbed wire, and cultured shrubs were replaced with tall pine trees and drooping willows.

Tyner Gillies

Unwilling to speak while he tossed Mac's words around in his mind, Jake did not pay attention to where they were going. He had never considered himself particularly imaginative— always he had been practical and realistic. Everything he had experienced in the last day—his own death and apparent rebirth; the battle against a bunch of crazy, chanting freak shows; Mac telling him he was somehow singled out for this second chance; everything—drove over his concepts of reality like a dumptruck, then backed over them for good measure. As he rode in silence, staring out the window, trying to make sense, he felt something crack inside him.

"Pull over," he said, and groped in the dark cab for the door handle.

"What?" Mac asked.

"I said pull this fucking jalopy over," he said, finding the door handle and yanking it.

Mac steered the truck to the shoulder of the road. Jake staggered out the open door while the truck came to a stop, and almost fell on his face when his work boots hit the ground. On a narrow road, with a wide ditch butting up against the gravel shoulder, Jake put his hands on his knees and vomited his twodollar burger into the yellowing grass.

When he was done with the twitching heaves, he stood upright and found Mac beside him. The older man's face, illuminated red by the truck's dim tail lights, appeared drawn with concern and sympathy.

He gripped Jake's shoulder hard in a powerful grip. Any other day Jake would have shrugged it away, but the pressure of Mac's hand felt like the only real thing in a world that had become very un-real.

"I know this is hard, Jake," he said. "But it will get easier. And you are not alone, in this or anything else."

Jake met Mac's gaze, and the care in the man's face made him feel ill again. He was mad at himself because he wanted it, that he was weak enough to need it. He shrugged away from Mac's touch, harder than necessary, and stalked towards the stillopen door of the truck. He wiped the back of his hand across his mouth as he climbed in and slammed the squealing door. Beside him, Mac did the same.

48

Jake rolled down his window and cocked his elbow out. He started to speak, but had to stop to clear his throat and spit noisily out his window. "You mind telling me where we're going?" he asked. "This doesn't look much like my neighbourhood."

"We are going to see the leader of our clan," Mac said, as he performed another careful shoulder check on the dark road and pulled the truck away from the shoulder. "And we are almost there."

"What is this clan you keep talking about?" Jake asked. "Isn't that like a family thing?"

"The clan is our family, Jake. The only one I've known since I died in the war. The Fates have a way of bringing people like us together."

"With family who break into your house and steals your beer, who needs enemies?"

Mac ignored him as he turned from the narrow road into an even narrower driveway. The pines and cedars closed in on each side, as they rumbled down an unpaved driveway. As they came around a bend, the driveway opened wide and Mac stopped beside two other cars—a small, new, foreign compact and an old Mercedes—in front of a huge, sprawling, rancher-style house. Mac killed the truck's engine and opened his squealing door. Reluctant to get out of the truck, Jake sat still for a moment, looking at the house through the windshield. He'd had quite enough of entering strange places and making new friends for one day.

Mac stood at his open door and looked at Jake. "You'll be safe here."

Jake glanced over at him. He had the horrible feeling, a burning certainty, that he would never be safe, anywhere, ever again. He tamped the feeling down and slowly opened his own door. "Yeah, whatever."

They slammed their doors. Mac led the way to the front of the old house, probably build in the late sixties or early seventies. The paint on the wooden siding appeared new and the round river-stones that surrounded the front door in an arch were clean. The house had an expensive, polished feel and it made Jake feel out of place in his, torn, bloody clothing and scuffed work boots.

"Nice place," Jake said, grudgingly.

Mac turned the knob and stepped into the house. "When you've had two hundred year's worth of experience to build your life, you might have a house like it as well."

"This guy is two hundred years old?" Jake asked, wonder making his voice airy.

Mac nodded.

The foyer glimmered with white marble, the walls warm and inviting with polished wood; out of date, but, once again, expensive. It looked like something out of a 1960's television show.

"This the new guy?"

Jake turned to see a woman, black hair hanging past her shoulders, wearing snug blue jeans and tight, black v-neck t-shirt, standing in the entrance to a hallway, one hand on her slender hip.

"Isabelle," Mac greeted the woman with a nod and a smile. "This is Jake Ross."

"I thought you said he was a fighter," she said, her tone flat, almost disinterested. "He doesn't look like much."

Jake felt like he was at an interview for a job he didn't want, but he tried to be polite and nodded in greeting. She only crossed her muscular arms and eye-balled him up and down.

Mac grinned. "He put down two of Taber's clan and then saved my bacon. He can hold his own."

Isabelle huffed. "Yeah, we'll see."

"Is Morgan here?" Mac asked. "He's expecting us."

Isabelle glanced over at Mac, then back at Jake, one dark, slender eyebrow lifting a little above her blue eyes. "He's in his study." She turned down the marble hallway and cast a glare over her shoulder. "Try not to bleed on the floor."

Jake looked down at his torn, bloody leg, finally seeing it in the light. "This was my best pair of jeans," he said as he pulled up the thick fabric to look at his calf. "The only pair without holes in…" He trailed off mid-sentence, as he looked at his leg. He'd expected a jagged wound, complete with infection from the dirty teeth of a homeless drug user, but found instead a scabbed over mark that looked several days old. No meat was missing from his calf, and while tender to the touch, the searing pain had faded to a throbbing ache.

"You heal quick now, Jake," Mac said, his creased smile appearing. "It's not a gift we all receive, but there are some benefits to this life, eh?"

Jake continued to look at his leg then stood up. He sniffed, an exaggerated sound. "Yeah? Well my jeans are still fucked."

Mac rolled his eyes. "There really is no pleasing you, is there?"

Jake shrugged and glared at his jeans.

They followed Isabelle down the broad hallway, past several closed rooms, around a corner, and through a set of open double doors. The scene that greeted Jake was something his imagination could barely conceive. The walls of the huge room were lined with floor to ceiling shelves, and each was filled with books of every size and description; from huge leather-bound tomes, to small, common paper-backs. A fireplace against one wall had wide leather chairs horseshoed around it. A massive wooden desk stood near the back. Behind the desk, holding a magnifying glass and examining an ancient-looking book, sat a slim, red haired and bearded man.

As they approached the desk, the bearded man glanced up at them and broadly smiled. He set the magnifying glass down beside the book and marked his place with a red ribbon before standing up and coming around the desk with his hand extended. "You must be Jake," he said, grasping Jake's hand in both of his. His hands were warm and smooth, his grip firm, but not crushing. He smiled easily, as he met Jake's eye.

Despite his misgivings, Jake felt himself smiling in return.

"I see you made it through your first battle. Mac told me on the phone you did well. Dropped Taber with one blow. Good work tonight."

"Uh... thanks."

"Jake Ross," Mac said, "this is Morgan Caron."

Morgan let go of Jake's hand and slapped his head in a mock gesture of forgetfulness. "Proper introductions. I always forget about them. Thanks Mac." He stepped back and clasped his hands in front of his chest, looking at Jake expectantly. "Can I get you anything?"

"Uh... no. Thanks." Jake's stomach had settled and, now empty, had begun growling again. Even he, who was not much for social graces, didn't think it would be appropriate to ask for a sandwich.

"He's got a fine gift for the conversation, this one." Morgan walked back around his desk and sat down in the high, leather, wing-backed chair he'd recently occupied. He studied Jake for several moments, stroking his short beard. "You look worried, Jake. Are there any questions I can answer for you?"

A firm believer in never asking a question you didn't want the answer to, Jake asked, "Yeah. Like what the fuck I'm doing here?" He crossed his arms and put a little growl in his voice to show the grinning man he wasn't particularly impressed.

Morgan's smile faltered a little. "Well…"

"How about why did a crack-head bite a piece out of my leg? Or you could go into why a gigantic hairy dude was chanting over some little kid with another rotting in a bathtub. I've definitely got a couple questions that need some answering."

Morgan held up his hands in a gesture of surrender, his smile returning. "Slowly, Jake. There are answers to all your questions, but they'll take some time to explain." He held out a hand, indicating two low-backed leather chairs that sat at angles in front of the desk. "Have a seat, please."

Jake had absolutely no interest in sitting, and dropped his chin a little, giving Morgan his best ring-glare.

Moran continued to smile. "Please, Jake. I'd appreciate it."

Originally planning on telling Morgan to go fuck himself, Jake was surprised to find his ass in a chair. He shook his head slightly and looked around, wondering why he was having such a difficult time being himself. He fixed an angry scowl and tried to remember he was pissed off. Mac took the seat beside him. Isabelle wandered around behind Morgan's desk and put one hand on one of the wings of Morgan's chair. Her body seemed at ease, but the look she gave Jake was all full of cold tension. He was a little surprised there weren't icicles forming in his hair.

"Why you're here, Jake," Morgan said, "is a deeply complicated question. The short answer is, you were chosen. Why or how you were chosen is a conundrum that only the Fates can answer. You understand the idea of a conundrum?"

"Yes, I know what a conundrum is; an unanswerable riddle. I'm a fighter, not a moron."

"Right, well I can certainly see that," Morgan said, his smile still fixed. "A fighter of no small ability as well. Anyway, none of us is sure why we were chosen for this life, but we find ourselves here nonetheless. We, here, hope to guide you, as we ourselves were guided when we were given this second chance."

The look on Morgan's face was all empathy and deep concern. Despite the honesty in his face and his open manner, Jake felt a reluctance to believe him. He'd been screwed enough in his life to make his trust a rare and elusive thing; something given to almost no one since his father died shortly after Jake started his professional boxing career. He was nothing if not taciturn and suspicious of everyone—traits he took a certain amount of pride in.

Despite his instincts, Jake found himself wanting to trust the man across the desk, but his ridiculously stubborn streak rallied behind his righteous indignation. He maintained his scowl. "Yeah, and what exactly am I supposed to be doing with this 'second chance'? Spend my time stabbing drug addicts and rescuing small children?"

Morgan sat back in his chair, crossing his legs as he steepled his fingers. "Incidents like tonight are only a small part of who we are, Jake. It's up to you to learn what the Fates have planned for you when they gave you this opportunity. It's up to you to embrace it."

"I don't want to embrace anything," Jake said. "I don't want anything to do with you people. I don't want to go on grand rescue missions, and I sure as hell didn't want to kill anyone. What do I have to do to get rid of you?" Jake felt vaguely guilty for being so angry. He was proud of what he'd done in rescuing the boy from those chanting freaks, but he didn't like being manipulated, and that was certainly what was going on here.

"There is no getting rid of us, Jake. You're part of the clan now."

"No," Jake said, the thin ice of his patience cracking beneath Morgan's words. He stood and looked down at the man. "I'm not part of anything."

Isabelle stepped away from Morgan, her hand dropping to the small of her back. She stopped pulling whatever was there when Morgan raised his hand.

Jake stood still, his breaths coming heavy, as the glared at Morgan and ignored Isabelle. "I never wanted to be part of this. I never wanted to be chosen for this second chance. I just wanted to be a fighter and be left alone."

"You are a fighter, Jake," Morgan said, still smiling, his voice even and infinitely reasonable in the face of Jake's biting fury. "You fight with us now. You fight for the people we protect—the people of this city."

Jake snorted. "I might as well be talking to myself. I'm done here." He turned from the desk and started walking towards the doors.

"What do you think will happen, Jake, if you leave here alone?"

The boxer stopped and turned. "You gonna come after me?" he asked, his voice low, slow. "Any time you think you're up to it." He shrugged his shoulders and flexed his hands.

"It's not us you need worry about, Jake," Morgan said. "Those two sentries you let go? The two bodies you left broken, but not dead, with Taber. Don't you think they might talk about you to the elders of the clan they serve? Don't you think our enemies now know you exist? If they don't, they soon will, and even if they don't know your name, they'll know your face. How long do you think you'll last without our protection? You killed one of their most powerful soldiers tonight. Do you not think they'll seek retribution? There is safety in numbers."

"I didn't kill anyone. Mac killed him."

"You had a hand in it. That is all they need to know."

"So you're telling me that you roped me into this shit and now I can't get out 'cause this Taber guy has friends who want to kill me?"

Morgan shook his head slowly, a wan, patient smile on his face. "You were roped into nothing. You made a choice, as a grown man, to do what you did. I'm just explaining the realities of this life to you. You've come to us while we're in the middle of a war. The dark clans are as powerful as they've ever been and we are called to challenge them at every turn. You cannot hope to face them alone, and if you leave here, abandoning us, that is exactly what you'll be doing."

"You mother fuckers." Jake gritted his teeth and clenched

his fists until his knuckles cracked and his arms trembled.

Morgan sighed and rubbed a hand over his short red hair. "This," he said, shaking his head again, "is not how I wanted our first meeting to go." He pressed his lips together and rubbed at his beard.

Jake crossed his arms again and waited.

"Okay," Morgan said, looking up. "No one is trying to force you into anything here, Jake. But you've got to accept the situation as it is and understand we're not trying to hurt you. We're welcoming you into our fold. Offering you support and protection. Something that you've never had in your life, unless I miss my guess."

Jake kept his face as smooth as he could, but his jaw tightened. It was true he'd been alone for the better part of his forty years, doing nothing but fighting and working a string of shitty jobs, but he was used to it. He even liked it that way, or so he told himself.

"And by your reaction I think my guess was dead on," Morgan said and paused, studying Jake's face like one of his leather books. "You can walk out of my house and never look back if you want. We'll leave you alone and you won't hear from us. But know you'll be dead inside a week, and that would be a tragic loss; both to us, because you'd be an asset to the clan, and to the greater good, because you'd never fulfill whatever purpose the Fates had in mind when they chose you."

Jake said nothing, hoping he looked like he wasn't worried.

Morgan opened the top-centre drawer in his desk, pulled out a small card and slid it across the surface towards Jake. "Here is my number. If you need anything, want to talk, or have any questions, please call me. Mac will take you home." He turned and looked over his left shoulder. "Isabelle, will you see them out, please." He picked up his magnifying glass and continued studying the pages of the book on his desk.

Jake had the distinct impression he'd just been dismissed.

Mac stood up and walked towards the doors. Jake stayed where he was and glared at the top of Morgan's head. Jake waited, but Morgan gave no sign he noticed the stare, nor cared if he did.

"I have questions, now, Morgan," Jake said.

Morgan looked up from the book. "You're angry now, Jake. I can understand why, believe me. I was shocked myself when I woke up and someone I didn't want to talk to was telling me the same things I'm telling you now. But I'll not sit here and be abused by you when you're in a snit. Call me when you've had some time to yourself, to get used to the ideas you've been given, and we'll talk some more." He looked back down at the book.

A slow anger burbled in Jake's gut at being chastised like a school boy. He opened his mouth to give vent to that anger, but Mac reached up and squeezed his shoulder. He wanted to press the issue, but was afraid he'd really lose his temper and punch Morgan in the face. It had to be bad form to punch a two hundred year old man. He uncrossed his arms, glared at the business card on the desk without touching it, and turned to follow Mac from the room.

Isabelle quickly stepped past them, her footsteps tapping on the marble floor. As she passed, leading down the hallway, Jake couldn't help but notice the way her hips swayed in her snug blue jeans. When she reached the outer door, she turned abruptly and caught Jake's eyes below her waist. She gave him a look that froze the air. He gave her his best grin—which likely wasn't saying much with his scarred lips and bent nose—but it did nothing to melt the ice. She yanked open the door, her blue eyes boring into him, as he and Mac walked by. The door slammed behind them.

"Not exactly friendly, is she?" Jake commented, as he climbed into Mac's truck.

Mac grunted, as he yanked his door closed. "She's not bad once she warms up to you. But she's fiercely loyal to Morgan, and anyone challenging him is a direct insult to her. Looks to him like a father." Mac coaxed the old truck to life, and then guided its rumbling way along the bumpy driveway.

The drive into north Surrey was silent, as Jake sat looking out the dirty window. He wished he had a better understanding of what was happening. But he could wish all he wanted, while his doubt got into a fist fight with resignation, and anger slid to sucker punch the winner.

CHAPTER FIVE

ake opened his eyes and looked out his bedroom window to see the falling rain. He sat up in his narrow bed, looked at the clock on his night stand, and realised he'd slept most of the morning. Apparently, fighting crack-heads and rescuing children made a man almost as tired as getting murdered in a parkade.

He swung his legs out of bed and stood, then lifted one foot back onto the mattress to check the wound on the back of his leg. Most of the scab had fallen away to reveal new, healthy, pink skin. There were definite evidence of teeth marks, but faint.

One thing Jake did notice, however, was the lack of his usual morning pain. His shoulders didn't crackle and pop when he rotated his arms. His arthritic fighter's hands weren't swollen and sore with the wet weather. Even the air through his oft-broken nose didn't have quite the same whistle. He hated to admit it, he felt fantastic.

He picked up his bloody and ruined jeans off the floor from where he'd dropped them in exhaustion the night before. He held them up to the light from the window and glared at the torn leg before throwing them into the corner in disgust. As he threw them, he noticed a sliver of white sticking out of his back pocket. He grunted in curiosity and bent down to pick it up. The sliver proved to be the corner of a folded envelope. When unfolded, he saw a single line written across the front in tall, looping letters: 'For new jeans. We don't let family go cold. -Morgan.' He opened the envelop and saw a collection of bills, all bearing the number '100'. With the money was a business card identical to the one Jake had refused to accept the night before.

His first instinct was to throw the bastard's money out the window—because Jake Ross could not be bought—followed immediately by wondering how Morgan had slipped the envelope into his pocket. Once he counted the bills, all ten of them, he began rationalizing that he'd more than earned the money, and double, for his work the previous night. He dropped the envelope onto his dresser and tossed the bloodied jeans into the trash bin beside the narrow door.

He wandered through his apartment, dressed only in his skivvies, looking at the sparse contents; the worn out couch, the tiny television with rabbit ears that got two fuzzy channels, the shelves filled with dog-eared paper-back books. Even if he did believe all the nonsense about the 'clan' that Mac and Morgan tossed at him, why would they want some guy who'd had his ass kicked too many times and lived in a shit-hole with nothing to show for his life. It didn't make any sense at all.

After several moments of pacing around and scratching at the hair on his flat stomach, he decided he needed to go where he could clear his head and do some thinking.

Jake hitched his gym bag up higher on his shoulder as he rounded a corner and his destination came into view.

Tartan Boxing was a run down, damp, smelly shit hole run by Warren Boyd. It was a crappy building in a crappy west Surrey neighbourhood, but Jake trained there because Warren let him train for free and it was close to a bus stop.

He pulled open the steel door and was greeted with the stench of stale sweat and the sound of heavy metal music. It was a Sunday afternoon and the gym was mostly empty except for a couple of pre-teen kids in one of the rings, enthusiastically beating on each other. Another group of young men were yapping more than training. Jake walked through the gym, past the rows of worn, heavy bags, towards the locker room at the back of the building. Warren's office door was open and the man had his bulk stuffed into a cheap, faux-leather chair, as he tapped away at a broad calculator, peering at it through narrow reading glasses. He looked up when Jake passed.

"Ross? Is that you?"

Jake stopped and leaned in the door to the office.

"You come to work out?"

"Yeah, something like that." Really, he'd come here to think, but he'd be moving around while he did it.

Warren grunted and looked back at his calculator. "Good. I got you a fight, two weeks from now, down in Bridgeview. I would have called you, but you ain't got a fucking phone." Warren looked up at him again, over the top of his glasses. "This kids a cooker, Ross. Only been pro a few months and he's got two knock outs already. Won every fight as an amateur. You beat him, I'll put you on my next casino card. He beats you, he goes."

Jake nodded and continued to lean against the door.

Warren took his glasses off and dropped them onto his desk. "All I gets a fucking nod? I thought you'd be happy. This is what you wanted ain't it?"

"Yeah, Warren, it's what I wanted. I got a few things on my mind just now, is all."

Warren grunted again and looked back at his calculator, squinting until he remembered to put his glasses back on. "Well, whatever those things are, tell 'em to fuck off. You got a choice to make, Ross. Either you get on this chance and ride it like it's your last, because it is, or you hang up the gloves and take up knitting. You decide." He jabbed viciously at the calculator with one thick finger, his squint pulling his top lip up to show his yellow teeth.

Choices. Jake had to make all kinds of fucking choices. "Okay, Warren, I'll be ready."

The promoter grunted his assent, as he picked up the calculator and slapped the side of it, glaring at the numbers beyond his bulbous nose.

Jake changed quickly into his workout gear: worn boxing

boots, a stained tank-top, and an old pair of fight trunks too blood-stained to wear back into the ring. He went back out onto the gym floor and dropped his bag in a corner and rummaged around for his skipping rope. Taking some deep breaths, he stepped into the big open space in front of a wall of mirrors and started twirling the rope, warming up. The cord of the skipping rope cut through the air with a faint whistle, punctuated by the tick-tick of it hitting the cement floor. It was a sound dearly familiar to Jake Ross. He took comfort in it and let his chaotic thoughts fall into the rope's rhythm and come to some semblance of order.

Slowly, as the sweat first beaded, then ran down his face, he was able to bully his thoughts around and get them where he could look at them. He replayed the incidents of the last several days, going over them, looking for the holes in his opponent's defense, poking at the gaps in his own game, trying to figure where he went wrong, or what he'd done right. The more he looked, the less he liked.

He spun the rope faster, his feet thumping out a rhythm on the floor.

He felt as though he was being corralled, like an obese heifer, by Mac and Morgan. They claimed he'd had the freedom to choose his own actions during this process, but the choices they talked about were not really choices at all. Follow the girl into the parkade, or do fuck all while she gets raped or murdered. Get in the truck with Mac and fight the freaks in the shit-hole house, or let them kill a little kid. Take the glass of water from the Devil himself, or die of thirst in the desert. All the choices were loaded, presented to him with the knowledge of what he would do before he knew himself. They pulled him around on a chain, like a half-witted dog too dumb to bite, and he didn't like it one bit.

He looked up at the clock above the mirrors and frowned. He'd been skipping for more than half an hour. Usually his knees started to ache and his ankles swelled up, but they felt light and springy. He was barely breathing heavy, even though he'd been pushing the rhythm. He let the rope stop, slapping lightly against his shins, and felt vaguely satisfied with himself. Gathering the rope in a coil, he tucked it back into his gym bag and dug around for his hand wraps and bag gloves.

He'd just started hammering into one of the long heavy bags, reveling in the way it jumped when his punches connected, when Warren came out of his office.

"Hey, Ross."

Jake turned and looked at him.

"You busy?"

Jake looked down at his gloved hands, then at the still-swinging bag, with exaggerated slowness. "Not at all, Warren. I was just standing here doing fuck all."

"That's what I thought. Got something useful for you to do. Wanna do some sparring today?"

"Not particularly. I was just gonna get a sweat going on my own and then take care of some things."

"Oh," Warren said as he walked past Jake with his heavy shuffle. "I wasn't really asking 'cause I give a fuck what you want. I need you to move around with one of the guys I manage. He's got a big fight in the States in a couple of weeks, and you're the only guy here in his weight class. Besides, you could use the work." Warren looked over his shoulder, as he laboured towards one of the rings. "I'll make sure he goes easy on you."

Jake sighed and put out a hand to stop the swinging of the bag. He had a strong desire to tell Warren to take a flying fuck at a rolling donut, but the fat man was right. If Jake was going to work his way back up the ranks, he needed all the training he could get. He walked over to his gym bag, pulled off his gloves, and started digging around for his mouth guard and head gear.

When he had all his gear on, he turned and walked toward the ring. His opponent appeared ten years younger, four inches taller, and covered with a lot of angry, angst-filled tattoos.

"Jesus, Warren," Jake said, as he stopped and gazed at his opponent, one of the yapping young men he'd seen when he entered. "I thought you said he was in my weight class."

"He is," Warren grunted, as he struggled up onto the side of the ring and leaned on the ropes. "He's a heavy weight, you're a heavy weight."

"Yeah, if by heavy weight you mean fucking massive. He's gotta out-weigh me by fifty fucking pounds."

"Don't exaggerate." Warren waved dismissively. "It's twenty

at the most. Now, are you gonna get in this ring and move around? I'm not getting any younger, and I didn't climb my fat ass up here for nothing."

Reluctantly, Jake stepped up onto the ring apron and swung a leg through the ropes. The fighter opposite him showed off an evil, gap-toothed smile, and stuck in his mouth guard, which was styled to look like a row of fanged teeth.

"Okay, Robbie," Warren called from across the ring. "Let's just move around a little. The old guy is out of shape, slow, and nowhere near your ability, so try not to kill him."

Jake dropped his hands and turned. "For fuck sakes, Warren. I can hear you. And I'm not that old. I'm only 43."

Warren shrugged. "As far as fighters go, you're fucking ancient, and George Foreman, you are not." He pulled a stop watch from the pocket of his baggy jogging pants and peered at it, holding it out at arm's length and squinting. "Okay, time."

Jake turned back to his opponent, Robbie, who began shuffling quickly across the ring as soon as Warren spoke. The kid grinned with arms clenched tight. Jake had a sneaking suspicion Robbie had no intention of going easy at all.

The first flurry of punches came hissing towards Jake and he was forced to slip, duck and jump backwards to keep from getting his head knocked off. The kid's punches were hard and looked like they carried all the power his towering body could generate. Jake pivoted smoothly out of his way, letting the bigger man's forward momentum carry him past, and poked him in the jaw with a sharp jab. The kid's head snapped sideways, almost losing his footing.

Jake allowed himself a smug, grin. Old, am I?

Robbie came forward again, with a little more caution this time, not so willing to get tagged. He threw a crisp combination of sharp, focused punches. Jake had to grudgingly admit that the kid was pretty good, but he was able to either block or avoid the shots. Jake came back with a few of his own, his hands getting through his opponent's guard, crashing into head and body. A hard overhand right slammed into Robbie's chin, and the big man staggered backwards to fall onto the ropes. When he regained his balance, his eyes were wide, the cockiness gone, replaced with a healthy dose of fear.

Jake pressed forward now, feinting and throwing jabs to soften up his opponent's guard. Robbie back-pedaled, his hands up high, trying to block Jake's punches, and he wasn't even making a vague pretense at an attack. Jake threw a series of soft punches at Robbie's face, drawing his guard up higher, then uncoiled his body and sunk a hard right hand into the middle of Robbie's solar plexus. The air whooshed out of the kid's lungs and his knees buckled. Robbie sagged to the canvas. He stayed there, on knees and elbows, head pressed into the ring mat, as he struggled to find the breath that had deserted him.

Jake turned from him and walked to his corner, then stopped when he saw the look on Warren Boyd's face.

"What?" Jake asked, his speech slightly distorted from his mouth guard.

"Where the fuck did that come from, Ross?"

Jake stuck one gloved hand under his arm and yanked it off, then pulled out his mouth guard. "What do you mean, Warren? Your kid ain't that good."

Warren leaned his elbows on the ropes and shook his head. "Oh, he's that good all right. Best I've trained in ten years. And you just beat the shit out of him in…" Warren looked down at the stop watch, "… Ninety-eight seconds."

Jake looked from Warren, to the kid on the mat still searching for his breath, then back to Warren.

"Jesus Christ, Ross. If you fought like that in some of your bouts you'd be back on your way up the chain. Hell, you'd be at the top of it."

Jake pulled off the other glove and his headgear, then walked over to where Robbie was still on hands and knees, sucking in great sobbing breaths. He bent down to help the bigger man to his feet.

"Come on, kid. You'll feel better if you stand up."

Slowly, with a great many painful groans, Robbie climbed back to his feet and looked at Jake with obvious respect.

"Thanks, Mr. Ross," Robbie gasped.

The title of 'mister' almost startled Jake, and he shook his head. "Just Jake, kid."

Robbie nodded. "Any chance you'd be able to work with me a little, Jake. Before my fight."

Again, Jake was startled. He'd been coming to this gym for years and any of the young guys stopped asking for his advice long ago. "Yeah, sure," he said with a grin. "I'd be happy to. I'll see you in here in a couple of days."

Robbie nodded, attempted to push a smile through his grimace, and turned to stagger towards the ropes.

Jake stepped to the edge of the ring, and Warren shuffled next to him.

"Are you on the juice, Ross?"

Jake looked at him, confused. "The what?"

"The juice. You know, steroids. Are you taking that shit?"

"What? Fuck, Warren. No, I'm not taking steroids."

"Humph," Warren said, as he struggled to get off the ring and back down to the floor. "A couple days ago you were slouching around the ring like a monkey humping a football, and now you're thumping the piss out of damned good fighters, fifty pounds heavier than you."

"I thought you said he only had me by twenty pounds."

"I lied like a sidewalk," Warren huffed, as he got back to the floor and stopped to catch his breath. "I'm gonna use you in that fight, still. But if they piss test you and you fail, you'll never fight with me again. You got me?"

Jake rolled his eyes. "Okay, Warren."

The fat man grunted and waddled towards his office.

Jake pulled off his sparring gear and unwrapped his hands, as he walked towards the locker room, following the bulk of the boxing promoter.

He went into the locker room, showered in the moldy stall , and quickly dressed. As he washed and dressed, his mind churned and reeled over the events of the past hour. The ability with which he fought, the rediscovered endurance and speed he thought had been left behind with his youth. Was this part of the "gifts" Mac had talked about?

When he left the locker room, Jake was determined to make his way back down to Morgan's house to put some more questions to the man and see if he could pry out some answers. Thoughts of answers were cast aside, as Jake stepped into the wide space of the gym and saw a familiar figure standing in the door to Warren's office.

Jake ducked back into the locker room on instinct, hoping he hadn't been seen, and peered around the corner. In heated discussion with the fat promoter was the shorter of the two thugs he'd fought only days before; the man who had killed him.

The thug was talking animatedly, his hands waving about in apparent anger. Warren sat and gave him a bored look, thick arms folded across his bulging gut. Eventually, the thug threw up his hands in exasperation, yelled several colourful threats at Warren, and stormed out the door. When he was sure the thug was gone, Jake stepped into Warren's office.

"What the fuck was that all about?" he asked.

Warren jabbed at his calculator again. "Some dip shit who thinks he's somebody, pointing his finger at me and whining. Wants him and his 'crew'," Warren made quotation marks in the air with his fingers, "to be allowed to train here for free. Says it'd be in my best interest to do as he asks. I told him it'd be in his best interest to go fuck himself. He didn't like that so much."

"So, who is he?" Jake looked out the office door, towards the entrance of the gym.

Warren shrugged. "Gang member, I guess. Or at least thinks he's a gang member. Call themselves the Surrey Soldiers. Stupidest name I ever heard. I was in the fucking army, and we didn't have any assholes looked like that."

"You know his name?"

"I called him 'fuck face' a couple of times. He seemed to respond to that."

Jake shook his head and laughed. "Okay, Warren. I'll see you at the fight."

Warren grunted in farewell and glared at his calculator.

Jake trotted towards the exit, wondering if the thug would still be there. If he could, Jake would lay hold of the murderous prick and see if he could beat the guy into answering a few of the numerous questions Jake wasn't accustomed to asking. The blonde girl from the parkade, Veronica by her stripper name, had said something about 'your boss' when she'd been screeching at Jake the night before. If he could figure out the identity of the 'boss' the thugs worked for, he might find the answers to a couple of his questions.

When he reached the door, Jake opened it slowly and looked out. The thug, his murderer, stood smoking a cigarette beside a black, run down, shit box Honda Accord. In the driver's seat of the Honda sat the bigger thug. Both of them showed evidence of the fight they'd had with Jake in the missing teeth and purple bruises marking their faces.

Jake tossed his gym bag onto a bench just inside the gym, slipped out the door and behind a rusted pickup truck to watch them. He didn't dare approach them where they were now. It was too open and he'd have no chance at surprise. They'd most likely run once they saw him, realising he wasn't dead. He couldn't risk losing them.

After a few minutes, the smaller thug threw his half-finished cigarette on the ground and climbed into the passenger seat of the Honda. Jake desperately looked around for a means to follow them, because he sure as shit couldn't run after them through traffic.

As his head swivelled, he caught sight of a yellow beacon of hope; a taxi, the driver talking on his cellular phone, parked by the curb in front of the gym. Jake trotted over to the cab, pulled open the back door and tumbled in.

"Follow that car," Jake said and pointed behind him, at the Honda, now pulling away from the curb.

The taxi-driver, an East Indian man in his mid-forties, sighed in an exasperated fashion. "Hang on," he said into the phone in a clear British accent, "I got some asshole in my cab, thinks he's James Bond." The driver turned and fixed him with a scowl. "Look, mate, you see the little light on the top of the car? It's off. I'm not bloody working. Now, fuck off." He lifted the phone back to his ear and resumed his conversation. "So, like I was saying before this mad fuck got in my cab..."

Jake looked around desperately while the rusted-out Honda neared the end of the street. He lifted his ass off the car seat and dug into his hip pocket where he'd stuffed three of the bills from Morgan's envelope. With gritted teeth, he pulled one of the bills free and held it over the taxi driver's shoulder. "Here, this'll get us started. And," Jake pulled in a pained, hissing breath, like he'd just hit his thumb with a hammer, "another one like it when we get where we're going."

The driver studied the bill for a moment, then, at the phone. "I'll have to call you back." He dropped his phone into the empty seat beside him and plucked the bill deftly from Jake's fingers. "You're the boss, my friend. Where're we going?"

"That Honda," Jake pointed down the street behind him where the black car was disappearing around the corner and into traffic. "Follow it."

The taxi driver looked in his side mirror, nodded once, dropped his car into gear, made a smooth u-turn and accelerated sharply down the street. Once at the corner, he checked both directions and pulled quickly into the flow of traffic. A couple of quick lane changes and there was only one car separating them and the black Honda.

"You a cop?"

Jake, peering intently at the Honda, wasn't paying attention. "Uh, what?"

The driver made eye contact with Jake in the rear-view mirror. "Are you a cop? A flat foot? The fuzz?"

"No, I'm not a cop."

"Then what you want with that car so bad?"

Jake shrugged. "I need to talk to the guys driving it."

The driver nodded and focused on the road.

They drove in silence for several minutes, following the black Honda through the Surrey traffic, working their way from the industrial flats up into the city centre.

"You a fighter?" the driver asked.

Again, Jake wasn't paying attention. "What?"

"You a fighter? You come out of the Tartan, didn't you?"

"Oh, right. Yeah, I'm a fighter."

"You any good?"

Jake looked intently at the Honda, now two cars in front of them. "We're gonna find out."

The driver nodded again and looked back to the road.

They twisted and turned down several streets. The taxi driver followed skillfully, always keeping them in sight, but never getting too close.

"You're good at this," Jake said.

The taxi-driver nodded. "I used to do it for a living. I was a cop, a detective, on the New Delhi police force. If you can tail a car through that kind of traffic, you can follow anyone any-where."

Jake grunted. "I've never met a brown guy with a British accent before."

The taxi driver smiled. "My mum was born in London and had an arranged marriage with my dad. I grew up in the UK and then went to India with my Dad's family when I was done school. I ended up staying. When the police force found out I could speak English, they hired me without an interview."

"Then what the fuck are you doing driving a cab."

The driver shrugged. "It's the only job I could get here. Well this, or working in a 7-11."

Jake laughed, and the driver grinned.

"Those blokes in the car ahead, what you want to talk to them about?"

Jake thought for a moment, wondering how much he should tell a well-educated ex-policeman who he'd paid to chase down a car. "I gotta ask 'em about a girl."

"Judging by the look on your face, those'll be some hard questions."

Jake nodded once. "Yeah. You might not wanna be around when they get asked."

The black Honda pulled onto 108th Avenue and then into a side street not far from the Whalley strip area. The old Honda pulled over to the curb next to one of the new office high rises that had been popping up in the area like shiny black pimples. Jake saw the reverse lights flash briefly, as the driver put the car into park. The taxi driver pulled the cab over, several parked cars away, and Jake watched the Honda. After a few moments, the two thugs got out and began walking down the sidewalk, away from the front doors of the new building.

"I think this'll do, man. Thanks." Jake reached into his pock-et and pulled out another hundred. It killed him to hold it out to the driver. But, despite being a cheap bastard, Jake Ross was a man of his word.

The taxi driver eyed the bill a moment. "This girl you're asking about. These guys hurt her?"

"They tried," Jake said, still holding out the bill.

"You stop 'em?"

Jake looked at the driver in the rear view mirror and nodded. The driver rubbed his stubbled chin and nodded. "Keep it," he said finally. "Consider it a contribution towards the questions you have to ask."

Jake held out the bill a moment longer, waiting for the man to change his mind, fervently hoping he wouldn't.

The driver turned in his seat and looked Jake full in the face. "Go ahead, mate. One good guy to another."

Jake smiled, clapped the man on the shoulder, and slipped out of the cab. Maybe not every person he'd ever meet for the rest of his life was going to be an asshole.

He trotted over to the edge of the building and tried to act inconspicuous. He'd never actually tried to follow anyone without being seen before, and he wasn't entirely sure what he should do. The guys in the movies always hid in doorways while they 'tailed' someone, so he figured he'd give it a try.

He ducked into the doorway of a store front, peered around the brick framing and down the street, watching the two thugs as they walked towards the end of the massive building. He waited, hiding in the doorway, trying to see where they would go.

The door beside Jake opened and slammed into his ass. Jake stood upright and looked through the glass door at a young woman trying to force a stroller through the door Jake blocked.

"You mind getting out of the way?" she asked, exasperated.

Jake sighed. This never happened in the movies. He stepped away from the entrance, exposing himself to the street, and held the door open so the woman could push her stroller through.

"Jackass," she said, as she walked by and fixed him with a glare.

When she was past, Jake let the door go and looked down the street. The two thugs had reached an alley leading behind the building and started down it. They still hadn't noticed him.

He ran after them, his coat flapping beneath his arms, as his heavy work boots slapped the sidewalk. Several steps from the alley he slowed to a cautious walk, then leaned to the side to look carefully around the corner.

The two thugs, heading down the alley, came to a stop and stood on either side of a steel door in the building. The smaller of the two pressed a white button on the wall, presumably a door-bell, and they waited. Jake ducked back behind the wall, as the bigger thug looked up and down the alley with exaggerated care. When Jake looked back, the steel door opened. The two thugs had company.

The man who joined them wasn't the biggest man Jake had ever seen, but he was up there. His shoulders filled the black leather jacket he wore and he stood inches taller than the bigger of the two thugs. His bare scalp—bent towards the two thugs while he looked to be giving them instructions—was spider-webbed in black tattoos and what looked like a black star-burst surrounded his left eye. The newcomer's big hands made small, efficient gestures as he spoke, and the two thugs nodded in apparent understanding. They were too far away for Jake to hear the conversation clearly, but it looked like the tattooed man said 'the girl' several times.

"And the Lord will keep us all to His bosom, so long as we repent."

The voice behind him made Jake turn. He saw a man dressed in filthy jeans and what appeared to be a long, ragged lab coat. The man walked up and down the sidewalk, his finger stabbed into the centre of an upside-down Sears catalogue as though he were a Pentecostal minister giving a sermon to his flock. Jake knew the man; a fixture in the Whalley area since Jake was a teenager. He didn't know the man's name, but everyone called him the Preacher.

The Preacher studied the catalogue as though he were reading from it. Jake could see it was open to the camping section. "And the Lord said unto me, go forth and tell the people of this land what assholes they are, so that they might give up their ways of foolery, fornication, fuckery, and know Me better."

The Preacher's sermons seldom made any sense, and were never polite.

Jake turned away from the homeless man and gazed back down the alley. The two thugs were still nodding. As the big man in the leather jacket spoke, he reached into his pocket and pulled out a white envelope. The smaller of the two thugs took the envelope with what appeared to be cautious reverence and slipped it into the inner pocket of his ridiculous, sequined jacket.

A cluster of people came up the sidewalk and, to avoid looking too suspicious, Jake turned from his post at the mouth of the alley and leaned against the building, hands in his pockets. He glanced up and down the sidewalk and tried to look like he was waiting for someone. How that was managed, he wasn't quite sure, but he gave it his best shot.

Several more people filed past Jake, presumably coming from the Sky Train station, making their way to whichever destination called them that day. The stream was steady and Jake did his best to look casual, studying the tops of his boots as the people passed him and dodged around the Preacher, who shouted random insults at them as he gestured with his catalogue.

"I see before me a man of the fates. A sinner in need of a good, honest beating. A lost sheep that needs to be sheared and its wool turned into a stout cord to be promptly used to deliver the aforementioned beating."

As the Preacher's semi-religious proclamations reached his ears, Jake looked up to discover, to his great horror, that the filthy man stood a few feet from him, a dirty finger pointed at him accusingly while his other hand held aloft his Sears catalogue.

"You, my son, are in need of guidance. Guidance I will happily provide!"

"What?" Jake said, incredulity bending his voice, any pretense of stealth forgotten. "Get the fuck away from me."

"Now is not the time for refusal. Now is the time for repentance. You will learn the ways of the fates and their trickery. You will learn now before it's too late."

"I don't want to learn anything, you crazy bastard," Jake said, waving at the man as though he were a wasp at a barbecue. "Go away."

The Preacher stepped closer to Jake, his accusing finger rigid and pointing. He was still five steps away, but Jake could smell the reek of his unwashed body and filthy clothes, causing bile to climb up his throat.

"Repent of your foolishness, I say. Take off your blind-fold and see the truth, you silly fucker. Release it. Be rid of it. Repent!"

Several people passed between Jake and the Preacher, all of

them looking at the boxer with a combination of pity and amusement. Jake realised the situation would be funny if it weren't happening to him.

The sound of footsteps, barely heard over the preacher's ranting, brought Jake's attention to the mouth of the alley, his heart leaping in his chest. He'd been so busy trying not to look obvious, and then being yelled at by the homeless man, that he'd forgotten to watch the two thugs and their new friend. As Jake looked over, his murderers stepped out of the alley and onto the sidewalk.

Jake was about turn away to try and blend into the crowd, when the Preacher dropped his Sears catalogue and lunged forward with uncanny speed. The homeless man closed the distance between them before the catalogue hit the ground and grabbed the back of Jake's head. The Preacher gave a sharp pull and Jake found himself on one knee in front of him, head bowed as though in prayer. The Preacher stood close to him, his filthy lab coat flapping about Jake's head, covering his face. The stink of the man almost caused Jake to puke on the Preacher's worn out running shoes, but he managed to keep his last meal down and kept his eyes on the ground.

"Yes, my dear sheep of below average intelligence," the Preacher shouted, "kneel before your glorious and ridiculously handsome shepherd, and repent your sins of imbecility and ignorance."

Below the hem of the Preacher's coat, Jake could see the shiny gym shoes of the two thugs stop, and he heard mean-spirited laughter. "Look at these two fucking freaks," one of them said. Jake thought it was the smaller of the two, by the sneer in his voice. "Why don't you give him a blow job while you're down there?" The bigger thug laughed, and the shiny shoes moved away down the side walk.

Jake stayed on his knee for several more moments, holding his breath while the Preacher's voice rang ridiculous in his ears.

"And so the lost goat, for he is too stupid to be counted a sheep, receives his guidance." The filthy hand released Jake's head. "Rise, my bleating goat. Rise like a new man to face the world. Rise and see the fates for what they are. Know they are no longer honest. Know they have been bent around you."

Jake stood and looked down the sidewalk. The two thugs were lost in the throng of people, but at least they hadn't seen him. He had the advantage of them thinking he was dead, but he almost gave that advantage up by being stupid and exposing himself. He looked the Preacher up and down. The reeking vagrant had actually helped him.

That didn't mean, of course, Jake had any idea what he was talking about.

Jake rubbed at the back of his head, where he imagined there might be a large dirty hand print. "Uh, thanks," he said. "I think."

The Preacher smiled broadly, and stooped to snatch his catalogue off the ground, the wrinkled pages rustling stiffly. "We men of the fates must stick together, my tender goat. Someone must keep them honest."

Jake shook his head, as he rubbed at his short hair. "Yeah, okay. Whatever you say, man."

Again, with that same uncanny speed, the Preacher moved up to Jake and grabbed the lapel of his coat, close enough so that he could count the pimples on the homeless man's face. Jake almost gagged again, as the stink of the man clogged his nostrils, his vision filled with yellowed teeth and greasy hair.

"No, goat," the Preacher said, his voice low and clear, his eyes focused on Jake's face. "It is not whatever I say. It is whatever the Fates say. But they've been tricked into making speeches they never planned. Keep your feeble wits about you."

The Preacher thrust Jake away from with enough force that Jake bounced off the stone wall. The filthy man lifted his catalogue high in the air and jabbed an accusing finger at a girl who rapidly typed on her cell phone. "And lo comes a fornicator! Making dirty words with her fingers on her shiny hand phone and sending them to boys. Sending them that they might read those lewd, filthy messages. Read them and touch themselves!"

Jake stared at the man, his mouth open. For a moment, he thought about dragging the Preacher into the alley and shaking him until he explained what in the blue fuck he was talking about and why he had helped Jake go unseen by the two thugs. Perhaps find out how the man knew Jake didn't want to be seen in the first place. He quickly discounted the idea. The moment of clarity in the Preacher disappeared. The focus with which he'd spat his last words into Jake's face had passed and he was a crazy bastard again.

The Preacher moved down the sidewalk, following a rotund man who ate a hot dog. "Before us we see another sinner, committing the cardinal sin of being a fat bastard! Likely is he to drop dead of being a fat piece of shit, only to make those of us who fill our bellies with nothing carry his fat ass to an apothecary. My back, children! My back fears this bovine fool already!" The rotund man dropped his hot dog on the ground and started to cry.

As the Preacher's voice began fading down the sidewalk, spreading abuse and bad advice as he went, Jake turned back to the mouth of the alley. It was deserted, the steel door closed and the man in the leather jacket gone. Jake walked cautiously down the alley, and stood where he'd seen the thugs. The featureless grey steel door had edges studded with heavy rivets and the bright steel doorknob had a heavy lock immediately above it. There were no markings on the door, and when Jake tried the knob it didn't budge, not even so much as a rattle.

As Jake examined the door, he looked up and noticed the camera mounted above it. He quickly turned his face away and cursed. So much for being sneaky and undetected.

He turned and headed back to the alley's entrance and stepped onto the sidewalk. He looked in both directions, unsure of where to go, and stuck his hands in the pockets of his ragged jeans. He could go back to the gym and collect his bag, but he wasn't particularly inclined to catch the bus to go down there. It felt like he would be going in the wrong direction. He could go home to his one bedroom shithole and sit around with his thumb in his ass; another idea he didn't find appealing.

Jake paused in his thoughts, tilting his chin towards the grey sky. Something tickled his mind from the interaction he'd witnessed between the two thugs and the large new-comer. It may have only been his overwrought imagination, but Jake thought he saw the big man say 'the girl', more than once. Jake couldn't read lips, and despite being a little faster today than he was yesterday, he hadn't actually developed super powers so there was no way he could have heard the conversation. It was entirely possible he'd only imagined 'seeing' the words come from the big man's mouth. But, it was also possible he'd imagined nothing.

Decision made, Jake turned in the same direction as the two thugs and walked towards the city centre.

CHAPTER SIX

everal hours later, Jake found himself standing in the dark, shivering his ass off, and wishing he'd thought harder about just going home. The neon lights of the Crimson Curtain's gaudy sign were starting to hurt his eyes. He was hungry, and he dumpster he hid behind while he watched the strip club must have been filled with some exceptionally putrid shit.

He sighed, then coughed up some of the stink, and wished for the hundredth time that he owned a watch. He rubbed his eyes and continued watching the front door, waiting for either Veronica Rains or the two thugs. Neither had materialized in the long hours he'd be standing in the dark.

"Enjoying the scenery, Jake?"

The voice, close to his ear, made Jake jump out of his skin as he whirled, fists raised instinctively.

"Holy fuck," Jake said, glaring at Oliver MacKinnon. "Don't you people ever come out during the day, or do you just prefer to harass the fuck out of me in the dark?"

Mac showed Jake his creased smile and shrugged in his denim coat. "It's a condition of our cause, Jake. Those who walk in the dark come out at night. That's when we need to be about as well."

Jake turned away from Mac and folded his arms. "I suppose you talk like a character in an old pirate movie 'cause that's what the dark understands too, huh?"

The older man ignored the caustic comment and folded his own arms, while he took in the sight of the strip bar. "Why are we here, Jake? You come back to get some more popular culture?"

"I don't know why you keep saying 'we'. And how the hell did you know I'd be here."

Mac shrugged again. "I had a feeling."

Jake rolled his eyes. "How'd I know you were gonna say that?" The boxer took one hand from under his arm, made a fist and breathed warmth on it. "If you had a 'feeling', shouldn't it tell you why I'm here?"

"Don't quite work like that," Mac said, one finger coming up to scratch his leathery cheek. "I get feelings. They come when they're inclined and won't be called when they're not. I don't get to watch your entire life like a movie. If I did, I'd have to watch you dropping a shit in the morning, and no one needs to see that."

Jake grunted in agreement and continued to watch the front door of the building. Mac stood in silence for a few moments before clearing his throat. "In earnest, Jake, why are you here?"

Jake opened his mouth to make a smart-ass comment, and then closed it again. The truth was he didn't really know why he was here. The only thing that had him standing beside the reeking dumpster was a vague hunch based upon an imagined lip reading of instructions given to two men who'd already killed him. Instructions possibly concerning a girl whose life he'd saved, but seemed to have a good hate on for him and tried to have him beaten by a juiced-up bouncer. None of the circumstances that had brought him here made any sense at all, and so he didn't see any harm in sharing them with the man next to him. "Remember the two guys who killed me?"

Mac nodded.

"They were at my gym today, trying to intimidate the owner into letting them train for free. I followed them up to one of those new high rises by the sky train station and they met with a guy who might have said something about 'the girl'. I assumed they were talking about the girl they were attacking when I ran into them, so I came here."

"That girl," Mac said, his thin eyes narrowing further, "she's here?"

"Yeah. You didn't know that?"

"You never told me, Jake."

"Well, I figured you, with your funny feelings and all, would figure that shit out."

"I keep telling you, Jake, I'm not a bloody mind reader."

Jake shrugged and continued to watch the door.

"So you're here," Mac surmised, "because you think the two men you fought might go after that girl again?"

"No, I'm here 'cause I like the colour of the rats in this particular alley." Jake watched the other man's leathery face, hoping for some kind of reaction. Mac gave none and waited, stone-faced, for an answer. "Yes, Mac, I think they might come after her again."

"Hmmm… " Mac rubbed his chin.

"'Hmmm?'" Jake repeated. "What does that mean?"

"I didn't see this."

"Didn't see what?"

"I didn't see the girl having any significance. I thought she was merely your opportunity for your second chance and entrance to the clan. I didn't expect we'd see her again."

"Right. I'm still not sure why you keep saying 'we'."

Mac turned from Jake, taking long, thoughtful steps around the items of trash in the alley. "The man you saw your attackers talking to," Mac said, turning back to face Jake, "what did he look like?"

"I don't know," Jake answered, uncrossing his arms and sticking his hands in his pockets. "He was a big dude. Shaved head. Dumb looking tattoos on his face."

Mac scowled. "How big was he, Jake?"

"Fuck, I don't know. He was big. Bigger than me. Thick as a bastard, too, like one of those strongmen you see on TV."

Mac leaned toward Jake, his body rigid. "The tattoos on his face; was there a many-pointed star on his left eye?"

"Yeah. How'd you know?"

"Kast," Mac said with a grimace, clenching his fists.

"Cast what?"

Mac shook his head. "No, the man you saw, I think it's someone we know. A servant of the dark called Kast. Taber was a puppy in comparison."

Jake thought of the massive man who'd been chanting over the child the night before and had a hard time imagining someone who might be worse.

"So," Jake said, "what about this guy?"

"He's bad, Jake. Bad on a level you've never known. And, if he is here, he won't be alone."

"Okay," Jake said slowly. "This Kast guy bring some friends with him?"

"Kast, as powerful as he is, is a minion. A bodyguard. He serves a man called Ethan Drake. And, as far as any of us knows, he is the leader of the dark."

"The leader?" Jake asked. "You mean, like the grand poobah? The big cheese?"

"The worst of the worst."

"Great." Jake said, crossing his arms again. "This day just keeps getting better."

"I must speak to Morgan about this." Mac turned towards the rear of the alley, where he'd come from. He stopped and turned back to Jake. "If you see Kast again, do not challenge him. He is too much for you. Don't even let yourself be seen. Go back to your home, and I will find you there."

"Yeah. Right."

"I'm not fooling, Jake." There was an edge in Mac's voice, almost pleading. "A meeting with Kast will be the end of you. Watch over this girl if you must, but if Kast comes for her, consider her lost." Mac turned and jogged down the alley, away from the club, disappearing in the wet murk.

Jake watched Mac go and then turned back to the building, a dismissive smirk on his face. Wasn't anything lost until the bell rang, and Jake didn't hear shit.

As he watched the front of the building, he sighed wearily. While he was more than game for a fight with this Kast guy, or anyone else who wanted to step up and try their luck, this waiting and doing fuck all wore on him. He seriously considered packing it in and going home, but something, down in the pit of his stomach, kept him rooted to the spot, like he needed to be there. So, he rubbed his eyes and continued to wait.

The night wore on and grew colder. Jake watched numerous patrons come and go from the small bar, most of them arriving sober and leaving drunk, several making their exit when the bouncer, Danny, showed them the way out by planting their faces on the dirty sidewalk. Jake kept well back from the mouth of the alley, away from the meager pockets of light from the street lamps and watched the foolishness with cold hands jammed into the pockets of his jeans.

Gradually, the flow of customers slowed and then stopped, and the last taxi parked at the curb, hopeful of a drunken fare, pulled away. The front door opened and Veronica Rains stepped onto the sidewalk.

Her long hair was loose about her shoulders and sat on the lapels of her black pea-coat. She looked up and down the street, her breath misting about her face and drifting up in the sparse, artificial light. Jake took a step back, further into the alley, to make sure he wasn't seen. He just wanted to see her safe, not start another confrontation. She looked up and down the street again, eyes carefully scanning. Once she appeared to be satisfied, she walked down the three concrete steps that led up to the door and turned to Jake's right. She stepped briskly down the sidewalk, the stiletto heels of her pointy shoes heralding her departure.

Jake waited several heartbeats before coming out of the alley to follow her. He stayed well back and on the other side of the street. Veronica looked around, checking over her shoulder, several times, but Jake kept his head down, his hands in his pockets, and was careful not to show any interest in her or her destination. He could almost feel her eyes stop on him the first time she looked back, but she turned forward again and kept walking. Her pace quickened and Jake let her pull ahead of him, only going fast enough to keep her in sight. Her head swivelled constantly, never resting, never looking to the ground, watching out for someone. She appeared to be scared.

She stayed on the street for several blocks and then turned onto a side street, into a low-income residential neighbourhood. Jake waited for several seconds before crossing the street, following her. She was well ahead of him now, but he kept track of her as the regularly spaced streetlamps shone off her bright hair as she passed under them. In those spaces, she looked like a golden haired specter, shifting away from him in pools of light.

It was well past midnight and there were very few cars out on the road, even in a city like Surrey, and even fewer in these small residential neighbourhoods. So, when Jake saw distant headlights reflected in the rear view mirror of the parked car he was passing, he ducked behind a tree and waited, a tingling sense in the back of his head lending him warning.

After a few moments, the headlights came even to where Jake hid, and then passed, moving slowly. He felt a hot bloom of adrenaline when he saw the familiar shape of the run-down Honda roll down the street towards where Veronica passed under another street light.

The driver of the Honda must have seen her, because he accelerated, the dilapidated car churning forward and screeching feebly. The noise from the engine caused the stripper to turn and look back. When she saw the car chugging towards her, she broke into a run, her shoes clicking rapidly on the wet concrete. As she started running, so did Jake.

The Honda passed and then swerved in front of her, front tires bouncing up onto the sidewalk. The two miscreants, still dressed in their ridiculous, sequined jackets, scrambled out of the car and charged at her. Veronica tried to change the direction of her flight, but she stumbled in her high heels and the two thugs were on top of her before she could regain her balance.

"Where you going?" the smaller of the two said, his words distorted by the fat, broken lips Jake had left him. "You think you're gonna get away again, bitch? Get in the fucking car."

He grabbed a handful of her pale hair and yanked her head sideways, as the bigger man grabbed her around the body. Veronica let out a scream of pain, and kicked and thrashed as much as she could in the big thug's crushing embrace.

"No one is gonna save you now, cunt," Shorty said, apparently enjoying the sound of his own voice and ridiculous commentary. "I took care of that motherfucker from the other night. He can't help you—

"What the fuck?" The man ceased his yapping, as he looked up, wide eyed shock painted on his face.

Jake lost sight of Shorty's shocked expression, as he drove his fist into the same mouth he'd recently bashed. The boxer took pleasure in the pained cry loosed by the thug, as he felt teeth give way and the man crashed to the ground.

The bigger man also wore a surprised expression. He stood straight, the thrashing stripper still locked in his grip, and gaped at Jake. "You're dead."

"And you're an asshole," Jake replied, as he lunged at the bigger man and drove a calloused thumb into his eye.

The big man reeled backwards, twisting his face away from Jake's gouging thumb, releasing his grip on Veronica, who tumbled heavily to the sidewalk. The boxer pursued his unbalanced foe and pummeled him with punches, driving the big man to the ground, kicking him in the torso to keep him down.

Jake whirled to see Shorty getting to his feet and reaching into his coat. Jake kicked the smaller man in the ribs as hard as he could with his heavy work boot. The air rushed out of the thug with a choked grunt. He collapsed to the ground again. Jake hauled him up by the back of his stupid jacket and rammed his head into the side of the old Honda. Jake let go and the man slid bonelessly into the space between the Honda and the curb.

Jake looked over at Veronica, who gaped up at him from the ground, fear warring with surprise on her face. He took a step towards her and she winced and held up her hands defensively, like she was expecting to be struck. Jake knelt beside her and took her scraped hands into his, and waited for her to open her eyes and look at him.

"Are you all right?" he asked.

She nodded, her blond hair shimmering around her face.

"Can you stand?"

She nodded again, and Jake grasped her under the arms to pull her to her feet. The bigger man tried to get up as well, but Jake kicked him in the side of the head with the toe of his boot and he slumped down again.

"You're not with them, are you?" Veronica asked, looking up at Jake.

"No. I'm not."

"Were you following me?"

Jake nodded. "I was. I thought these two fucks might try something again, and wanted to keep you safe."

She shook her head. "Why? I don't even know you."

Jake frowned. "I have no idea, to tell you the truth. This guy I know would say it's the will of the Fates."

"The what?"

He shook his head. "Never mind. Can you make it home from here?"

She nodded.

"Okay. Go where you need to go and meet me at your bar tomorrow night, okay? I wanna talk to you about these two assholes." He looked down at the two groaning men. "Right now, they're gonna answer some goddamned questions."

She didn't say anything, but looked up at him, tears gathering in her eyes. Jake didn't know if she was starting to cry from relief, gratitude, or anything else, but it made her blue eyes look even bigger. His breath caught in his chest.

"Get out of here," he said, his voice thick. "I'll talk to you tomorrow."

She nodded once more and turned down the sidewalk, her blonde hair waving behind her.

Jake watched her go, shining in the street lights.

A groan caused Jake to turn and look down. The smaller of the two miscreants stirred, trying to get his hands underneath his shoulders and moaning in obvious pain. Jake reached down, grasping the man's shoulder, and flipped him onto his back. Jake rifled through his pockets, checking to see what he'd been reaching for and found a small gun—a silver revolver—tucked into the waist of his pants.

"Stabbing me last time wasn't good enough? You gonna shoot me now?" Jake thumbed the released to the cylinder and dumped the cartridges into his palm. He tossed the bullets into the shrubs of a nearby house and snapped the cylinder shut.

Jake stood for several breaths, looking down at the thug who rocked side to side on his back, moaning. Jake tapped the revolver against his leg and thought very carefully about what he should do next. Questions needed answering and this piece of shit at his feet would likely have a thing or two to say, but getting him to say those things might prove a little difficult. Jake wasn't sure if he was up to kind of asking that might be necessary.

The memory of the girl, Veronica, screaming in pain and fear under the hand of this man, more than once, turned a page in Jake's mind.

"Okay, asshole, get up." Jake reached down with one meaty hand and hauled the smaller man upwards, tossing him bodily over the hood of the car. He lay there, still moaning, with his face pressed against the metal of the hood and blood pooling around his mouth. Jake grabbed the man's wrist and stretched the arm out across the hood. Jake pinned the hand in place with his own arm and leaned his weight onto the thug so he couldn't get up.

"Why are you after that girl?" Jake asked.

"Go fuck yourself," the bleeding man replied.

Jake grimaced. He flipped the revolver around in his hand so he held the barrel and cylinder, the handle protruding from the top of his fist.

"I'm only gonna ask you once more. Why are you after that girl?"

"I ain't afraid of you, you piece of— "

The insult broke off into a scream of agony, his body going rigid with shock, as Jake smashed the butt of the revolver down on the centre of his hand. The scream carried on in the still air and eventually trailed off into a sob.

"My hand! My hand! You broke my fucking hand. I'm gonna kill you, you mother—" The smaller man screamed again as Jake smashed his hand with the gun once more.

"Again, why are you after that girl?"

"I don't know," he said between great, shuddering breaths. "This guy, he hired us. Said he needed to talk to her, but she wouldn't come. We were just supposed to bring her to him."

"Why didn't he just do it himself?" Jake asked. "Why did he need you?"

"I don't know. He just said he wanted to talk to her."

Jake could feel the lie in the man's voice, a live thing in the air. He gripped the man's hand in his fist, squeezing it so that the thug cried out in pain, but also so the index finger stuck out by itself on the hood of the car. Jake gritted his teeth, his stomach churning, as he hit the digit with the gun. There was a wet popping sound and blood squirted across the dull metal.

"Okay!" the man screamed. "Okay. He said he couldn't be seen. Didn't want anyone to know he wanted the girl. Said he wanted to insulate himself."

"Where were you supposed to take her?"

Shorty struggled for breath, sounding like he was trying not to vomit, his words a gurgling slur. "That new building. The high rise. By the sky train station."

"This guy who wants her, who is he?"

"I never met him before a couple days ago. Big fucker, lots of tattoos. Told us to call him Kast."

Jake nodded, remembering the man he'd seen the thugs talking to earlier in the day, as well as Mac's warning.

"Okay. So, what's he want her for?" Jake asked, as he straightened out the thug's middle finger on the hood of the car.

"I don't know."

Jake gagged, his throat spasming and bile surging up from his stomach, as the gun cracked against the finger. It took several seconds for the screams to stop.

"What does he want her for?" Jake asked again, struggling to keep his voice even, doing his best to insert menace.

"I swear, man! I swear I don't know. He just gave us each a thousand bucks to bring her to him. It was good money, so I didn't ask questions."

This time Jake believed him and let him go. The thug slithered off the hood and fell to a heap on the asphalt, clutching his ruined hand to his chest.

Jake heard sirens in the distance. He looked around. Several of the houses now had lights on. The small man's screams must have woken the neighbours and they called the police.

Jake crouched down and yanked the smaller thug's face up to his. "You listen to me and listen careful. If I ever see you near that girl again, I'll fucking kill you. Do you understand?"

Shorty nodded, his eyes wide and rolling like a frightened horse. Jake thrust him back to the ground.

Jake stood and checked his surroundings. The sirens only seemed to be coming from one direction. He wiped the gun off with the bottom of his shirt, He had no idea if that would actually make a difference, but he didn't want the cops getting his fingerprints off the gun and coming to ask him questions later, and dropped the revolver on the concrete beside the thug. He looked around once more to see if anyone was watching him and fled down the street, away from the pools of light.

CHAPTER SEVEN

Jake walked through the front door of his small apartment and stopped, the skin on the back of his neck prickling and his heart lurching with a surge of adrenaline. There was a light on in his kitchen and another in the living room. He hadn't left them on. He was always very careful about turning things off; electricity was damned expensive. He slowly shut his door, turning the knob and easing it into place to minimize the sound, and then stalked down the hallway into the kitchen. He gripped his keys between his fingers, so they stuck out like claws, and readied himself for the scrap he was about to get into.

He relaxed when he realised the light came from the open fridge, the contents of which were busily being rummaged through. Jake couldn't see the intruder, concealed by the open door, but he 'had a feeling' who it was.

"I didn't buy any more beer for you to drink, Mac," Jake said.

"I don't drink beer," Isabelle said as she stood up from behind the door and turned to look at him. "And if I did, I certainly wouldn't drink the piss you buy."

Jake took a step back, surprised to see the black haired

woman. "What the fuck? What are you doing here?"

"She came with me," a voice said from the tiny living room.

Jake turned to see Morgan, an open book on his lap, sitting on Jake's threadbare couch beside the small floor lamp Jake had dug out of the dumpster behind his building.

A flushing sound from the bathroom made Jake turn again. Mac walked out, wiping his hands on a small towel. He smiled wide, the lines from the corners of his mouth traveling up to infect his eyes, and nodded. "Hi, Jake. I hate to tell you, but you are now out of toilet paper."

"Well, the gang's all here," Jake said, ire in his voice. "If I'd known you were coming, I'd have laid out some finger sandwiches."

"That's a lie," Isabelle said, holding up a jar. "All you have in here is pickled herring and some expired ketchup."

Jake sighed, exasperated. "How'd you get in here? I don't recall having a key cut."

Isabelle put the jar back and closed the fridge door. "That lock you have is shit. I picked it with a paper-clip."

"Great, my lock sucks. Duly noted." Jake looked over at Morgan. "Now what the fuck do you people want?"

"This is some interesting reading, Jake," Morgan said, holding up a weathered copy of 'Man's Search For Meaning', by Viktor Frankl "for a man who drives a forklift and punches people for a living."

"We can start a book club if you want," Jake said, dropping his keys on the kitchen counter. "Is there something I can do for you, or did you just come to comment on my library."

Isabelle snorted as she walked past Jake's bookshelf. "A handful of dog-eared paperbacks hardly counts as a 'library'." She cocked out one hip and ran a finger over a row of books, then rubbed her fingers together as she looked at them distastefully.

Jake pulled his coat off, gritting his teeth to keep from shouting in frustration, and threw it over the back of one of his two kitchen chairs. "We can't all afford mahogany bookshelves and overstuffed chairs." Jake folded his arms and did his best to look obstinate. "Let me ask again; what do you want?"

Morgan closed the old book. "Mac brought us some

interesting news, Jake." He put the book down on the coffee table and stood up, grinning. "I understand you've met Kast."

Jake shrugged. "I saw him, I guess."

"Where did you see him."

"That new high rise, by the sky-train."

"Hmmm… And what was he doing?"

Jake felt his mouth open to answer the man's questions, and then he shook his head and closed it. He was angry, wasn't he? Why would he answer this asshole's questions when he was so pissed off? It was like the guy's grin made him forget he was angry.

"Why does it matter?" Jake asked, trying his best to sound furious, but it came out sounding petulant.

"It matters a great deal, Jake," Morgan said, reasonably. "He is a powerful enemy of our clan, and we need to know what he is doing in our city."

"Here you go with this 'we' shit again," Jake said, forcing anger into his voice. "There is no 'we', and I don't give a fiddlers fuck about your 'clan'."

Morgan stepped forward and placed his hand on Jake's arm. Jake glowered down at the man, who was significantly shorter, but found his glower fading to match the friendly smile Morgan gave him. The bearded man's hand was also exceptionally warm, comforting even. It made Jake think of a favorite uncle, if all his uncles weren't assholes, or what it might be like to have a well-respected mentor.

"You do care about the clan, Jake," Morgan said, his hand moving up Jake's arm to rest on his shoulder. "We're your family now. And we need to know what you saw."

Jake felt himself nod agreeably and start to answer Morgan. Then he remembered he wanted to be a prick and was working very hard to be unreasonable.

Jake took a step back and shook his head. When he looked back at Morgan, the smaller man's brow was drawn together, like a father whose wayward son would not listen to reason.

"Jake," Mac said, stepping out of the bathroom door and closer to the boxer. "Just tell him what you saw."

Looking back at the bearded man, whose reasonable grin was again fixed on his face, all trace of annoyance gone, Jake shrugged. Mac would have relayed the story to Morgan already, so there wouldn't be any particular harm in telling him. Quickly, Jake re-told the story.

As Jake spoke, Morgan nodded and ran his long and delicate fingers through his neat beard.

"And what happened after Mac left you tonight, Jake?" Morgan asked, when Jake was done.

"I was right," Jake said, allowing himself a triumphant smirk. "The two assholes I saw talking to this dude you're so interested in went after the girl once she left the bar."

Morgan clasped his hands in front of him and waited a few moments before saying, "And…?"

"And I stopped them," Jake said, casting another smirk at Mac. "I don't think they'll be bothering the girl again."

Morgan nodded. "Well done, Jake. And the girl? What happened with her?"

Jake shrugged. "I told her to take off, that I'd deal with the two piss-ants that were harassing her."

"Yes?" Morgan asked. "And where did she go?"

Jake was about to tell Morgan he didn't know, but he'd be meeting up with her tomorrow, but something stopped him. It might have been petty and childish, but Jake felt more secure having information Morgan didn't; like he was holding back a fight-ending punch his opponent wouldn't see coming. This whole ordeal seemed like a big game, one Jake didn't know the rules to, and having even this little tidbit made Jake feel like the field was just a little more even.

"I don't know," Jake said after a moment's hesitation.

"Will you see her again?"

"I doubt it. She's just some girl, after all."

Morgan's eyes narrowed subtly, like he could read the lie in Jake's voice. "Hmmm… she's probably unimportant," Morgan said, his mouth quirking up at one corner after examining Jake's face. "Still, it would be nice to know why Kast is interested in her." He turned away, tapping his chin in thought, and then turned on his heel to face Jake again. "The two attackers, did they say anything."

Jake swallowed, his throat feeling thick, remembering the sound of the thug's fingers popping beneath the butt of the revolver. "I tried to ask him a few things, but he told me to fuck off," Jake lied.

Isabelle snorted from behind Morgan. "You're too soft, Ross. I'd have gotten some answers from him, I promise you."

"Yeah," Jake agreed, "but I wasn't willing to show him my tits."

Her blue eyes flashed and her top lip lifted in a snarl, as Isabelle reached to the small of her back. Morgan held up a hand and she ceased her reaching for the second time since Jake had known her, but her teeth stayed bared and she glared death at Jake.

"Really, Jake," Morgan said, shaking his head like a vaguely disappointed, exasperated parent. "We're only here to help you."

"I never asked for your help. And what have any of you done for me besides get me in a fight with a bunch of child murdering psychos?" Jake looked at Mac. "Or drink my beer?"

Morgan sighed, a sound that Jake found deeply satisfying. "All right, Jake. You still have the card I gave you? And the money?"

If the guy was trying to lay a guilt trip on Jake, he'd picked the wrong target. "Yes, I have the money, and I earned every cent when I went into that shit-hole house with Mac. The card... I think I used it to wipe my ass." He looked at Mac again. "Since, apparently, I'm out of toilet paper."

Morgan sighed again and reached into the interior pocket of his finely cut leather coat. He produced another card and slid it onto the kitchen counter, beside Jake's keys. "Here's another one, in case you need to call."

"Won't do any good," Jake said, folding his arms and leaning against the wall beside the fridge. "I don't have a phone."

Morgan looked around, brow furrowed as he checked the counter and the walls for evidence of a phone, and found none. He shook his head again. "Okay, Jake. We'll be by to see you soon."

"Yeah," Jake sniffed. "Don't strain yourself."

Jake did his best to look disinterested, as Morgan walked past him towards the door. Isabelle glared at him, blue eyes narrow, as she walked by, and Mac gave him a friendly slap on the arm and his creased grin. When the door closed behind them, Jake turned the deadbolt and looked out the peephole to make sure they were gone. Then he got a chair from the kitchen and wedged it underneath the doorknob and checked the peephole once more.

He went back into the kitchen and opened the fridge. Isabelle hadn't lied when she said there wasn't anything besides some pickled herring and ketchup. Jake shrugged, pulled out the jar of herring, and twisted the lid off.

There was something about Morgan Jake didn't like, he thought as he pulled out a piece of fish and stuck it in his mouth. Morgan had been all right and hadn't done Jake any harm that he could notice, but he did not like the way he'd been steered in directions he never planned on going, only to find he couldn't turn around even if he wanted to. Morgan might not be full of shit when he said he wanted to help, but he'd slid Jake into place as smooth as any old guy playing chess down at the park.

These people, this 'clan', claimed they were the good guys. Jake had witnessed Mac's intervention in saving the child from the house down in the Flats, but what other altruistic acts had he seen? If not for Jake, would Mac have let the two thugs molest Veronica in the parkade the night Jake was killed? Would the wrinkled man have stood by while they did the same an hour ago in the lonely street? How good were these people, really?

Jake reached into the jar and found it empty, the last piece consumed as he thought. He put the empty jar in the sink and looked at the clock on the stove. It was nearly five o'clock in the morning, the night lost in violence and thought. He sighed wearily and slouched towards his bed. He'd best get some sleep because he had a funny feeling the coming night would be interesting.

Jake stood in the damp night, eating a street-vendor hotdog, as he waited in his favorite alley across the street from the Crimson Curtain. He'd stood there long enough, he decided, that he should name the giant rat living behind the dumpster at the mouth of alley. Murray would be a good name, but he would have to give it a while and see if it stuck.

Murray, an uncommonly huge rodent that might pass for an underfed German Shepherd, made an appearance from under the dumpster and stood on his hind legs a few feet from Jake, fearlessly regarding the boxer. Jake took the last inch of his hot dog and tossed it towards the rat.

"Yeah," Jake said, still chewing. "I know you were here first. Consider this down payment on this month's rent."

The rat picked up the end of the hotdog, sniffed it appraisingly, and then disappeared behind the dumpster. Jake watched him go, wishing for a moment he'd stayed around a little longer. This whole watching strip bars thing was lonely work.

"And so a wayward goat keeps a lonely vigil, doing his duty in the dark."

The voice behind him, almost in his ear, made Jake jump. As he spun to face the voice's owner, he made a mental note to get his hearing checked. He dropped his fists, as he looked at the man behind him.

"What the fuck is it with people sneaking up on me in this alley?" Jake said to the filthy Preacher, the smell of the man reaching him even through the stench from the dumpsters.

"Goats have terrible hearing," the homeless man said with his fists on his hips, holding back his lab coat like an old west gunslinger. "Especially the ones who are uncommonly foolish."

"Yeah, yeah," Jake said, turning back to watch the strip bar. "Whatever. Fuck off."

"Hmmm…" the Preacher said in response.

Jake stood for several heartbeats, trying to ignore the man, but his curiosity and ire got the better of him. "Okay, what the fuck does 'hmmmm' mean?"

"It has several meanings, my little bleating friend. In this case, it is an indication that I am wondering why you are standing here in here this alley, giving away food to rats who obviously eat better than you do. Even the good Lord cannot show me the way to your redemption, when idiocy so clouds your actions."

"What the fuck are you on about?" Jake asked, arms still crossed, while he turned to glare at the man.

The Preacher clicked his tongue. "Tisk, tisk, goat. Such foul language does not befit a guardian of the city."

The phrase made the angry retort he'd been planning stop on Jake's tongue. "What do you mean, 'guardian'?"

The Preacher threw back his head and laughed, deep from his belly. "It is written on you as plain as the stupid expression on your face, Goat. The gifts you've received are easy to see, if you know what to look for. Easy to spot in your kind."

"My kind?" Jake said, slowly, his arms uncrossing. "What do you know about my kind?"

"Ah, the Lord giveth, and the Lord maketh you a moron." The Preacher rapped his filthy knuckles against Jake's forehead; a movement so swift that Jake didn't think to try and avoid it until after it was done. "You've received bounty, Goat. Bounty most can only dream of." The man stepped in close, his stench making Jake's newly-filled belly clench. "Remember, others have received similar, if not identical, bounty. You are not the only one walking under the good Lord's graces."

Several small pieces of thought began to click into place behind Jake's eyes. The Preacher, with his uncommon speed, his noiseless footsteps, his riddling comments, was like Jake: the recipient of a second chance, with all the freaky bullshit that came with it.

"You're one of them," Jake said, his eyes narrowing.

"'Them'? Which 'them', Goat? Is this a cosmic 'them'? Known only to the dear and glorious Lord, or did you have a more specific 'them' in mind?"

"That fucking 'clan'. You're with Morgan and his cronies."

The Preacher threw back his head and laughed again, his matted beard flapping with his mirth. "The good Lord does not bind me to any clan. He said unto me 'go forth and stop listening to bullshit,' and so forth I went, a man of my own means, with the good Lord guiding me to the riches I deserve."

"Riches, huh?" Jake snorted, looking the man up and down. "What riches might those be?"

"A goat such as yourself, so blind to the world around him, would not understand the Lord's bounty. So blind are you, Goat, ensnared by the evils of the common man, that you cannot even see a beauty among beauties, gliding towards us, like one of the good Lord's angels."

"What?" Jake turned, and looked up and down the street.

After a few heart beats, he heard the faint clicking of boot heels on the sidewalk and saw Veronica walk out of a side street and into the light cast by a street lamp. He turned back to the Preacher, to ask how he knew she was coming, but the man was well down the alley, scampering silently through the shadows, chasing Murray the rat, who still had a chunk of hot dog in his jaws.

Jake considered going after him, to ask what he knew about Morgan and the 'clan', and how he knew so much about the boxer himself, but he didn't know if the man would give a straight answer or just talk in biblical riddles all night. Veronica, however, who also had answers he wanted, was now walking into the bar. Jake figured a conversation with the stripper carried a higher likelihood of being productive, and was more urgent.

Veronica bounced up the three steps to the front door of the bar, her silky hair free and flowing. Jake waited for the space of a few breaths, then stepped up to the mouth of the alley and carefully scanned the street. There was very little traffic and no pedestrians. All the cars parked at the curb were empty, and he didn't see any movement. Satisfied Veronica hadn't been followed, he trotted across the street.

Opening the door, Jake found Danny, the muscle-bound bouncer, looking at himself in a full length wall mirror and flexing one of his comically huge biceps. When the bouncer realised someone was behind him, he lifted his hand like he had intended to scratch his nose all along, cleared his throat and reached for the metal detector sitting on a stool near the vacant coat check counter.

"Arms up, pal," Danny said, as he thumbed the power switch on the metal detector. Then he looked up at Jake for the first time. Recognition moved across his face. "What the fuck? You again? You come back for your beating?" Danny dropped the metal detector on the stool and took a menacing step towards Jake, muscles flexed and hands twitching.

Jake stepped away, his hands up, trying to come up with an excuse to avoid fighting the younger man, when a flowing wave of blonde hair appeared between them.

"It's okay, Danny," Veronica said, her hand on the man's massive chest. "I asked him to come."

Recognition lost an argument with confusion, and bewilderment snuck in and sucker punched confusion to assume control of Danny's face. "Uh… what?"

"It's all good," Veronica said. "Don't worry."

Danny looked from Veronica to Jake and back again. "So, what you're saying is…" his words were slow, as though he were talking through a complicated math problem. "You don't want me to kick his ass?"

Veronica nodded. "That's what I'm saying."

"You sure?" Danny looked disappointed.

"I'm sure."

"Oh," Danny nodded. "Okay, I guess." He regained some of his composure, stuck his chin out and gave an exaggerated sniff. "You let me know if you change your mind."

Veronica nodded again. "I will."

Danny puffed himself out some more, gave Jake a final glare, and then turned and stalked toward the centre of bar, chin cocked in the air, casting glares at the half-full tables as he went. When he was gone, Veronica turned to Jake and threw her arms around him, laying her head on his chest.

"Thank you," she said, as she squeezed. "I never got to say that last night."

Jake stood stiffly, as the girl hugged him, his arms out slightly, not quite sure if he should be hugging her back. His head swam with the smell of her perfume and the feel of her hair against his face. He suddenly felt too warm, sweat popping out at the base of his neck.

After a moment, she released him and stepped back, her hands on his chest. "Are you all right? Did anything happen after I ran away and left you again?"

Jake thought of the sound of the thug's fingers breaking, but shook his head. "Nothing you need to worry about."

Veronica nodded and then looked around the room. "Come on," she said, taking Jake's hand and pulling him away from the door. "Let's sit down. Over here."

She led him through the bar and towards a table at the back, away from any of the other patrons. As she walked, she shrugged out of her black pea-coat and draped it over one arm. Jake tried to stop thinking about her perfume and the way her hips swayed in snug black miniskirt she wore, as he glanced around the room. Plenty of gazes fell on her as she walked past, desire in every stare. A few jealous stares landed on Jake as well, taking in the hand Veronica held. When he saw that, he almost smirked.

They sat down on the plush seat at the table that faced out towards the open area of the common room. Jake waited quietly while Veronica hung her coat on a hook attached to the high back of the booth and waved to the waitress—the same slouch shouldered girl that had served him the last time—and held up two fingers. The waitress rolled her eyes and meandered towards the bar.

Veronica looked at Jake and smiled, and he blushed in the wake of it. It was an honest smile, not the same kind she gave to the patrons in the bar. The warmth of it brought colour to the boxer's face. He looked down at his rough hands on the black-finished table in front of him, and took deep breaths through his bent nose while he tried to find his composure and stop feeling like an adolescent boy with a crush on the babysitter.

"So," she said, as she smiled at him. "I'm... well, I'm really not sure what to say to you. Thank you, I guess, is a good place to start."

Jake felt himself flush further. "You don't have to thank me. I was just... I guess I was just helping out."

She nodded and looked up, as the waitress slouched up to the table, set down two slender bottles of beer without looking at either person, and stalked away without a word. Jake picked up the bottle and examined it. It was one of the ubiquitous brands trying desperately to pretend it was Mexican and tropical and ended up tasting like piss. He took a doubtful swig and wondered if he would be expected to pay for it.

"So," Veronica said again, rotating her bottle on the table without drinking from it, "what do we do now?"

Jake set his bottle down and pursed his lips. "How 'bout we start with you telling me why those two assholes from last night jumped you twice?"

She shrugged, picked up her bottle, studied it for a moment before setting it down again. "They've been coming around here for a few weeks. At first I didn't think too much of it, but then things got weird."

"Weird, how?"

"Well, they came in here, all polite and stuff, and asked me to come see their boss." She paused. She lifted the bottle, holding it a hairsbreadth from her lips for several heartbeats, still not drinking from it. "That's not such a big deal, really." She took a shallow swig and set the bottle on the table with a soft plunk. "I get requests like that all the time. Sometimes, if the money's right, I go."

She looked away, embarrassed. Jake didn't have to ask what she did when she answered those requests.

"So, I went with these two guys, even though there was something off about them, 'cause the money they were offering was phenomenal."

Jake waited for several breaths, giving her a chance to continue on her own. "And what happened?".

"They took me to that new high rise, by the sky train station. We went in through the back door and up some big service elevator. At the top was this big room, with the nicest view I'd ever seen in this city, and this guy... " She paused again, staring down at her beer bottle.

"Okay," Jake said, patiently. "What about the guy?"

"He scared me," she said and looked up. "He scared me like I've never been scared in my whole life. It was the worst feeling I'd ever experienced. He was dressed sharp, like some kind of business executive, and he was probably the best looking man I ever remember meeting face to face. But there was an ugliness in him. Like he was wearing someone else's skin and the guy beneath the face was bad." She paused again, pushing the beer bottle from one hand to the other while she thought. "It was strange, because he was beautiful but awful. Physically, he was perfect. Just looking at him turned me on like I can hardly remember ever being turned on before, but I could smell the bad coming off him, like he was wearing too much cologne. It terrified me, and made me want to run."

"And what did he ask you to do for his money?" Jake asked.

"Nothing," Veronica replied.

Jake's eyebrows climbed up his forehead. "Then what did he want?"

"He wanted to talk about my son."

"Your son?" He ran his eyes briefly over a body that bore no signs of having children.

She nodded. "Yeah, Gareth. He's seven." She noticed Jake looking at her hips and belly, and shook her head. "I had him when I was seventeen. You'd never tell, right?" A satisfied smile crept across her face. Jake felt himself flush and return her smile.

"What did he want to talk about your son for?" Jake asked.

Veronica's face turned serious. "This guy, he said he was from a school for gifted children. He said it was an 'institute'. I can't remember the name he used. He told me Gareth's scores on some aptitude test had been exceptional, and this school was interested in recruiting him. The guy said it would all be paid for, it wouldn't cost me a penny, but Gareth would have to live at the school, and they could take him as soon as the next day."

"But you didn't buy it," Jake said.

Veronica nodded. "It would have been so easy to believe him, to see a future for my son that I could never give him, but I couldn't let myself. It was too strange. Too good to be true. I asked why a fancy school would have two guys who looked like wanna-be gangsters show up in a strip bar to ask about Gareth, and why they wouldn't just call me to come meet them at his regular school?"

Jake took another drink of his beer. "And what did he say to that?"

"The guy was smooth. Smooth as any player I've ever seen, and I've seen some pretty slick douche bags in my time working here. He went into this story, seamlessly, of how the school was very exclusive, and they didn't approach children at other schools because they didn't want random parents coming to them and begging to enroll their kids. Blah, blah, blah. It was all bullshit.

"I stood up to leave, 'cause I'd heard enough, and the guy, with his weird attraction and repulsion thing he had going, was starting to seriously freak me out, and he holds out an envelope. He thanks me for my time and said that he was a man of his word, and wanted to give me the money that I'd agreed to. If he's gonna give me money, I'm gonna take it, but once I have the envelope he lifts up a black case, like the kind you'd put a laptop in, from beside his chair and unzips it. It's filled with money. He tells me that the school is so interested in Gareth that they are willing to pay me a yearly stipend, whatever the fuck 'stipend' means, to have him attend their program."

"They wanted your boy in a bad way," Jake said, a memory of a tiny body in a bathtub flashing into his sight.

Veronica didn't say anything for several moments, and then put her hand on Jake's scarred knuckles. "Are you all right?"

"What?" Jake asked, as he looked up and realised he'd been staring at the surface of the table. "Yeah, I'm fine." He took another loud slurp from his beer bottle. "So, what did you say to the money."

"I said no. It was a lot of money, more than I'd ever seen in my life, but it scared me that they wanted Gareth so bad. I might show people my ass for a living, but I'd never let anyone hurt my kid."

Jake nodded. "Never would have thought different."

She smiled, apparently grateful for the comment. "So, I told him no, and said I wanted to leave. He didn't miss a beat, told the two douche-bags to take me where I wanted to go, and thanked me for my time again. As I'm walking towards the door, he asks me for my address and phone number, so he could follow up with me in a couple of days to see if I'd changed my mind. Then I knew he was full of shit, 'cause if he'd heard of Gareth through his school, and knew where I worked, he would know all that stuff already."

"What did you say?"

"I asked for his card, so I could call him later if I did change my mind. He gave it to me, but got this real dark look on his face. I was more scared at that moment than I'd ever been in my entire life. Then he asked me, just out of curiosity he said, who watches Gareth when I'm working."

Jake nodded. "Of course he did. And what did you tell him?"

"I was shaking so bad I could barely talk, but managed to get out a line about a day care at night, or some fucking thing. It didn't matter 'cause I could tell he didn't believe me. The darkness around his face just got deeper, like a black hole swallowing all the light around him.

"It was all I could do to turn and walk towards the elevator, 'cause my knees were all watery, like I had a bad flu. When the doors were closing, he gave me the most awful smile I'd ever seen and told me he'd see me soon."

"Did you keep the card?"

She nodded and leaned over to slip her hand into the pocket of her coat. She produced a thick, creamy piece of card stock and held it out to Jake.

As he accepted it, he ran his finger over the textured paper and gold stamp lettering. The card was obviously expensive—a box of the bastard things probably cost more than Jake made in a full shift driving a forklift—but there was something off about it. It felt dirty, oily, heavy in his hand. There was a residue left by the man who had handled it, and an impression far deeper than the embossed lettering could ever suggest.

Jake held the card up so the gold letters caught the light and read the name Ethan Drake.

He dropped the card on the table, giving in a little flick with his wrist so it landed away from him. "Was there anyone with him, besides the two wanna-be's?"

"Yeah, this big guy. Way bigger than Danny. A tattoo like a star around his eye. He didn't say anything the whole time I was there. Just stood behind the Drake guy with his arms crossed, staring at me."

Jake sucked in a great breath through his nose, pulled down the rest of his beer in three long gulps, and plunked the bottle on the table. "Veronica, do you trust me?"

She pursed her lips and looked down at her almost full bottle. "Yeah. I don't know what your name is, but, yeah, I think I do."

He stuck out a rough hand. "Jake Ross."

She gripped his hand and looked into his face. "You can call me Emily, Jake. Veronica is the stage name I give to the jackasses who come in here."

"Okay, Emily," Jake said with a smile, standing up. "Put on your coat. I'd like to see your son."

CHAPTER EIGHT

As they walked towards the front door Emily shrugged into her black pea-coat and flipped her silvery hair over the collar while Jake wondered exactly what he figured he was going to accomplish by seeing the girl's son. It was the first time he'd ever wished Mac was around making his dumb comments and telling him what he should do.

When Danny saw them coming towards the door, he stood up off his stool and spread his arms out, giving his chin a little extra jut. "You okay, Veronica?"

She gave him a broad smile and laid a delicate hand on the bouncer's chest. "I'm fine, Danny. Just stepping out for a minute. I'll be back in a bit."

The bouncer looked down at her hand and his face softened a little. "Okay, I'll see you soon." He shot Jake his best glare.

Emily—Jake was having a hard time wrapping his head around her real name—turned towards Jake so Danny couldn't see her face and gave an exaggerated eye roll. Jake couldn't quite hide his smirk, but did his best to keep his mouth shut.

As Emily pushed open the door, Jake put a hand gently on her arm, holding her back, so he could walk out in front of her. He glanced up and down the street, checking for the presence of anyone who might be waiting for them. A vagrant rummaged about in the first dumpster of Jake's favorite alley, but otherwise the street seemed to be deserted. He kept still for a few seconds more, checking for movement, then glanced over at Emily and gave her a nod.

She smiled at him, warm and honest, not a hint of guile. "You looking out for me, Jake?"

He snorted. "I'm looking out for myself. Seems to be an abundance of boogeymen about lately, and it's made me paranoid."

"You and me both." Emily stepped through the door to join him on the steps. "You ready?"

"As ready as I'm gonna get."

She nodded, stuck her hands in her pockets of her coat and bounced down the steps. Turning left, she headed in the same direction she'd gone when Jake followed her the night before. They walked side by side in silence for a several minutes, as they both scanned their surroundings.

"So, where is your boy at?" he asked, after they'd walked several blocks.

"With my roommate," she replied, without looking at him. "Another girl, Jenny, works at the club and watches him on the nights when she's not working. I do the same with her daughter, who's a little bit younger than Gareth."

"She ever see these guys that keep coming after you? Or this Ethan guy?"

"No. We keep it pretty quiet that we know each other outside of work. Keeps people from talking, and I don't want anyone from that place to know what my real life is like. No one but Jenny even knows I have a son."

He nodded, thinking. He wondered how these guys who were after Emily, or more accurately, after her boy, would be able to find her randomly when she walked home, but wouldn't think to follow her to her house. Or, if they knew what school he went to, how would they not know where she lived. This whole thing grew weirder by the minute, and Jake didn't like it.

They turned onto the street where the two thugs had tried to jump Emily for a second time, and past the place where Jake had ruined a man's hand. He soon discovered how they'd not been able to follow her.

She turned onto a narrow, paved foot path between houses, came out into an alley, and then onto a different foot path. She did that several times until even Jake, who had lived his entire life in Surrey, was more or less lost. It would be impossible to follow her in a vehicle, and anyone on foot would have to be within several feet to keep from losing her as she turned down the different, intersecting, foot paths that honeycombed the residential neighbourhoods. They saw almost no one else, except for a few random people out walking their dogs.

The only person who acknowledged their existence was a reeking homeless man rummaging through a recycling bin that had been placed at the curb of one of the houses.

When the ragged man saw them walking by, he shuffled up, a filthy hand extended. "Can you spare some change, brother? I just want a cup of coffee."

Jake scowled at the man, who was a little too far off the Whalley Strip to be common-place in the neighbourhood. Emily shrank away and hid behind Jake's shoulder.

"Fuck off," Jake growled, turning his body to place himself between the man and Emily, as the beggar shuffled a little closer.

"Humph," the man snorted. "Cheap fuck. Can't even help a guy out."

Jake looked over his shoulder several times once they'd passed to ensure the dirty vagrant wasn't following them, but the man had dived back into the recycling bin and paid them no mind.

They carried on without speaking for several minutes, and as the silence grew strained Emily turned and looked up at Jake. "You know, you never did tell me what happened that night in the parkade, after I ran. Did anything happen to you? Did you get hurt?"

"I got stabbed. Does that count?" The comment was out of his mouth before he could think.

Her blue eyes went wide. "You got what?"

He carried on for several steps, thinking about trying to play off the comment as a joke to keep her from worrying, but he hated it with a passion when people fucked around with him, as he felt had been done plenty in the last couple of days. He decided to lay down the truth.

"The smaller guy, he had a knife and stabbed me." Jake reached under his left arm and poked a finger through the slit in his leather coat. Emily looked down at the hole in the leather, her arching eyebrows knitting together, as she stopped and grabbed the lapel of his jacket. She held it away from his body and looked at the interior, where the broad blood stain marked the lining and a faint light from a nearby street lamp showed through the knife cut.

"Oh, that's disgusting," she said, her lip curled in distaste.

"Yeah, the cowardly fucks can't handle a fair fight."

"No, I don't mean that. How can you wear this coat with all that blood on it?"

He felt his face get hot. He shrugged. "It's the only one I got."

She shook her head. "As a way of saying thank you, I'll buy you a new coat." She ignored his prideful frown and ran her fingers down his side, over top of his t-shirt. The feel of her hand, the closeness of her, made his breath catch and he shivered.

"Oh," she said, and looked up at him. "Is it still sore? Did I hurt you?"

Before he could stop her, she pulled up his t-shirt and looked at his side. It was her turn to gasp, and he shivered again as she ran her soft fingers over his bare skin.

"Have you ever lied to me, Jake?" she asked.

He shook his head. "No."

"And you're not lying to me about getting stabbed." It was a statement, not a question.

"No."

"There's a scar, but it looks old. Years old." She dropped his shirt and stepped back from him. "What the fuck is going on here?"

He took a few deep breaths, trying to clear his head of her smell and the memory of the tingle on his skin where she touched him. He jammed his hands in his pockets and started walking, and she fell into step beside him.

"How much do you want to know?" he asked, looking at the

toes of his worn boots.

"Could it have anything to do with Gareth?"

He shrugged. "I don't know. I'm still trying to figure some shit out."

She looped her hand through the crook of his elbow. "Tell me everything." They continued to walk, slowly now that Jake was sure they couldn't possibly be pursued, and he let Emily steer him through more foot paths and alleys.

As they walked, he told her what had happened to him since he'd first come to help her in the parkade. He started with his falling unconscious, apparently dying, then awakening to find Mac drinking his beer, and finished with the conversation with the Preacher in the alley before he'd come to meet her. He told it all and left out no detail.

"So what you're saying," she said, gesturing with her left hand, as her right still held his arm, "is that there is some kind of quiet war going on, here in Surrey, and these people, these 'clans', are fighting it?"

Jake shrugged, something he'd found himself doing a lot in recent days. "Yeah, that's what they tell me."

"And on the night we met, you were stabbed to death, but came back to life, and are now supposed to be in this clan thing?"

"As far as I can piece it together."

"You're also saying now you're as strong as you were ten years ago."

Jake nodded. "Yeah, that's what it feels like. Maybe even stronger. It's fucked up, right?"

She led him out of a footpath and onto a narrow residential street, stopped, and turned to him. "You know, it really is."

As she looked up at him, he found himself staring into her eyes. He felt his pulse quicken as he looked into their cobalt blue depths, pulling him in. He felt like a drowning man who'd accepted his fate and gratefully sank to the bottom of oblivion. He wanted to reach out to her, to gather her up and hold her to him, to keep her as his own. Then she smiled.

It was not a coy or knowing smile; it was a simple smile, one born of trust. A smile naive to the emotions its bearer stirred in others around her, a smile of innocence below a set of eyes that could no longer claim the title. For a moment, Jake felt a wave of shame for the base want that coursed through him, and he cleared the thickness in his throat and stepped back.

"Where to now?" he asked, his voice hoarse while he looked around the street.

She lifted one hand and pointed to a small, detached rancher. "We're here." She turned and walked towards the house. Jake followed.

The neighbourhood was poor, but above the poverty line, with small yards. He looked about the property, vaguely impressed; the trimmed lawn, the gravel driveway raked and clear of debris, and the wooden siding on the house looked like it had been painted in recent memory. It wasn't exactly the kind of house he imagined a dancer at the Crimson Curtain living in.

He followed Emily to the front door. She pulled a brass key from her pocket and unlocked a new deadbolt above the handle. She gave a solid knock before depressing the lever above the handle and stepping inside. An extremely alluring woman with long, raven hair sat on a butter coloured faux-leather couch, two children, a boy and a girl in their pyjamas, playing at her feet.

The woman looked up, a smile showing even white teeth. "Hi, Emily." Her smile faltered when Jake stepped in behind her. "Uh, who is this?"

The boy on the floor lifted his attention from the toy truck he was using to crash into the girl's Barbie doll, and his face split into a broad smile. "Mom!" he said, as he scrambled to his feet and launched himself at Emily, who caught him, stood with him in her arms and hugged him close.

"Hey, shorty," she said, as she held the boy.

The woman was on her feet now, hands on her hips, her smile completely gone. "Emily, I asked who your guest was." Her voice had a hard edge to it. "We've discussed this. You know the rules about bringing work into our house."

It dawned on Jake that the dark haired woman must have assumed him a patron of the strip club, who'd persuaded Emily to give him more than just a dance. He opened his mouth to discredit the idea, but Emily spoke first.

"Jenny," Emily said, and glanced at Jake, "this is the guy I met last night."

Jenny tilted her head, her scowl deepening.

"You know, the guy I told you about before? From the parkade? The one who's helped me out twice? This is Jake." She smiled at the boxer and continued to hug her son.

Jenny's face softened, and her smile returned. Jake, relieved he wasn't going to get chewed out by an angry stripper for the second time in a handful of days, stuck his hand out in greeting.

Jenny stepped past his hand, wrapped her arms around Jake's shoulders and pressed her cheek into his. "Oh, thank you," Jenny said as she squeezed him. "Thank you for helping her."

Jake, again at a loss for words, managed to grunt in reply and patted the girl hesitantly on the back.

As he received the embrace of a beautiful woman he didn't know, Jake was struck by a small realization; this woman, who pressed her body very firmly into his, smelled and looked just as good as Emily, perhaps even better. Jake had a particular thing for dark-haired women. But, as Jake looked over Jenny's perfumed shoulder, he was struck again, by something about the blonde girl that Jenny just did not possess. It was not a simple matter of appearance, it was something that could not be calculated with the eye.

Jenny finally released Jake's neck and moved her hand to his face. "We owe you," she said as she looked up. "And you are welcome here. What's mine is yours."

He felt his face flush, his skin burning under her fingers. "Uh, thanks."

She smiled all the wider, as blood rushed to his face, and patted his cheek with a soft palm.

He looked back at Emily, who gave him an amused grin as Jenny stepped away. The blonde girl stepped forward and turned so the boy in her arms was closer to Jake.

"Jake, this is my son, Gareth."

Jake knew he had a face that could frighten children, but gave his friendliest smile and reached out to touch the boy's shoulder. As he looked at the boy's face closely for the first time, he stopped still as stone. He instantly knew what Mac meant when he said he got "feelings." The boy possessed the blue eyes and pale hair of his mother. He looked like any other child, but

Jake could feel an energy pouring from him, like a static charge waiting to go off. The kid wasn't quite glowing, but Jake felt something obvious, a sense he'd never known before fill his vision, make his nerves tingle and his hair stand on end, as his hand neared the child. Even Jake, who had no knowledge of the powers Mac claimed were at play, could see with his layman's eye this child was special. He, inexplicably, had some understanding of why Ethan Drake wanted him, and understood even more clearly the dark man must not get his hands on him.

"Jake, are you all right?" Emily studied him, her slender eyebrows bunching together.

Jake shook his head, realizing he'd been staring at Gareth for several seconds. "Yeah, I'm fine," he said and put on his best, gap toothed smile. "Hi, Gareth. My name's Jake."

The boy smiled easily, his blue eyes lighting up, and stuck out a small hand. "Hiya, Jake," Gareth said as he put his hand into the boxer's calloused mitt and made his best attempt at shaking it.

Whatever it was about Emily that took her beauty and made it into something so desperately attractive, lay doubly thick about her son. Jake looked at Gareth and saw a deep charisma that even the strongest will would be powerless against. This boy, one day, would be a leader of men, someone that people would flock to. If shown the right way, Gareth would do much good in his life. If shown wrong, he would be extremely dangerous.

Still in awe, Jake shook the tiny hand. "I'm glad to meet you, pal."

The boy laughed, a rich sound that made Jake's scarred face split in a smile.

Gareth looked at his mother. "Did you take the night off?" he asked hopefully.

"We'll see," Emily said, and set the boy down. "Why don't you take Samantha and get some ice cream before bed."

Gareth gave a small hoot of triumph, reached down to take the hand of the small dark haired girl still sitting on the floor, and pulled her to her feet and towards the kitchen.

"That boy is special," Jake said, watching the two giggling children.

Emily folded her arms. "Yes, he is."

"He's one of those popular kids, isn't he? The one all the other kids like?"

The blonde girl looked up at him. "Yeah. Everyone loves him; his teachers, the other kids, strangers on the street, everyone. He has this way with people. I can't explain it. His mood affects everyone around him. If he is happy, he brightens up everyone in the room. If he's having a bad day, everyone has a bad day." She paused, examining Jake's face. "How did you know that? How did you know that from seeing him once?"

"Don't give me too much credit." Jake stuck his hands in his pockets, looking at the children as they clambered up a chair to open the freezer on the top portion of the fridge. "I'm not really very perceptive, I just got a feeling."

"Doesn't getting feelings about things make you perceptive?"

He looked at her and felt a smile turn the corner of his mouth. "Yeah, maybe."

"Okay, Jake, what does your feeling tell you we should do? What about these guys that want Gareth?"

Jake shook his head. "I don't know. I'm gonna have to ask Mac."

"The one who drank your beer?" she asked, smirking at Jake's frown.

"The very same, the damned thief."

"Can you trust him?"

Jake thought about that for a moment, rubbing his stubbled chin. Could he trust Mac? He certainly seemed like one of the good guys, saving the child in the shit-hole house and all, but could he trust him with the welfare of Emily's son? This was a game Jake had never played before, and he didn't know the rules. He didn't know whom he should trust.

"I think so," he said after several moments. "I guess I have to. It isn't just a random coincidence this Drake guy wants your kid. There's something else to it, and it probably sucks. I'm new at this whole thing and I need to ask someone before we can figure out what we should do?"

Emily's smirk was replaced by a small, honest smile. "What's with this 'we', Jake?"

Jake snorted, trying to appear nonchalant in the face of the saying he'd used so often in the last few days. "Well, I can't let these pricks keep harassing you, can I? What kind of guy would I be then?"

"You're gonna stick with me on this?"

"Yeah," he said. "Whatever 'this' is."

She blinked heavily, moisture glistening in the bottoms of her eyes. "Thanks, Jake."

The boxer shrugged, uncomfortable with her sudden show of emotion. "Yeah, don't worry about it. What are you doing for the rest of the night? Are you staying here, or are you going back to work?"

She wiped a manicured finger underneath her eyes to keep her half-formed tears from marring her makeup, and then looked at the boy happily eating ice cream from a small bowl. "I'd love to stay here with him tonight, but if I don't work then I don't get paid. If I don't get paid, we don't pay rent and we don't eat. So, as much as I hate that place, I need to go back."

Jake nodded his understanding. "Okay, I'll walk you back to the bar, and then see what I can figure out about your boy."

Emily nodded and walked over to Gareth, bending down to speak in his ear. The easy smile Gareth wore became a frown, complete with bottom lip sticking out, but he nodded in as much understanding as a seven year old can possess.

"Okay, let's go," Emily said as she walked past Jake and opened the front door.

Jake followed her out the door and paused to shut it. When he turned back, he ran into her. Emily had stopped dead on the walkway, looking into the front yard.

Jake looked up and his breath stopped, his heart lurching in his chest. In the middle of the yard, a huge shape loomed. A many pointed black star framed an eye that was creased with a large smile.

"Hello, clansman," Kast said.

CHAPTER NINE

ake glanced around the yard, as Mac's words concerning Kast echoed in his mind; he is too much for you.

Thoughts of escape were quickly quashed as Jake noted several other figures in the small yard, spread out like a fan around Kast. Most were ragged and bent, like the so-called guards Jake and Mac had encountered at the house where they'd fought Taber for the child. There was one that stood out, though, to Kast's left: a man with a highly stylized beard, crafted into a long point that jutted from his chin, as well as pointed sideburns and long, slicked-back hair. A heavy gold chain about his neck and a long leather coat gave the man a showy appearance. Jake thought he looked like a misguided comic book character. He grinned at Jake and then leered at Emily in a way that made the boxer's skin prickle.

"How the hell did they find us?" Emily asked as she frantically looked around.

"We were followed," Jake said. A hot bloom of anger spreading across his chest, as he saw one of the homeless lackeys stirring restlessly behind Kast; the same man who had stopped them to beg for change on the way to Emily's house. With them, also, was the man who'd been digging through the dumpster in Jake's alley. "They were sneaky as fuck and the pricks followed us."

"We've come for the boy, clansman," Kast said from his position in the middle of the yard. The followers around him shifted anxiously. They reminded Jake of a pack of coyotes waiting for an exhausted deer to fall down.

Jake pulled Emily behind him and gave his best in-the-ring glare to the tattooed man. "Go fuck yourself." He had no doubt Mac would have made some kind of long-winded philosophical comment, or poetic challenge, but Jake didn't have much poetry in him.

Kast spread his hands, trying to appear reasonable, which would have been quite a feat considering his monstrous appearance. "It doesn't have to be like this," Kast said, his voice gravelly and hard. "We are men of honour, Jake Ross, you and I. We can discuss this."

Jake's eyes narrowed. "How do you know my name?"

Kast chuckled. "We all know the man who felled Taber, a dear friend to me and valuable comrade to our cause. Your name is on the tongue of every soldier in this war. Much praise will fall to the one who kills you."

"I didn't kill him. Mac did."

Kast shrugged. "Your hand didn't hold the knife in Taber's neck, but it was you who felled him. If not for you, Taber would be here now and MacKinnon would be rotting in a shallow grave."

Behind Jake, Emily shifted and he could feel the nervous tension rolling off her. "You didn't tell me you killed someone."

Jake gritted his teeth. "I didn't. Well… I guess I did, sort of." He watched the ragged people shifting closer to them. "I'll try and explain it if we ever get out of here."

"You have proven to be a man of skill, Jake Ross," Kast said, his speech carrying an odd formality. "You bested Taber and the two mercenaries I sent to collect the girl. You've interfered in my plans significantly." Kast flexed his massive hands. "For the valor you've shown, I give you leave to go, one warrior to another. Take the woman if you must, but you get only one opportunity to leave and not look back."

"We can't leave Gareth," Emily said, gripping Jake's arm.

He nodded, as he kept his eyes on the people inching towards them, most of which held knives or clubs in their hands. They couldn't run because Kast would just kick down the door and take Emily's son, and probably kill Jenny and her daughter just to make a point. He had to figure a way to get both Emily and Gareth away from there and draw these assholes away from their home.

"Is there a back door to this house?" Jake asked Emily from the corner of his mouth.

"Yeah, of course."

"When I say so, you go back inside, grab Gareth, and get the fuck out of here."

"What about you?"

"I'll be right behind you."

"You said that before and you got stabbed."

"I mean it this time." As the words left his mouth, he knew it was a lie. If he was going to try and hold this doorway long enough for Emily and Gareth to get away, he would not be following her.

"Ready?" he asked her and felt her squeeze his arm. He raised his fists and sucked in a deep breath to shout out a challenge, and give Emily the signal to run. Kast grinned and stepped forward, Jake's willingness to fight apparently pleased Kast, but the boxer's attempt at heroics were interrupted by a roaring engine and squealing tires.

Headlights appeared, approaching fast. Kast frowned, as the beams shone in his eyes. Jake saw the old Mercedes that had been at Morgan's place surge down the street and come to a drifting stop in front of the house, the front tires making long divots on the lawn.

Before the vehicle was fully stopped, the passenger door flew open and Isabelle rolled out, coming to her feet and making a throwing motion with her right hand. A small knife appeared in the neck of the nearest of Kast's men, and he went down. Mac climbed out of the driver's seat, his sword in one hand and Satan's drywall hammer in the other.

Kast pointed a finger at the newcomers. "Kill them," he shouted. His soldiers ran to obey. Kast turned to the man with the beard and pointed at Jake. "Naeven, take care of him and get the boy." The bearded man leered, as he sauntered towards Jake and Emily.

Mac slipped under the slashing knife of one of the soldiers and hacked into the man's thigh with his sword. As the man fell, Mac leapt over him. "Jake," he shouted, flinging the war-hammer with an awkward underhand motion. The heavy weapon pin-wheeled through the air, sailing over Kast's head. Jake managed to fumble it into his grip without getting brained.

Jake swung the hammer in a wide arc, and the bearded man—Naeven—slipped two long knives from beneath his ridiculous coat, his grin growing.

"Move, you idiot," Isabelle yelled from across the yard, as she closed with one of the ragged soldiers and another knife flashed in her hand.

"Get the girl out of here, Jake," Mac shouted, as he chopped into another of the screaming vagrants. "We'll find you later."

"MacKinnon," Kast said as he stalked towards the slim man, Jake and Emily apparently forgotten, "I was told you might appear, with one of your 'feelings'. You're like a rash that will never quite die, but I think tonight I've had my fill of you."

Isabelle dropped her opponent and reached behind her back, her hands flashing faster than Jake's eye could follow. Several small knives streaked through the air toward the tattooed giant. Kast lifted his hand before his eyes. like a man shooing away a gnat, and one of the knives sank into his palm. The other two struck him in the chest.

Jake expected him to go down, but Kast looked down at the knife in his hand, like it was an annoying splinter, plucked it out and tossed it casually onto the lawn. The two knives in his chest, he simply ignored.

"Holy fuck," Jake muttered, as he looked at the spectacle unfolding before him. "We have to get out of here." He swung the hammer towards Naeven again.

The bearded man leapt back, away from Jake's wild swing, and the boxer took the opportunity to spin past Emily and through the door to the house. He yanked the girl through and slammed the door, as Naeven regained his balance and jumped after them. Jake felt the jarring impact of a body hitting the door, as he threw the bolt. He dropped his hammer on the floor and dragged the living room's couch in front of the doorway. The door shuddered from another heavy blow, but held.

"What the fuck is going on?" Jenny said from the kitchen, a cordless phone in her hand. "I heard shouting and I was calling the police."

"Keep calling them," Jake said, as he walked past her. He scooped Gareth up from where he sat at the kitchen table, a spoon in his hand and a half-empty bowl of ice cream in front of him. "Does this place have a basement?"

"What? Yeah, a crawl space."

"Good," Jake said. He bent to pick up the hammer, Gareth's arms around his neck. "Take your kid and get into it, and don't come out 'till the police arrive. They probably won't even look for you, or care that you're here."

"They?" Jenny asked. "What 'they'? Who the fuck is 'they'?"

"Jenny," Emily said, as she took her friend's hand. "You really don't want to know. Just do what Jake says."

There were tears of fear and frustration in Jenny's eyes, as she flapped her arms helplessly, then grabbed her daughter's hand. She moved through the kitchen and towards a small mud room with a door to the back yard. She yanked back a mat in front of the door, and Jake saw a small square portal in the floor. Jenny grabbed a steel ring and lifted the door, revealing a set of narrow wooden stairs leading into the dark.

Jake passed Gareth to Emily and helped Jenny down the stairs, then lowered her daughter in after her. "Remember," he said, as Jenny hugged the small girl. "Don't come up for anyone but the police." He pointed to the phone in Jenny's hand. "Use that. Give the 911 person your number and make the cops call you before you come out. Don't be fooled by anyone else."

Jenny nodded and wiped her tear streaked face. "What are you guys going to do?"

Jake looked out the small window in the mud room door. "We're going to get the fuck out of here while the getting doesn't suck." He closed the crawl-space door gently, sealing away Jenny and her daughter, and then smoothed the mat back into place. You couldn't tell there was a door there by standing and looking at it. Jake hoped it would keep the two of them safe.

His inspection complete, Jake stood close to the back door

and peered out the window. He could see a small, neat yard, with a worn patio table and chairs, and a small plastic swing-set, but other than the furniture it was deserted. He waited several more seconds, looking for movement, but saw none.

"Okay," he said, looking at Emily who was hugging Gareth close to her. "When I open the door you run straight to the back fence, okay?" He thought about taking Gareth from her, but decided it would be better to have his hands free. "I'll be right behind you."

Emily nodded sharply, causing her blonde hair to sway around her face, and Jake was struck again by just how stunning she was. Even through the rank fear making her face pale and drawn, her beauty shone through as she struggled to keep herself together. He shook his head to clear it, hefted Mac's hammer, and yanked the door open.

Emily broke into a run, Gareth clinging to her neck. Jake noticed she'd changed from her stripper-heels into black, flat-bottomed shoes while he had helped Jenny into the crawl space. Jake closed the door with a bang and took off after her, searching the yard for any threat. He'd only made it a few steps when a heavy body slammed into him from behind and sent him tumbling across the yard, the hammer spinning from his grip.

Rolling to his feet, Jake searched for his attacker and found Naeven moving smoothly towards him. The man's hands were empty, his knives apparently put away, but those empty hands were up like he knew how to use them, and he moved towards Jake in a way the boxer would have admired if the bearded man had not previously been instructed to kill him.

Naeven attacked, fists and feet flying. Jake was able to either block or dodge the attacks as they came, but was being driven backwards. He couldn't find an opening to counter. A spinning back-kick, connected with Jake's mid-section and drove much of the wind from him as he tumbled to the muddy grass of the back yard. Naeven was on top of him instantly, knee across Jake's neck, the majority of his weight high on Jake's chest where he couldn't push the bearded man off.

"Jake!" Emily shouted from across the yard, as she stood, shifting anxiously from foot to foot, Gareth still held in her arms.

Naeven whipped one of his long knives from under his coat and pointed it at her. "Don't worry, bitch. I won't hurt him for long. You, on the other hand, I'm going to take my time with and hurt plenty." He looked down at Jake. "You hear that, clansman? I'm going to hurt her, a lot, for as long as she'll last, because once they have the boy, Ethan and Kast won't give a shit about her." He appeared to be waiting for a reaction from Jake, but the boxer refused to give the showy prick the satisfaction and continued to struggle. Naeven laughed and leaned down. "Don't you know when to give up? When you've met your betters? Don't you know you can't fight the dark? No   matter how bright you think you are, the darkness always falls around you. It falls as it pleases."

Jake gritted his teeth and struggled for air. "Don't you know you shouldn't wear a fucking handle on your face?"

Naeven tilted his head quizzically, just in time for Jake to reach upwards and grab Neaven's beard, yanking on it as hard as he could from his position on his back. Naeven let out a squawk, losing both his balance and his grip on his knife, as he closed both his hands around Jake's scarred mitt. Jake heaved, bridging with his hips and pushing with his other arm, while still gripping the long beard, and tossed Neaven over his head. Jake scrambled to his knees, refusing to release his hold, and punched Neaven several times in the face. Naeven's head bounced with the force of the blows, as far as Jake's grip on his beard would let it, and Jake kept hitting him until he went limp.

Jake released him, and the showy man lay supine and unmoving on the ground. Jake felt a stinging in his right hand and looked down at his knuckles to find one of Naeven's white teeth embedded in his flesh. Jake picked it out with a grimace and dropped it onto the muddy earth. "Asshole," he muttered, as he got to his feet and trotted towards the chest-high, cedar plank fence, stopping to pick up his hammer.

"Okay," he said, as he reached Emily and Gareth and held out his arms. "Give him to me and climb over."

She nodded and handed Gareth over. The boy's face was stiff, his small lips pressed into a thin line, but he wasn't crying. Jake gave his best grin, and the boy returned it. Jake watched

Emily as she jumped and threw her foot up onto the top of the fence, but his grin turned into a shout of warning, as a dirty fist reached up to grab her silky blonde hair. She yelled in surprise and tried to pull away, but the hand, and the dirty face attached to it, yanked hard and pulled her halfway over the fence, away from Jake. Jake lunged forward, Gareth still gripping his neck, and grabbed the hand that held Emily's hair. With a grunt, he brought all his weight down in a crouch, smashing the grasping arm against the top of the fence, producing a satisfying crack and a scream of pain. The hand released its grip and Emily tumbled free, back towards Jake, and rolled across the damp lawn.

Jake stepped to the fence and peered over. The man who'd grabbed Emily lay at the base of the fence, clutching his shattered arm and moaning pitifully. He wouldn't be much more of a problem, but he had friends running down the alley towards them and they looked inclined to be a massive pain in the ass. Jake counted at least five more bodies running through the dim alley, too many to fight.

"We can't go this way," Jake said, as he turned from the fence and pulled Emily to her feet. "We'll have to go out the front."

Emily looked up at him, eyes wide, as she rubbed at her scalp. "But that guy, with the tattoos…"

"Let's hope Isabelle put enough knives in him that he falls down," Jake said as he ran across the yard, stepping on Naeven's moaning form.

When he reached the corner of the house, and a small gate that led to the front yard, Jake slowed and looked around the corner. He could hear yelling and see shadows thrashing through the headlights of the old Mercedes. If they were exceptionally lucky maybe they could sneak past them all without being seen. Jake reached up and undid the latch on the fence, and swung it toward him with a squeal of rusted hinges.

"Come on," he said, over his shoulder to Emily, and started creeping around the edge of the house.

The scene that met him, as Jake stepped into the light cast by the car's headlights, was something out of an old war movie. Limp, twisted bodies littered the lawn, many with small knives sticking out of them or broad slashes carved into their flesh. But this war was not over, and was still being hotly contested.

Kast fought both Isabelle and Mac and was not close to losing. The giant had the older man pinned by his neck to the hood of the car with one hand, while he held Isabelle by the lapels of her leather Jacket, off the ground and shook her like she was a dusty rug. Mac beat ineffectually at Kast's forearm with his fists, while Isabelle kicked and thrashed like an angry cat, all of which did nothing more than make the tattooed man laugh.

The giant's back was towards them and Jake saw a chance. He pointed towards the other side of the street, in the direction he'd come with Emily on their walk from the Crimson Curtain. "Run for that alley," he said. He pushed Gareth back into her arms. "Keep running, and I'll catch up."

"No," Emily said and gripped his arm as she accepted her son. "Every time you say that you leave me. What are you going to do?"

Jake looked over to where the figures still struggled against the car. Mac's blows slowed as Kast squeezed his neck tighter, and Isabelle screamed out in pain, as the giant slammed her back against the side of the Mercedes. Jake had thought about leaving them and running with Emily, but something niggling at the back of his mind didn't sit right. It felt suspiciously like a conscience, and Jake didn't like it at all.

"I can't leave them to die," he said as he looked back at her. "I'll be right behind you. I mean it."

Without waiting for her to answer, Jake turned and sprinted across the yard, Satan's drywall hammer held up, ready to swing. He tried to soften his steps so that the giant wouldn't hear him coming, and hoped that one blow to the back of the tattooed head would end the fight.

Once he was within range, Jake leapt into the air and made a whistling slash with the hammer. Kast, without looking at him, pivoted smoothly out of the way, and the momentum of Jake's swing sent him tumbling across the lawn. The words *he is too much for you* flashed through Jake's mind, as he sprawled on the churned, muddy earth.

He was on his feet in an instant, turning and raising the

hammer again, as he spit out a mouthful of mud and grass, but Kast tossed Isabelle at him, almost casually, and the impact of her body drove the air from him and sent the hammer spinning into the night.

Jake wheezed, as he lay on the ground, his limbs tangled with Isabelle's. He tried to find his breath, which had departed with both haste and great enthusiasm. He shoved at Isabelle, and the dark haired woman slid bonelessly off him, and he struggled to sit up. He was hammered back into the ground, as Kast stepped forward and slammed his heavy foot onto Jake's chest.

"You're almost as stupid as MacKinnon, Jake Ross," Kast said, as he glared down. "You could have gotten away, but chose instead to help these fools. You and your clan will do nothing but lose if you so quickly forget your goals to save the weakest among you. Now you will fall and they will die." Kast tilted his head, a look on his tattooed face that could only be described as confused.

"You could have been something, Jake Ross, if you'd not been fighting for the wrong side. Pity you'll never get the chance." Kast's expression didn't change, as he reached up and pulled one of Isabelle's knives from his chest, sliding the slender blade out of thick layers of muscle.

Jake heaved at Kast's foot, but he might as well have been pushing at a house for all the give he found in it.

Kast leaned down, the knife loose in his fist, and placed it casually against Jake's neck, using all the care he might if he were deciding where to carve a pumpkin. "I really do regret this, Jake Ross. I wished we'd had an opportunity to meet in combat as honourable men, one old warrior to another, and see how the fates would have measured us."

He gave a melancholy grin, appearing genuinely regretful, and his grip tightened on the knife. Jake gritted his teeth and waited for the bite of the steel.

There was a dull thud and Kast's massive shoulders jumped up towards his ears, and his grin shifted into a grimace. The giant stood upright and turned, lifting his heavy boot off Jake's chest, allowing Jake onto his side to suck air into his battered body. Kast brought his empty hand up to the back of his head and Jake saw blood seeping through the thick fingers. Behind Kast stood Emily, Satan's drywall hammer gripped in both hands.

Kast pulled his hand away from his head and looked at the blood, then at Emily.

"Ow," Kast said.

"There's more where that came from, fuck face," she spat.

Kast shook his head sadly, Jake apparently forgotten, and took a slow step towards her. The savagery that had been painted on Emily's face was quickly replaced by a look of profound fear.

"You're another example of someone playing for the wrong side," Kast said, conversationally, as he examined his fingers and then rubbed them together. "This could have been so easy for you. Now, it's only going to end in pain."

"Yes, it is," Jake said. He surged off the ground, fear of what the giant would do to the blonde woman shocking life into his tired limbs. Kast started to turn, but Jake leapt onto his back, one arm clamping around the giant's neck. Kast grunted in surprise, dropped Isabelle's slender knife in the grass, and reached up to grab at Jake.

Jake squeezed as hard as he could on Kast's neck, pushing his wrist towards his biceps like a pair of scissors, hoping to choke the giant unconscious. Jake found it was much like squeezing a tree trunk, and produced a similar reaction.

Kast got a hold on the collar of Jake's leather coat and started to drag him off. Jake hung on as hard as he could, but felt himself being lifted free nonetheless, the seams on his jacket digging into his armpits. As he looked down on the top of Kast's head, still scrabbling for purchase and trying desperately to hang on, he felt the handle of Isabelle's other knife sticking out of the giant's chest. Jake ripped it free and Kast gave no indication that he noticed. Jake looked at the short knife, gripped awkwardly so only the last couple of inches of the short blade protruded past the heel of Jake's hand.

If I don't do something to end this, Jake thought, we're all going to die.

Jake gritted his teeth, his stomach twisting, and rammed the knife into Kast's eye.

This, the big man noticed very well.

He let loose a roar of pain and heaved Jake off his back and into the air. Jake flew, his arms and legs pin-wheeling, to land heavily on his back, the air driven from him, again. The boxer rolled onto his hands and knees, his head spinning amid the bright flashes of light in his vision, and looked back at the wounded giant.

Staggering around the yard, Kast flailed and howled in agony, swinging his massive fists at the air while blood streamed down his tattooed face from his ruined eye.

Jake struggled to his feet and felt a sharp, stabbing pain in his side. He'd had a rib broken in the ring before and recognised the sensation. He gritted his teeth and shuffled over to where Emily clutched the hammer to her chest and pulled it from her grip. She didn't look at him, her eyes fastened to the bellowing giant. She nervously wiped her hands on the front of her skimpy dress, as she released her hold on the wooden haft.

Pain lancing through his side, Jake held the hammer like a batter ready for a pitch and waited for Kast to turn towards him. The giant had his remaining eye open, bloodshot and furious, and his massive head whipped about as he searched for Jake.

"Ross!" Kast roared. He pulled the knife from his eye socket. There were gobs of bloody pulp hanging from the short blade. "Ross, I'm going to use this knife to carve the litany of my clan into your hide! I'm going to cut out your heart and wear it like a pocket watch! I'm going to skin your slut and turn her into—"

Kast's rantings came to an abrupt end when Jake swung the heavy hammer, pain from his broken rib slashing through his body, and smashed it into the giant's jaw. Kast's head snapped sideways, and he crumpled to the ground with a grunt. The force of the swing, and the pain through his body, unbalanced Jake, and he fell to his knees in the churned mud of the yard.

As the huge man fell, Jake wondered if he'd killed him, fervently hoped for it, in fact. But Kast didn't stay still for long, and began stirring almost at once, a slow moan leaking from between his teeth.

"Won't this fucking guy ever die?" Jake asked no one in particular.

"Get up, Jake," Mac said, as he came out of the dark at Jake's side. The grey haired man bled heavily from his nose and mouth. He grabbed Jake's arm and heaved him to his feet. Once Jake was up, Mac picked up the limp form of Isabelle and slid her past the open front passenger door of the old Mercedes, to lay unconscious beside the driver's seat.

"Quickly, Jake, you need to go," Mac said, as he closed the door on Isabelle.

Jake opened his mouth to reply and was stopped by distant sirens; likely the police responding to Jenny's 911 call. He looked around the yard, littered with the bodies of the dead and dying, and realised that Mac was right. They all needed to get the fuck out of there.

He limped towards the rear passenger door of the Mercedes and opened it. He waved to Emily, who still stood in the yard, staring at Kast, frozen with fear. "Grab Gareth and get in," he said, the breath needed to form the words causing a searing pain in his side.

Emily nodded and beckoned to Gareth, who had been hiding behind a shrub while his mother took on Kast. The two hustled across the yard and dove into the back seat. Jake moved to follow, but stopped at Mac's hand on his arm.

"No, Jake, you need to drive and get them somewhere safe."

"Me?" Jake asked, and winced. "Where are you going?"

"I'm going to run from the police when they arrive. Lead them on a bit of a chase so you can get away."

"Run from the police? Won't they catch you?"

Mac chuckled. "I've been sneaking far longer than you've been alive, Jake. Those boys won't catch me. Don't you worry."

"Where do we go?"

Mac shrugged. "Somewhere safe. Where no one would expect you to be. Not your apartment. It's a safe bet if Kast knows who you are, they'll know where you live. Just lay low for a while. Isabelle will know how to contact Morgan and me."

"Yeah, if she wakes up."

The older man pressed his lips into a thin line and looked at the unconscious woman. "Just get her out of here."

Indecision gripped Jake. He'd come to Emily's house to get a look at her son and get an idea of why the people who'd been menacing her had been so insistent. Looking around helplessly, wishing hard he was elsewhere, he sucked in a deep, startled breath. Kast was gone.

"Where the fuck did he go?" Jake asked, looking at the spot in the yard where the monstrous man had laid.

Mac followed his look, his face grim. "Kast is a soldier, not a fool. We will see him again, and sooner than we like." He gave Jake a small shove. "You must leave, Jake. You must keep them safe."

Jake looked at Emily, who watched him from the back seat, the same fear he felt mirrored on her face; a deep numbing fear, that soured his gut and made his knees feel like over-stretched rubber bands.

Alongside the fear in Emily's face was another emotion Jake had trouble identifying. It had been a long time since he'd seen it: trust. She watched him, trusting that he'd know what to do, and he did not have it in him to let her down.

His decision made, he nodded, and hobbled around the front of the car to the driver's door and collapsed into the seat of the still-running Mercedes. Mac picked up his sword from the churned earth and waited calmly in the middle off the yard where the police would be sure to notice him when they arrived.

Closing his door with some difficulty, Jake dropped the car into drive and slammed his foot down on the accelerator. The back end of the car swung sideways as the rear wheels carved a swath in the soft earth, then surged away from the curb and down the street. He didn't see any sign of the wounded Kast, which was a pity. He would have liked to hit him with the car.

"Where are we going, Jake?" Emily asked from the back seat. Jake glanced at her in the rear-view mirror. Her blue eyes, framed by silken hair, looked back. His heart caught in his throat again, as he saw the trust, the faith she'd placed in him.

"I gotta get us somewhere safe."

She nodded, as she stroked Gareth's hair, his head buried in her chest. "Any idea where?"

He smirked at the thought of the angry face that was going to greet him. "I have an idea."

CHAPTER TEN

ake pulled the Mercedes into the dingy alley behind Tartan Boxing, slid the gear shift into park, and switched off the engine. Warren Boyd's car, a run-down Lincoln with a peeling vinyl roof—exactly what you would expect an overweight, balding boxing promoter to drive—was parked in the same alley, out of the light and well hidden from the street.

"Where are we?" Emily asked as she looked out the window, distaste painted on her face.

"We'll be okay here for the night." Jake opened the driver's door. "An old friend lives here."

"An old friend?" Emily looked doubtful.

Jake paused, half-way out of the car. "Well, not so much a friend as a miserable old fuck, but he's about as close to a friend as we're gonna find right now."

Emily did not look at all assured.

Jake walked around the hood of the car and checked the back door to the gym. As expected, since Warren didn't trust anyone, it was locked. Jake walked the dozen feet to the edge of the building, and slipped into the crevice between the gym and the warehouse next to it. He squeezed himself into the opening, shuffled a couple of steps, and reached up to a narrow ledge, onto the brick trim of the building, and found the spare key Warren had been keeping there for twenty years. Jake was unsure why it was in that particular spot, since Warren couldn't get into the crevice without the aid of a shoe horn and bottle of Vaseline, but Jake had used it once or twice when he was a kid when his old man was pissed at him for something and he needed a place to sleep.

Slipping out of the crevice, Jake hurried back to the door, unlocked it and pocketed the key. "Come on," he said, pulling open the door and waving to Emily, who struggled out of the car with Gareth still clinging to her. Jake opened the front passenger door of the Mercedes and bent down to slide his arm under Isabelle's knees. He grimaced at the pain of his broken rib.

"Get your hands off me, you idiot!"

Jake pulled back in surprise, smacking the back of his head against the top of the door sill. "You're awake," he said, rubbing the back of his head.

"Yes, I'm awake," Isabelle said sourly, as she slowly shifted her legs out of the car and onto the dirty concrete. "Where are we?"

"A safe place." Jake reached down a hand to help her up.

She waved him off, an annoyed look on her face, and pushed herself up with a grimace and stood unsteadily, one hand against the car. "Don't be vague, Ross. I asked where the fuck are we."

Jake sighed. "At my gym. I don't think they'll look to find us here."

"Yes, well you're not much of a thinker, are you?" She limped past him towards the open door of the gym, shuffling past Emily without even glancing at her.

"So, this is one of your 'clan'?" Emily asked once Isabelle had disappeared into the dim interior of the gym.

"So they keep telling me."

"Not very friendly are they?"

Jake shrugged and put his hand on Emily's back to guide her into the building.

Inside, Jake found Isabelle leaning against one of the metal pillars that supported the upper floor, her eyes closed and her dark hair covering her lowered face.

"Are you all right?" Jake asked

"I'm fine," Isabelle said, her chin tilting upwards. "This place stinks."

"Yeah, but it's a good stink." Jake put on a smile that only made Isabelle's scowl deepen. Jake shrugged again. "Come on, let's go upstairs and get cleaned up."

A narrow wooden staircase stood attached to the wall furthest from the front door and, as they reached the bottom of it, Jake heard movement above them.

"Who the fuck is that?" Warren Boyd called down, his bulk filling the entrance at the top of the stairs. There was what looked like a sawed-off shovel handle in his hand, and he was wearing only a pair of baggy boxer shorts and a white t-shirt.

"It's me, Warren."

"Ross? What the fuck are you doing here?"

"I need a place to lay up for a while." Jake waved his hand up the stairs, like a bell hop showing the way. Emily put Gareth down and held his hand, as they walked up the creaking wooden steps.

"Lay up? You in trouble with the cops? And who are all these strays you've brung?"

"No, Warren, no cops," Jake lied. "Just a little trouble. And these are... new friends, I guess."

"Friends huh? I guess if you're bringing friends for tea I better put some fucking pants on." Warren disappeared back into the entrance, his shuffling steps loud on the wooden floor.

"Some hospitality you get here, Ross." Isabelle grunted her way up the first few steps.

"Are you sure you don't want some help?"

"No, I don't want your fucking help." As she said it the leg she stood on buckled and she fell backwards. Jake caught her and, pain arcing through his side, heaved her up like a groom carrying an angry, bleeding bride.

"I thought I said I didn't want your help," she said as Jake started thumping heavily up the stairs.

"I thought you said you were fine," he said between gasps.

She only huffed in reply, but swung her arm around Jake's neck and held on as he carried her.

The top of the stairs led into a narrow hallway with a small bench and several pairs of shoes, presumably Warren's, as well as a coat rack with several garments hung neatly on it. The hallway opened into a small, clean apartment. An old couch sat on a worn oval rug in front of a modest television, beyond which sat an old table in a tiny kitchen. Jake laboured over to the small couch and set Isabelle down as gently as he could.

She looked around. "It's filled with old crap, but at least it's clean."

Jake shook his head and painfully stood upright. He pressed his hand to his battered side, as Warren came out of a doorway on the far side of the kitchen, this time wearing a pair of old, but recently pressed, dress pants and a button up flannel shirt. He'd even straightened out his comb-over.

"Okay, Ross, what the fuck is going on? You've been acting all weird, and now you're bringing people into my house? You haven't done that since you were eighteen, got drunk after a fight, and had to sleep it off here so your old man wouldn't belt you one."

"Jesus, Warren," Jake said, looking the portly man up and down. "You always dress up for company?"

"You bring ladies to my house, Ross, I dress accordingly. If it were just you, I'd walk around in the buck and fart as often as possible." He gave his best smile to Emily. She smiled, uncertainly, in return. "Now, the fact they're ladies notwithstanding, Ross, why did you bring them here, of all godforsaken places. You trying to show them the high life?"

"We ran into a little trouble, is all, Warren. We'll be gone in the morning."

"A little trouble, huh?" Warren pulled his glasses out of his shirt pocket and slipped them on his face, then took Isabelle's chin in his hand and tilted her head up to peer at a bloody gash in her scalp below her hair-line. "Looks less like a little trouble and more like ten or twelve stitches."

Isabelle pulled her chin away and slapped at Warren's hand, giving him her best annoyed glare. Warren ignored her and shuffled into the kitchen.

Jake followed the pudgy man. "I'm serious, Warren, we'll just be here 'til the morning. Then we'll be gone."

"Jesus, Ross." Warren halted and turned to face Jake. "You're the one making a big deal of this. Did I ask you to go? Did I tell you to fuck off? Did I reach for the phone to call up the cops? No. I just wanted to know why you're here. You need to stay? Fine. Fucking stay. Just quit your sniveling. It's unbecoming in a man of your height."

Jake stood, speechless, while Warren turned and opened a cupboard above the kitchen sink and pulled out what looked like a red fishing-tackle box.

"Warren," Jake said. "If I didn't know better, I'd suspect you were getting friendly in your old age."

Warren only grunted and peered at Jake over the tops of his glasses, as he grabbed one of the kitchen chairs and set it down beside Isabelle on the couch. "Be certain, Ross. You don't know any better."

He set the red tackle-box on the end table beside the couch, opened it, and took out a small sealed package containing a curved needle.

"What do you think you're doing?" Isabelle asked, moving away as far as the couch would let her.

"I'm gonna put a couple stitches in your melon so you stop bleeding on my couch." Warren pulled on a pair of latex gloves.

"Like hell you are." Isabelle tried to get up.

Warren pushed her back with one finger. "Listen, missy. I've been stitching up fighters since before you, or lumpy here," he jerked his thumb over his shoulder towards Jake, "were even alive. And I'm damned good at it, and if you don't sit still I'm gonna mess it up, and your pretty face will be ruined. So, quit your crying and don't twitch."

Isabelle opened her mouth to protest again, but Warren grabbed her chin again and started cleaning the area around the gash. He took a small syringe and gave Isabelle a few brief injections. Within another moment he had the curved needle and surgical thread in hand and making small, neat sutures, his thick fingers working deftly.

Without taking his eyes off his work, Warren spoke to Jake. "That boy looks scared and hungry, Ross. Take him into the kitchen and feed him something while his momma cleans herself up." He looked over the top of his thick glasses at Emily. "You hurt?" Emily shook her head. "Okay. Bathroom is over there." Warren tilted his fat chin towards an open door next to the bedroom he'd recently come out of.

Emily looked down at Gareth, who clutched her dress with both hands, and smoothed his tousled hair. "Can you stay with Jake while I use the rest-room?"

The boy looked up at Jake, doubtfully, then back at his mother.

"He's our friend," Emily said. It looked as though the boy was expending a mighty effort not to cry, and then nodded slowly while his bottom lip protruded, just a little.

Jake held out one scarred hand and gave Gareth a grin. The boy looked at the hand for several heartbeats, then released his grip on his mother's skirt and hooked his small hand into Jake's. In his gentle grip, Jake could feel the boy's hand trembling.

Jake knew the child was terrified, but he had no idea what to do about it. He didn't ever recall holding a child's hand before tonight, and was not a man used to lending comfort. He'd never had anyone to give it to.

He tried to think of something to say as they walked towards the kitchen, but his mind gave him nothing but a dial tone. Once they reached the kitchen table, Jake tried to pull his hand free of Gareth's grip, but the boy wouldn't let go.

"Uh, Gareth?" Jake said softly, looking down at the top of the boy's head.

No response.

"Are you hungry? You want something to eat?"

A pause. Then a small nod.

"Can you let go so I can see what we have to work with?"

Another pause, then a slow release of the small hand. Unsure if it was the right thing, Jake hooked his hands under the boy's arms and hefted him up so he was sitting on one of the kitchen chairs. Gareth didn't look at him, but kept his eyes on his small hands, clasped tightly in his lap.

Turning with a sigh, Jake examined the small kitchen. There was a short fridge in the corner, one of the kind that was likely still lined in lead and had been made about a thousand years ago. Jake pulled the lever-like handle and opened the door to find actual food on the shelves, far more than he'd expected; milk in an old-school glass bottle, sliced ham in butcher's paper, a block of hard cheese, and a loaf of bread free of any green fur.

In the times he'd been in the gym, after-hours, he'd snuck in and slept on the stained canvass of the ring he had never been into Warren's little apartment. The chubby man was boorish and rude, and always looked a bit of a mess, but his living space was far different. It caused Jake to look at him with a different eye.

"Whatever it is you're fooling around with over there," Warren called from across the room, "make me some, too. This playing doctor shit is hungry work."

Jake grinned. Hearing Warren at his foulest lent a sense of normalcy to the fucked up day. "Okay, Warren," Jake said, laying out pieces of bread for sandwiches.

"Are they coming back?"

Jake stopped and turned at the small voice behind him. Gareth had raised his head and stared at Jake, his blue eyes red and teary.

"What's that, pal?" Jake stepped close to the boy, crouching down so they were eye-to-eye.

"Those people you were fighting, are they gonna come here? Are you gonna have to fight them again?"

"No, Gareth. They aren't gonna come here."

Gareth paused and looked down at his hands. "But you're gonna have to fight them again."

The kid was sharp, Jake had to admit. "I'm not sure. But, yes, I might have to."

"This is about me, isn't it?"

It was Jake's turn to pause. How was he supposed to answer that? How did you tell a seven year old that people had been killed fighting over him? Jake didn't know, so he did the easy thing and lied through his bent teeth. "No, of course not, Gareth. Why would you think that?"

"The big man, the one even bigger than you, he kept talking about 'the boy'. That's me isn't it?"

Lying to a child wasn't near as easy as Jake might have thought. He nodded. "Yeah, pal, he was talking about you."

The boy huffed, tears starting to flow down his face as his small voice cracked. "But, why? I didn't do anything wrong."

"No, Gareth, you didn't. You didn't do a thing wrong. Don't

think that. I'm gonna find out what they want. Don't worry."

"Are you gonna let them take me?"

The fear and sorrow in the child's voice cracked through the decades old shell around Jake's heart. The fighter felt a stinging at the corners of his eyes. "Never," he said, fighting to keep his own voice steady. "I won't let them get anywhere near you." The words were free of his mouth before Jake had time to think about them, but as they crossed the distance of years and generations to the boy, Jake knew them to be true. This child was important, and there was no way he was going to let that greasy fuck or his tattooed boogey-man get their miserable hands on him. Gareth slid off the chair and threw his arms around Jake's neck. The boxer hugged the boy back, without hesitation this time, his calloused hands catching on the soft material of the boy's pajamas.

"I thought you were gonna make something to eat."

Jake looked up to see Warren peering down at them, as he peeled off his surgical gloves.

"We're getting to it, Warren." Jake stood.

Warren gave his usual grunt. "You mind getting to it before I'm dead? I'm old, Ross, and I'm wasting away to nothing." Warren tossed his used gloves into a trash can next to the wall and began washing his hands in the kitchen sink.

Jake rolled his eyes, again, and set Gareth on the counter beside the sink. Quickly, the boy giving pointed instructions, Jake put together several sandwiches, cut them into quarters and slid them onto a plate he found in a cupboard above the sink. Jake carried the plate and several glasses to the coffee table in front of the couch, while Gareth followed, clutching the bottle of milk.

Isabelle sat on the couch, a small, handled mirror in her hand, examining Warren's handiwork. Jake didn't have to look to know the job was well done; Warren had put stitches in his own face more than once, and the old trainer did as good a job as any emergency room doctor.

"How do you feel?" Jake set the plate down.

She looked up at him, then back at the mirror. "Like a gigantic freak threw me into an idiot and ruined my day. Thanks for asking."

"You always so nice to people?"

She put the mirror down and flashed him a bright smile, her hard face actually turning pretty. "Only the dumb ones."

Jake gritted his teeth and grabbed several pieces of sandwich, then sat down in the chair Warren had been using.

Emily came out of the bathroom, her face slightly red from a fresh scrubbing, her makeup gone. Jake studied her, as she came around the end of the couch and sat on its arm beside her son, who sat at Isabelle's feet and munching on a ham sandwich. Jake marveled, yet again, at her appearance. Even without makeup and with dark circles standing out under her tired eyes, Emily was still stunning. The very sight of her made Jake's heart thump. He wondered if she had this effect on all men, or if he was just a bigger sap than most.

Warren came out of the kitchen and grabbed a triangle of sandwich off the plate. "So, you wanna tell me anymore about this trouble, Ross?" he asked around a bite of food.

Jake looked up at Isabelle who had stopped examining her forehead in the small mirror and glared at him. The dark-haired woman gave a very slight shake of her head. He trusted Warren, but had to wonder how much to tell the man for his own welfare.

He cleared his throat. "How much do you want to know, Warren?"

"How bad is it gonna be?"

"It ain't good."

Warren took another bite of sandwich and chewed quietly for a moment. "Is anyone going to be coming here looking for you? Anyone I should worry about?"

"If someone shows up looking for us, you'll need to worry about them. But I don't think anyone will."

"You sure about that, Ross? No one knows you're here?"

Jake looked over at Emily and Gareth, both who studied him. Could he say for sure that Kast and Drake would not come here looking? They knew his name, and knew his face. Would they know where he trained? He decided the odds were very long they'd come to the gym to look for him. He shook his head, hoping his hesitation didn't leave too much room for Emily and her son to doubt.

"Yeah, Warren, I'm sure no one knows."

Warren grunted again and popped the rest of his sandwich into his mouth. "If you say so, Ross, I'll take it." The chubby promoter looked up at the clock above the kitchen sink. Jake followed his gaze and saw that it was nearing midnight. Warren sighed and ran a hand over his balding pate. "Okay, I'm old and need my beauty sleep. You do what you like, but keep it down to a dull roar. There are a couple of cots in the spare room, and the sheets should be clean. I'll see you in the morning." The portly man turned and shuffled through the kitchen and into his small bedroom.

Turning from Warren's closing door to the couch, Jake smiled. "I don't think he's the only one who's tired." Gareth was listing to port, his head against his mother's hip and a half-eaten sandwich in his hand, with his small mouth open as he slept. Jake stood and easily scooped the boy up. His ribs still ached when he lifted the boy, but the throb began to lessen, his new ability to heal was kicking in. He walked around the couch, Gareth cradled to his chest, and into the small room Warren had pointed out.

There were two cots in the room, one against each wall, wide enough for one person to sleep on comfortably, both made up with white sheets and wool blankets. Jake crouched awkwardly and pulled back the blankets on one of the cots, and gently laid Gareth onto the narrow mattress. He pulled the blankets up to the boy's chin and reached out to touch his golden head, but stopped as a shadow moved through the light coming from the open doorway.

He stood and saw Emily stepping into the small room, closing the door behind her. They were in near darkness, the only light coming from the meagre glow of a street lamp, filtered through the thin curtain on the window. Jake moved away from the bed Gareth lay on, expecting Emily to walk past him and check on the boy, but she surprised Jake by stepping up to him instead.

She slid her arms around his neck and pressed her delicate face under his jaw. His breath caught in the back of his throat and a rush of blood made the skin of his face feel tight, as her slender body pressed against his.

"Thank you," she said against his skin. "Thank you for helping us."

Hesitantly, he put his hands on the small of her back and she pressed closer against him. His mouth went dry and he couldn't find any words to respond. He stood still while he felt his heart beating so hard that she must have been able to hear it crashing against the inside of his chest.

She pulled back and looked up at him, her body still pressed against his, the light from the street lamp falling across her face. He felt more than just the muscles of his body stiffening, as he looked down at her, and she gave him a hint of a smile.

"No one has ever done anything like this for me, Jake." She kissed the corner of his mouth. His pulse pounded in his ears so hard that he could barely hear her words. "No one has ever been this kind without wanting something from me first." She reached one arm behind her and slid down the zipper of her short dress, then shrugged it off her shoulders. The dress caught on the curves of her hips and Jake gasped as he looked down at the silky black bra she wore that barely covered her firm breasts. "I want to thank you." She leaned up to kiss him again and he turned his face so that she got the side of his chin instead of his mouth.

Jake's desire thrummed in him like a guitar string on the verge of breaking. Emily's scent made his mouth water, and he had a vital, uncomfortable tightness in him that cried out to let her relieve it. But, he'd seen something in her face as she tried to kiss him, and it wasn't a mirror of his desire.

He saw gratitude, certainly, in her features, and tenderness. But most of all he saw sad, and tired. She didn't want him the way he wanted her, but she was willing to give herself to him to thank him because she thought it was what he wanted from her. It was what all men wanted from her, and paid her for, and she was willing to give it to him. The thought of the girl before him servicing him like he were any other man, out of an obligation she felt, stamped out his lust and left him feeling empty.

He took his hands off her back and she arched towards him, presenting her body to him. Instead of groping her like she ex-pected, he pulled her arms from his neck and pulled her dress up to cover her chest.

"You don't have to do this," he said, as she looked at him, puzzled. "I'm going to help you no matter what. You don't have to do anything for me."

"I know I don't have to," she said, and reached up to touch his face. "I want to."

He put his hands on her hips and pushed her away slightly. "I know you want to. But you don't want me, and it's okay." He leaned forward and kissed her softly on the forehead, his scarred lips pressing against her smooth skin. "You should get some rest. I need to check on Isabelle." The last was a lie. The dark-haired woman wanted his care about as much as she wanted to eat broken glass, but Jake needed to get out of dark room and away from Emily's scent.

She dipped her head forward, then looped her arms through the straps of her dress and zipped it up. When she lifted her face again there was a tear running down her cheek. "Thank you," she said again, her voice hoarse, choked and unsteady. "Really. I've never met anyone like you before, Jake." She reached up and touched his face again, but without any sexuality in it. "You're a good man."

Jake nodded, not trusting himself to speak. He'd been called many things in his life, but a 'good man' was not among them. He felt his own emotion running, and tried to keep it from his voice as he cleared his throat and tilted his chin towards the empty cot. "Really, you need to rest."

She nodded and took her hand from his face. Before she could say anything else, he turned and pulled the door open, then stepped through. As he closed it, he heard the springs on the empty cot squeak with her weight.

He stood with his back to the closed door for a few moments, his head hanging, catching his breath and willing his heart to slow. His head knew he'd done the right thing, but other parts of his body called him an idiot.

He saw a shadow move across his feet and looked up. Isabelle leaned on the back of the couch, her muscular arms folded across her chest, her eyes narrow.

"What?" Jake asked, after a few strained moments of silence.

"She offered herself to you, didn't she?"

Jake scowled. "How would you know that?"

Isabelle shrugged. "She seems the type to give herself up out of gratitude to an idiot." She glanced down. "That and there is a bulge in your jeans."

Jake looked down, his face growing hot, and turned towards the kitchen. Isabelle limped forward and put a hand on his arm. He paused, and lifted his gaze to her.

"I'm sorry, Ross." She looked down at her own feet and then back up. "I can feel the draw of her and the child just as much as anyone else. She has a power she scarcely realises, and for a man to resist her, well, it's something. I just wanted to say I may have misjudged you. You might have something to you after all."

Jake was unsure whether to take the hard woman's words as a compliment and be done, or wait for the jibe to come. "Thanks."

She grinned slightly, a lifting of one corner of her mouth. "I still think you're an idiot. But you might be a salvageable idiot."

Jake smiled in turn, and then looked down at Isabelle's hand on his arm, noticing she hadn't removed it yet. The dark-haired woman looked at it as well, and then shifted a little closer. Jake inhaled and held his breath, waiting for her to stab him or toss him across the room or something, then was surprised when she looked into his face. The hard lines around her eyes and mouth—the ones that gave the impression she was permanently pissed off about something—softened and faded. He breathed in again and her scent filled his head. Where Emily smelled of perfume and sexuality, Isabelle smelled of honey soap and honest sweat. She moved closer still and Jake felt the press of her body, all taut muscle and hard lines, against him.

"What are you doing?" he asked, his mouth going dry again.

She tilted her head and looked, for a moment, to be a pretty girl instead of a hardened fighter. "If a man can resist such a temptation as that woman, perhaps he is strong enough to provide a little comfort." She pulled him around the end of the couch then shoved him, hard, so he fell backwards and sat heavily. She pulled her shirt over her head, then unbuckled her jeans and pushed them to the floor. The light from the lamp beside the couch lighted one side of her body and accentuated the lines and valleys of her muscle, making her hard curves stand out. Jake sat and stared at her, his brain not quite able to comprehend what was happening.

She crouched and put one knee on the couch between his legs, then reached for his belt buckle. "Know one thing, Ross," she said as she yanked at his belt with one hand and ripped his shirt over his head and off his arms with the other. "I am not offering myself to you. I'm borrowing you for a few minutes."

Jake thought it best to say nothing as she climbed on top of him and reached between his legs. As he was learning, more and more as the days went on, some things you really should not question.

CHAPTER ELEVEN

ake lay on the couch, panting and staring at the ceiling, as
Isabelle stood, stretched, and ran her hands through her
black hair. He could not remember the last time he'd been
touched by a naked woman, let alone so thoroughly used,
but there wasn't an ounce of complaint in him.

The lamplight fell across the stitches in Isabelle's forehead.
"Do you want me to take those stitches out for you?" he asked
as he struggled to sit up and pull his pants on.

She looked at him like he'd just asked if she wanted to eat
shit. "Why would I want you to do that?"

"Won't they be hard to take out once they heal over?"

She looked at him, clearly not comprehending, for a
moment, then rolled her eyes and shook her head. "No, Ross.
We don't all heal like you and Mac. That's an individual gift just
like all the others. I'll have to leave those in for a few days, just
like anyone else." She grimaced, putting a hand to her ribs as she
bent, stiff and slow, to pick up her shirt from the floor. "In fact,
you might have to find me a wheel chair."

As she reached her arms above her head again to pull on her
snug t-shirt, Jake saw the faint white lines of old scars criss-
crossing her body. One long line led from the bottom of her rib

cage, down her hip, and close to her knee. He reached out to trace one finger along the line, touching it softly.

Her head snapped down as he touched her. "What are you doing?"

He pulled his hand away. "Sorry, I didn't mean—"

She moved away from him and stepped awkwardly into her jeans. "This life is hard, Ross. So we take our comfort where we can, and a soft touch goes a long way. But you and I," she pulled her jeans over her taught hips, "are not lovers, and we are not friends. Take what you've been given, be happy with it, and don't go looking for anything else."

Jake folded his hands in his lap. These were strange people he'd fallen in with. "Right. So, can I ask where you got the scar?"

She frowned slightly, doing up her belt buckle. "That," she said, "was what killed me." She sat down on the couch beside him and started pulling on her boots. "A piece of shrapnel about the size of a tennis ball tore me open." She finished the laces on one boot and started on the other.

"Shrapnel?"

"Yes, from a road-side bomb in Pakistan. I was a field medic, and was trying to hold in the guts of an eighteen year old boy while he was carried on a stretcher. One of the soldiers carrying the stretcher stepped right on it and it killed us all." She picked up a belt of knives Jake hadn't noticed before, several of the small sheaths empty, and began buckling it on. "I woke up the next day, all torn to hell but still alive, and hobbled back to a base where they patched me up and sent me home. It wasn't until Mac met me at the airport and took me to Morgan that I realised I'd actually died, and been given this second chance."

Jake sat, rubbing his chin. Something tickling at the recesses of his brain. "You were in the army?"

She shrugged. "Yeah, sort of. My mother was born here, but my father was American. I was a nursing student and decided to join up to make my father happy. Within a few months I was in a foreign country changing bloody bandages and listening to men scream."

Jake crossed his arms, the tickling in his brain growing to a full on itch. "Have you met many other people like you? I mean, like us?"

She looked at him, her mouth turned down in a frown. "Not many, but a few. Even you must understand these second chances are not common."

"The people who get these second chances, what did they do before?"

"What are you on about?"

"Well," he stood up, and picked up his jeans from where they were heaped on the floor. "Mac was a soldier, and you were a medic in a war zone. What was Morgan before he died?"

Isabelle pursed her lips. "He doesn't speak of it much, but Mac told me he was a detective in a police force. In Toronto, or something, when the city was young. What are you getting at?"

He pulled on his jeans, buckled them up, and then pulled on his dirty t-shirt. "You were a medic, Mac a soldier, Morgan a cop. All of you did something useful, performing some kind of service, before you were given this second chance. Before you were... chosen. So what happened with me?" He looked at the floor, letting the question hang between them. "I'm nothing but a washed up fighter who runs a fork lift to pay my rent. I never did anything to help anyone in my entire life until the day I was killed in a parkade, in a fight I never wanted to be in."

The words stung because he wasn't just making self-deprecating comments to make himself look modest. They were true. Jake didn't go around beating up people, or robbing old ladies, but he'd spent the majority of his life carefully avoiding other people's messes and staying out of their business. He never asked for any help and certainly never offered any. He'd been on his own since his father died shortly after Jake turned pro, and his mother before that, in his barely remembered childhood.

"I'm not like you people," he said. "I've never done anything good in my life. I don't belong here."

He expected Isabelle to jump in and agree, tell him he was an idiot and he didn't deserve the gifts he'd received, but instead she sighed heavily. He looked up at her.

"I don't know why any of us were chosen for this, Ross, but the Fates don't make mistakes. They saw something in you," she looked him up and down, "for whatever reason, and picked you for this chance. I cannot explain it."

"The Fates," Jake said, snorting. "What the fuck are these 'Fates'? Where are they? Are they hiding on a mountain top? Do they buy their socks at Walmart? Can I phone them up and ask them what the fuck they were thinking? You people are always talking about the mysterious Fates." Jake waved his fingers in the air, making a gesture of mock wonder. "But, no one has told me what they are yet."

She sat on the couch, leaned back and crossed her legs and arms, as Jake paced on the other side of the coffee table. "The Fates," she said, then tilted her head to one side and sucked her teeth, "are hard to explain."

He stopped pacing, put his hands in his pockets, and waited for the apparently difficult explanation.

"They are a consciousness," Isabelle said after a few moments, "that tries to keep some semblance of order in the world. They give us our gifts, and present us with opportunities, and leave it up to us to decide what to do with them."

He lifted his shoulders. "Whose side are they on?"

She shook her head. "I'm not sure there is any side for them. They might be good, or they might be bad, but it seems their goal is balance. For whatever reason, it always seems our enemies have the upper hand, Morgan says it's because the dark can always see into the light, but not the other way around, so the Fates help us out once in a while. To tell you the truth, I don't know how they help us, other than giving us a new member for the clan on occasion."

"Okay, so the bad guys, they have their clans too, right?"

She shrugged. "In a manner of speaking, yes."

"So do the Fates give them gifts, too? Are they killed once and then given a second chance to be a bigger asshole?"

"No, for them it's different. The dark seems to be able to recruit who they want, and their strength, their gifts, are gained through ritual. A man like Kast is the result of many dark acts, the power of each piling on the last. Our side, who stand against people like Kast, are chosen whether we like it or not."

Jake had more questions, but paused. "'Whether we like it or not?' I thought all you people in this clan were excited about this shit. I thought you wanted to be here."

Isabelle looked away, silent for several moments. "I never

wanted this, Jake." Her use of his first name surprised him. "I had a life at home and a boy waiting to marry me when I got back. I didn't want to die in the desert and then be told I was needed for some kind of cosmic struggle. It's worse than the war." She sighed, the sound filled with weariness. "I am here because I need to be. Because there is no one else to do this work if not me. Believe me when I say I was chosen for this, just like you, but I never wanted it."

Jake pulled his hand out of his pocket and rubbed at his chin. "Did anyone ever explain to you why, exactly, it was you who was chosen?"

She shook her head. "No. I asked questions of Mac and Morgan when I was first brought into the clan, but neither one of them could tell me. Mac seems to think it's some kind of calling and a great gift to be chosen for this life. Morgan is more like a college football scout trying to make his team stronger and glad of anyone who shows up to bolster the numbers. Almost twenty years I've been fighting this war, with nothing to show for it but a bunch of scars and a room in Morgan's house, and I've never been told why."

Jake slowly walked around the coffee table and sat down on the couch beside Isabelle. He was stunned at the raw truth in her words and the amount of herself she'd shared with him. "Why do you keep doing it if you don't know why?"

"Because of nights like tonight. Because when a man like Drake sends his dog to snatch a child, someone has to be there to stop him. Someone has to be willing to hold up a light and face the dark."

Jake nodded. That was the first thing he'd heard that made sense since he'd been stabbed to death in a dingy parkade.

He still had questions, though. He still felt like he was shadowboxing in a dark room, fumbling at specters, punching at nothing. Isabelle was the first person who'd given him a straight answer about anything.

"You ever heard of a guy called the Preacher?"

"The Preacher?" she asked, looking at him. "You mean that stinking freak that carries around the Sears catalogue?"

He nodded.

"Yeah, I've heard of him. Why?"

"He knows what we are."

Isabelle rolled her eyes. "You really have been hit in the head too many times, Ross. How would a homeless psych-patient possibly know what we are?"

"Cause I think he's one of us."

She stood up, her expression incredulous. "You really have lost it."

"No, I haven't. When I was following the two guys who killed me, he seemed to know what I was doing and helped me. The next time he saw me, he was talking about the Fates, and how they'd been bent. And he moves like you do; way faster than he has any right to."

"No, Ross, that's not possible. No member of our clan, or any clan for that matter, would be allowed to rot away in an alley. It would be too big a waste."

He shrugged. "What if someone wanted him to rot away?"

"What does that mean?"

"I'm not sure, but the guy knows something." He stood up. "I think, if I can get him to stop yelling at me about the Lord, he might be able to tell me what is going on. About why Drake wants the boy," he pointed at the room where Emily and Gareth slept, "and why he wants him so badly." He chewed at his bottom lip. "Have you ever known them, the bad guys, to take children before?"

Isabelle appeared to be thinking for a moment, and then shook her head. "It was a practice from the old days, before my time, but it brought too much attention to have children go missing, so they stopped doing it and found other ways to perform their rituals."

"When they did do it, what was it for?"

"Power, Ross," she said. "It's all, always, about power. The energy to be found in the life of a child is significant and can be used to accomplish great things, or very dark things. The darker the purpose, the more harm you have to do."

"The night I first helped Mac, Taber was trying to sacrifice a kid and had already killed another. Now they want Gareth. I wonder how many others they grabbed that Mac didn't know about." He scrubbed a hand over his short hair. "What are they doing that they needed so much power?"

Isabelle shook her head. "I don't know. I hate to admit it, but you might be on to something. I need to call Morgan."

Jake stood. "Okay. I'm going to go ask some questions."

"Ask questions? Where?"

He stepped towards the staircase and stopped to look back at her, then nodded at the closed door. "Watch over them. I'm going to find the Preacher."

Jake closed the door to the old Mercedes and looked up and down the filthy street. The Whalley Strip, the dirtiest street in all of Surrey, was still alive even at this late hour, as figures barely resembling humans shuffled along the sidewalk going about their addicted business.

This was not a place Jake wanted to be, even if it were broad daylight. The denizens of the street, be they the staggering crack zombies in their stained and ragged clothing or the strutting drug dealers in their designer jogging pants and Cadillac Escalades, would all happily kill him for the keys to the Mercedes or the stained jacket on his back. He needed to find the Preacher, and this late at night, the man would be around people; he needed someone to mock.

Wondering if he was making a mistake and wasting time, Jake started walking slowly down the street. The questions burning in his mind seemed so important while he stood in Warren's little apartment with Isabelle, but now, in the dim glow of the street lamps, they seemed hollow and useless. He wondered where Mac was, if he'd made it past both Kast's minions and the police, and if he would be better off trying to find the older man. Or, perhaps, Jake should talk to Morgan. He still didn't like the red haired man, but he was one of the good guys in this freakish war the boxer had gotten himself into, and he was running short on friends.

A deathly skinny woman, wearing black leotards and mismatched high heels veered towards Jake, as she shambled down the sidewalk.

"Hi," she said, as she rubbed a dirty hand under her nose and then scratched at her scraggly hair.

"Uh, hi," Jake replied, taking a step back.

The woman looked Jake up and down, and wiped her nose again. "So, I'll suck you off for five dollars."

He had been propositioned by prostitutes before, but never quite so blatantly, or anywhere near so cheap. "Uh, no thanks," he said, and took another step backwards.

The woman's eyes went wide and buggy. "Well, fuck you, then, you fucking fuck!" the woman screamed, as she leaned towards Jake, spit flying from her lips and her arms flailing. She stood back, wiped at her nose again, and shuffled away down the sidewalk as though nothing had happened.

"This fucking place." Jake turned and carried on down the sidewalk.

The occupants of 'The Strip' looked at him warily, as he walked by. Anyone who wasn't in one of the two predominant categories, dealer or user, was almost always a cop. Half the people he passed hurriedly stuffed things into their pockets and looked like they were ready to bolt. Jake kept looking for the Preacher, hoping that he hadn't misjudged the fact he would be here, yelling abuse and ridiculousness at an apathetic flock.

Jake's gamble paid off. He found the man sitting on his Sears catalogue, in front of a closed mechanic's shop. The windows of the shop were so heavily barred one might think they kept gold inside instead of tools.

"Lo comes a goat, a lost expression on his face," the Preacher said without looking up from an old McDonald's wrapper, as he busily picked at old cheese with a long, dirty fingernail.

"I have a couple of questions." Jake wondered if he wasted his time.

"Oh?" The Preacher said, and looked up from the wrapper. "The goat comes and seeks knowledge from the shepherd. The good Lord has guided you far, my hoofed little friend." The Preacher suddenly stood with fluid ease and stuffed the wrapper into the pocket of his filthy pants. "What can a humble man tell such an enlightened ungulate as you?"

Jake, never an articulate man, was already having a hard time sorting his thoughts, and decided to put them as simply as he knew how. "What the fuck is going on?"

"Ah, the sixty-four thousand dollar question, Goat. What the fuck is going on, indeed?" The Preacher looked away, down the street and sighed. It was an honest, weary sigh, without any sarcasm, ridicule or theatrics in it. It was the sigh of a man who was very, very tired. "I have been asking myself the same question for twenty years, Goat, while the world shifts around me and I hide among these streets."

"What are you hiding from?"

"I hide from the iniquities of man!" The Preacher turned and shouted at a street light, all the weariness gone, replaced once again with lunacy. "I hide from the foolishness of goats who cannot even see the beards dangling from their chins and the collars around their throats."

"No!" Jake shouted, stepping close, heedless of the man's stink and grabbed his arm. "No more riddles. No more bullshit. You know what is going on. You're one of them." Jake hesitated. "One of us. Now drop the fucking act and talk to me."

The Preacher looked down at Jake's hand, then up into his face. The lunacy was gone, his eyes clear and sane. "I hide from lies, Goat. I hide from men who would use their gifts for unintended purpose. I hide from subtle tyranny that would make honest men into fools, and harmless souls into tools of deception. I hide from those who would use the lives of innocents to bend the Fates and meet their own ends."

Jake released his grip and threw his hand in the air. "What does that even mean?"

"It means, Goat," the Preacher said, as he bent down to pick up his catalogue and dust it off with a hand that was dirtier than the sidewalk, "that nothing is as it should be, and good men can only take so much. I was a good man, once. I stood much where you stand now, but I was cursed with eyes that were open and could look on no more. I could not stand and see the cause I had shed so much blood for be perverted and twisted. I could listen to no more rubbish. So I removed myself and sought purpose elsewhere, where I would not be troubled."

Jake let his chin fall to his chest. The events of the long night and the struggle to make sense of the Preacher's rambling caught up to him. Weariness trickled into his bones, filling them to bursting. It was only with an immense force of will that he didn't slump down and sit on the sidewalk. He lifted his head with an effort and looked at the Preacher. "What are you talking about, man? What am I supposed to do?"

"You must open your own eyes, Goat. You must know the truth in what you've seen and not allow yourself to be led where you're not supposed to be."

"What? Then where is it I'm supposed to be?"

The Preacher looked up at the street light and said nothing.

Trying to get answers out of the man was like trying to solve a Rubik's cube, fucking near impossible, but you heard about someone, somewhere once who had done it, so you kept trying. Jake rubbed his chin. "What were you before you were… this? Before you got your second chance."

The Preacher opened the Sears catalogue to a section with pictures of men in pyjamas, and ran his finger down the page, nodding, then looked up at Jake. "I was a soldier, Goat, in a war long past, and near to forgotten."

Jake nodded. "Just like Mac and Isabelle. You served something before you got this, well… whatever the fuck this is. So what about me? I'm nothing like you people. Why was I given this thing?"

"The Fates choose carefully." The Preacher flipped through the catalogue, as though looking for the answer to Jake's questions. "Their gifts are not given lightly, and in this case, they did not make the choice themselves. It was made for them."

Jake scowled. "What do you mean 'made for them'?"

The Preacher said nothing, but looked at a picture of a home gym and nodded.

"Are you saying these Fates, whatever the fuck they are, didn't want to pick me?"

The Preacher closed the catalogue with a snap and lifted it above his head while pointing at it dramatically. "Ah, the wayward goat comes to the Lord's truth, and finally sees the light!" He looked at Jake. "You can be taught, Goat. Perhaps you are worthy after all. Whether the Fates intended it or not."

"If it wasn't supposed to be me, then who was it?"

The Preacher shrugged. "Only the Fates know, and they don't do much talking, even to so learned and painfully handsome men as myself."

"How, then? Why? How did I end up getting this thing? This chance?"

"If you open your beady little eyes, Goat, you will see."

Jake sighed and rubbed at his face again. "How do you know all this? If you're here hiding, how do you know what these fucking Fates are doing?"

"Seeing is easy when your eyes are open, and the good Lord has blessed you with sight, and not cursed you with horns and a tiny little brain." The Preacher moved away from Jake, getting louder, pretending to read from the Sears catalogue. He started to slip back into whatever insanity he hid in. Jake was losing him.

Jake followed him down the sidewalk, trying desperately to think of the right question that would get a usable answer. "But, what am I supposed to do?" he blurted. "What do they want with that little kid and his mother? What should I do with them?"

The Preacher spun on his heel, one filthy hand streaking out and grabbing the front of Jake's coat. "You must take your gifts and use them the way the Fates want them to be used, though they weren't meant for you. You are a fighter, Goat. Do what you know how to do. Do not let the boy be used like the others."

As quickly as he'd grabbed Jake, the Preacher let him go and pointed a dirty finger at a car that slowed so the occupant could take a look at the sniffling prostitute that had offered to service Jake. "The Lord sees you and your filthy desires, fornicator!" The Preacher screamed, as he ran towards the car. "He sees what you would do with this unfortunate creature."

The car sped up and the Preacher chased it, waving his Sears catalogue, while the prostitute sniffed and screamed at him for scaring away a customer.

Jake pinched his ruined nose and shook his head. Sighing, he turned and walked back towards the Mercedes.

The conversation with the Preacher had at least given him a few things to think about, but the questions in his head still outnumbered the answers. If these Fates, whatever they really were, hadn't planned on picking him for this second chance, then who had they planned on picking. And if they didn't want him, who did? And why?

He reached the Mercedes and stuck the key into the door

lock, when a scrape behind him made him turn. He looked over his shoulder to see a bloody figure stumble out between two buildings and come shambling towards him with a sword in its hand. He left the keys in the lock and raised his fists, wishing he'd brought Satan's drywall hammer with him instead of leaving it on the back seat of the car.

"Hello, Jake," the figure said, as it fell towards him.

Reflexively, Jake grabbed the falling body. It took him several heartbeats to realise it was Mac.

"Holy fuck, man," Jake said. "What happened to you?"

"I ran into a little trouble getting here."

Jake looped an arm around Mac's waist, opened the driver's door to the Mercedes, and hit the power door lock button. He dragged the wounded man to the back door, leaned him against the car so he could open it, and then dumped him in.

"What kind of trouble? You look like you've been run through a wood chipper."

Mac held his side and breathed through clenched teeth, his eyes squeezed shut, as he pulled his legs into the car. "I got clear of the police fine, but Kast's people were everywhere and a few of them caught up to me."

"A few of them?" Jake asked. "How many?"

"Seven. Maybe eight."

"Eight? Where are they now?" Jake fumbled Mac's sword out of his limp hand and gripped it as he looked around.

"They are where I left them, and will go no further."

Jake looked down at Mac, taking in a ragged cut in his hairline and the blotches of blood on his clothing. He couldn't decide if he respected him, or was terrified of him. "You're a hard man, Mac."

"Fear and desperation make men hard, Jake. Where are the boy and his mother? Are they safe?"

"They're fine." Jake closed the back door before dropping into the drivers seat, slamming his own door behind him. "They're with a friend of mine, and Isabelle is watching them." He put the keys in the ignition and started the car. "How'd you even know I'd be here?"

"I had a feeling." Mac grimaced, as he lifted his hand from his side and looked down.

Jake followed Mac's eyes and saw a long rip in his denim jacket and a bloody gash in the skin beneath. "Holy Christ, Mac, you're torn up good."

"Yeah, but you should see the other guy." Mac chuckled and there were flecks of blood on his lips.

Jake dropped the car into drive and pulled away from the curb. "My friend, Warren, he'll be able to patch you up a little. Hopefully, close that cut enough to keep you from bleeding to death." Jake ruled out the idea of the hospital without even asking. Mac had killed several men that night, and if he showed up in the emergency room with stab wounds, the police would likely appear soon after.

"I'd be grateful, Jake. Then we have to call Morgan, tell him we have the boy safe. He will know what to do next."

"Isabelle said she was going to do that when I left. He probably already knows."

Mac nodded and laid his head back against the seat. "I had a feeling I'd find help on that street, Jake, and I was lucky it was you. What were you doing there?"

Jake pressed his lips together as he drove, thinking of his response. In the short time he'd known him, Mac had never given the boxer a reason to doubt him, but Jake wondered if he could trust him. He didn't know enough about this weird game he played to know what the rules were. It could be that Mac looked honest, but was really cheating like a mother-fucker. Was he asking what Jake had been doing because he needed the information to help the situation they were all in, or did he check to see if Jake had discovered something he wasn't supposed to know? If the Preacher was right, and someone had fooled these Fates, then who could be trusted?

"Nothing. I just had an idea and it turned out to be a waste of time," Jake said after a few moments, glancing at Mac in the rear-view mirror.

"Hmmm." Mac closed his eyes. "You've met the man they now call the Preacher."

Jake tried to pull in a steady breath, as the muscles in his back bunched and his face started to burn. "Uh," he said, thinking feverishly of what to say. He felt like a kid caught doing something he shouldn't.

"He is one of us, you know." Mac's eyes were still closed, and Jake didn't know how to respond. He wasn't sure if Mac was playing him on, testing him, genuinely imparting information, or a combination of all three.

"I kind of had that suspicion," Jake said, trying to sound like he didn't know too much.

"His name is Will Connors, or it was once, anyway. He was a good man. A good friend."

Jake opened his mouth and gaped for a moment, before clearing his throat and licking his lips. "You knew him?"

Mac nodded. "I did. He was a member of our clan."

"He was?" Jake asked, feigning complete surprise. "When was this?"

"He left our fold about twenty years ago, before Isabelle came to us."

Jake drove a few more blocks, waiting to see if Mac would volunteer any more information. The grey haired man said nothing, but rode with his eyes closed. "Why did he leave?" Jake asked when the silence had grown too long for his frayed nerves.

Mac opened his eyes and sighed. "He and Morgan had a falling out. A bad one, that came to the edge of bloodshed. Will took exception to the way Morgan led the clan, and Morgan could not tolerate Will constantly questioning his word. Will said he was leaving and Morgan was only too happy to watch him go."

"I thought you couldn't leave." Jake brows came together, as he remembered his first meeting with Morgan. "When I tried to walk, you told me that Taber's clan would come looking for me since I'd had a part of his death. How has the Preacher, or Will, survived without you?"

Mac took in a deep breath, wincing as he pressed his hand tighter to his side. "Will was better than most of us at hiding, blending in with the people around him. He could have walked through a gathering of a dark clan and not be noticed. When he left our clan, he hid, but he did it not by disappearing, but by hiding who and what he was. He created a facade to wear as he walked the streets and our enemies never recognised him." Mac paused and looked out the window. "Only he wore the facade too long, and it went a little too deep, and he truly lost who he was beneath the play-acting and the filth. He became what he was pretending to be."

"Have you talked to him?"

"Not in more than a year," Mac said. "He would seek me out, when he first left, try and explain his side of his dispute with Morgan, try and convince me he was right. As the years went on, our talks became less and less frequent, until one day I looked for him and the man I once called brother was no longer there; only the reeking shell he'd left behind." Mac sighed again and looked over at Jake. "You must be careful of what he says, for it is not always sincere. He is still angry with Morgan, and deeply lost. I believe he would say near anything to bring Morgan trouble."

Jake's feeling of being caught doing something he shouldn't flared up again. "How do you know I've been talking to him?"

Mac shrugged. "If someone new comes to the clan, Will always seems to find them, yell nonsense at them, call them names and tell them someone is deceiving them. I don't know how he figures it out, but he does."

Before Mac came stumbling out of the darkness, bloodied and torn, Jake had been sure he was onto something among the web of the Preacher's ramblings; sure he'd discovered something important about what was happening around him. If Mac was telling the truth, and the Preacher was only spewing shit at him to piss Morgan off, then Jake was left with what he had before: two thirds of fuck all.

One question still tickled at Jake's mind. Taking his eyes off the road for a moment, he glanced over at Mac. "When Will got pissed off about the way Morgan was running the clan, was he right?"

Mac pursed his lips, then grimaced in pain. He drew in a deep breath and blew it out through loose lips. "No leader is flawless, and no one will agree on every matter, but Will made some horrific accusations that couldn't possibly be true. There were things Morgan might have done different, other decisions might have been made, but in the end he was, and is, a good man and helps to keep this city as best he can. When events came to a head, when Will was begging me to leave with him, and Morgan was giving me the option to stay, I chose the level head and stayed where I could do the most good."

"Do you trust him? Morgan, I mean."

Mac nodded immediately, without hesitation. "With my life, Jake."

Grimacing, Jake pushed down a little harder on the accelerator. He didn't much like Mac's response, because Jake was convinced he'd soon be doing just that.

CHAPTER TWELVE

Jake drove the Mercedes slowly down the street in front of Tartan Boxing, as Mac spoke from the front passenger seat. "We have to move the girl and her son from here, Jake. We'll take them to Morgan's house, where we can marshal our strength, and call for friends to stand with us. Morgan might have gathered reinforcements already; that is what he was doing when Isabelle and I came to the girl's house. Yes, once we are strong again, and not running, we can decide what to do."

Nodding mutely, Jake turned into the alley behind the gym and pulled the car in beside Warren's old Lincoln. The boxer was not at all happy with the way the night was turning out. He wasn't sure he trusted Morgan. Hell, he wasn't sure he trusted Mac, and he had done nothing but steer him right and had saved his life at least once. There was something about Morgan that set Jake on edge; a hint of that fighter's instinct that tells you when your opponent is putting you on so he can give you a good shot in the liver. The man was too likeable. In his presence, Jake wanted to trust him, to like him, and Jake hated nearly everyone.

"Couldn't we just keep them here for a while?" Jake put the

car in park and switched it off, then turned in his seat to look at Mac. "They'll be fine with Warren. We can take Isabelle down to Morgan's, fill him in on what's happening, and get some of those reinforcements you were talking about."

Mac shook his head. "No, Jake. We must not leave them unguarded. Your friend may be a good man, but he cannot stand against what will come for them if our enemies discover where you've hidden the girl and her boy. You should not have left them to seek out Will either. They must be protected."

Jake hated to admit it, but Mac was right. If the giant tattooed freak came here, Warren wouldn't even be able to slow him down. He nodded. "Okay, man, we'll do it."

The words faded and died in Jake's throat, as he glanced out the passenger window to the back door to the gym. A sliver of orange light showed around the edges. Jake was sure he'd shut it and locked it tight before he left. His heart lurched in his chest, as he scrambled for the door handle. Mac, following Jake's gaze, looked over and cursed.

His heart thumping, Jake leaned over the back seat, groping around until he felt the handle of his hammer. Jumping out of the driver's seat, he ran to the gym entrance, not pausing to see if Mac followed, and slowed as he reached the door. The steel frame was ripped apart, the bolt shattered. Jake's mouth went dry as he saw a huge, dusty boot print beside where the bolt used to be.

He shouldered open the door and sprinted up the stairs. His heart dropped even further when he reached the top. The small apartment was in shambles, the furniture reduced to match sticks, and there was a thick spray of blood against one wall. Nothing moved. Jake felt a hot splash of bile surge up the back of his throat and his mouth took on a harsh, sour taste.

"Emily!" Jake shouted, gripping the hammer. He crashed through the debris and into the small spare room. The two bunks were turned on their sides, the blankets heaped in the corners of the room. His limbs felt numb, his vision swimming, as he searched the empty room. He turned and staggered back through the doorway. He looked up to see Mac limp through the entrance from the stairs.

"They're gone." His own voice sounded distant and hollow

in his ears. "I never should have left them."

Mac leaned against the wall, sword dangling from his right hand while his left was pressed to his side. "Oh, Jake," he said, looking at the floor beside the boxer's feet.

Jake looked down and saw a crumpled form lying under a broken kitchen chair. He bent and scooped the chair aside to reveal Isabelle, her clothes bloody and torn, her hair matted to the side of her head.

"Oh, Christ." He knelt beside her and cradled her carefully to his chest. Her head lolled and her eyes were part way open. Jake felt her neck for a pulse, then put his head to her chest and listened, hearing nothing. He felt his eyes sting and jaw tighten, as he pressed his fingers on her eye-lids, closing them for the last time.

Mac knelt down beside Jake, put one hand on his shoulder, and the other on Isabelle's forehead. Jake waited for him to say something meaningful or profound, but the older man just knelt there, looking at Isabelle's bloody face, his lips pressed into a thin line.

A rustling and a groan came from the other side of the room. Mac tried to leap up, but had to put a hand to the wall to keep from falling over. Jake set down Isabelle as gently as he could and picked up his hammer. A round shape, beside the tipped-over refrigerator, shifted and let out another groan.

"Warren?" Jake vaulted over the upside-down couch.

"Ross?" Warren asked, as he struggled to sit up.

Jake knelt beside the heavy man and helped him to sit upright and lean against the wall. There was a thick gash in his bald pate, both his eyes were blackening, and he was missing one of his upper teeth. "What happened, Warren?"

"I got up to piss and heard a crash from the bottom of the stairs, then the biggest fucker I ever seen came through the door." Warren winced and touched his head tentatively. "The girl, Isabelle, stabbed him a couple times, but it looked like he didn't even feel it, and he walked over her like she wasn't there. Smashed through the door to the spare room, came out carrying the little kid and dragging the blonde girl."

"Kast," Mac said, as he limped through the broken furniture. "Was he alone?"

Warren shook his head slowly. "No, he had a couple guys looked like homeless trash, and some freak who looked like a wanna-be rock star. The rock star had this funny beard, looked like it was half ripped off. Isabelle took down one of the homeless guys, but the rock star stuck her with a long knife when she was taking on the other two."

Jake clenched his teeth and hot rage burned up his face. If he met up with that man, Naeven, again, he'd do more than rip off part of his beard.

Warren coughed and spit again. "I tried to help. Hit that big fucker a good one in the head, but he just tossed me away like I was nothing. The showy guy, the rock star, danced a jig on me when I was already down."

"Did they say anything, Warren?" Jake asked. "Did they say where they were taking Emily and Gareth?"

The chubby man shook his head. "No, the big guy didn't say much, just came through here like a steam engine. The rock star did a lot of yapping about the dark prevailing and resistance would do no good, and blah-fuckity-blah. I didn't have a clue what he was on about."

"I never should have left." Jake rubbed his face with his hand.

"If you'd been here, you would only be dead too," Mac said. "You could not have stopped Kast. He is too much for you, especially if he had help."

Jake felt a fury building inside him at Mac's words. A fury he planned on introducing to Kast when they met again. They would see who was too much for whom.

"The boy and his mother were taken alive," Mac continued. "We may have an opportunity to get them back."

"That won't do Isabelle any good," Jake said.

Mac looked down at his sword and said nothing.

"I thought you were on your way back sooner," Warren said. "After your friend talked to you."

"What?" Jake asked. "After what friend talked to me?"

"The girl, Isabelle," Warren said. "I heard her talking on the phone while I was lying in bed, trying to decide if I had to piss or not. I assumed she was talking to you."

"She must have called Morgan." Jake looked up at Mac.

The grey haired man nodded. "Must have. At least he'll know about the fight in front of the girl's house and that we faced Kast. He will call for other members of the clan. He will be prepared."

Jake stood and helped Warren up, then stood a kitchen chair back on its legs and led the chubby man to it. "Warren, he's cut up pretty bad." He tilted his chin towards Mac. "Can you put some stitches in him?"

Warren looked at the bloody splotch on Mac's jacket, then looked around the room. He pointed past Mac. "Yeah, grab the kit." Jake looked where Warren pointed and saw the first aid kit half hidden beneath a couch cushion.

Jake fetched the kit while Mac sat in a chair in front of Warren and stripped down to the waist. Jake paused in the act of righting the kitchen table to stare at Mac's upper body: it was a roadmap of jagged white scars, front and back, the mark from the German bayonet foremost among them. It made Jake's old injuries look pitiful and mild in comparison.

He turned the coffee table the right side up, found it would stand on its own, and pulled it up to the two seated men and set the first aid kid on it. Warren opened the kit, then started to clean Mac's side with damp, cloth squares from a small, white package.

"What is Kast going to do with Gareth, now that he has him, Mac?" Jake asked, still taking in the sight of the scars.

"He will take him to Drake."

Jake fought the urge to punch the older man in the side of the head. "I guessed that. What is Drake going to do with him?"

"I don't know, Jake," Mac said. He hissed, as Warren jabbed him with a small syringe.

Jake paused. "Will he do to him what his people did to the kid we found in the bathtub?"

Mac hesitated, and Jake's heart lurched again. "Truly, I do not know, Jake. Perhaps he will, or perhaps he'll have other plans for the boy. Whatever he plans, we have to regroup with Morgan. We cannot go for them alone."

Jake turned away and rubbed a hand through his short hair. "What if there is no time, Mac? What if, by the time we get to Morgan and get help, Gareth is already dead?"

"Do I even want to know what you're on about, Ross?" Warren asked, as he squinted down at a curved suture needle in his hand.

"No," Jake said.

Warren grunted and carefully poked the curved needle into the rent in Mac's side.

Mac looked up at Jake. "We cannot hope to save him on our own, Jake. I am half dead, you are inexperienced, and we are both exhausted. If we seek him out now, even if we could find him, we will both be killed and the boy will surely die. We need aid."

"No." Jake scrubbed his forehead with the heel of his hand. "That can't be the answer, Mac." He crouched down beside the older man, their faces close and their eyes locked. "I know you can find him. I promised him I wouldn't let those pricks take him, and I've already let him down." He felt his voice catch and took in a long, unsteady breath. He had never been much for keeping promises, mostly because he'd never made many, and knowing he'd broken this one, cracked his stony heart. "I can't sit and do nothing."

Mac studied Jake's face for several long moments while the boxer seethed and Warren worked on Mac's side. "You've come a long way in a few days, Jake." A smile crept onto Mac's creased face. "You are not the man you once were."

Jake stood upright, his anguish turning into a slow burning anger. "What the fuck does that mean?" he grumbled, but he already knew.

He had lived on his own a long time, giving a shit for no one but himself. He kept his head down and minded his own business, and did his best not to fuck with anyone, or let them fuck with him. But now, after meeting Emily and Gareth, he found he didn't want to stare at the ground anymore. He'd found something better than himself to think of. He found something worth standing up for; someone who needed him. The world looked different to him now. Even the way his skin felt had changed.

He rubbed his chin. Perhaps there was more to this second chance than quicker hands and joints that didn't hurt.

"No, Mac," he said. "I am not the same guy anymore. Go

ahead and say you told me so, or whatever the fuck, but I made that kid a promise and I'm damned well going to keep it. You go back to Morgan and do what you gotta do, but I'm gonna get Emily and her boy. The bell for the last round is ringing and I'm gonna come out of my fucking corner and answer it."

Warren snipped off the end of his thread with a small pair of scissors and inspected Mac's side. "This thing stopped bleeding," he said, squinting through his glasses. "And it's not deep enough to hit anything important. But you do so much as try and wipe your ass, it'll split open far enough to drive a Buick through. You need a doctor, pal." Warren ran a hand over his head and winced, as he touched the gash in his scalp. "Fuck, never mind you, I need a doctor."

Mac stood up and slowly pulled his torn, bloody denim shirt back over his shoulders and started to do up the snaps. "You mean to go, regardless of what I say to you, Jake?"

"Fucking right, I do."

Mac nodded. "Very well. I cannot let you go alone."

Jake couldn't help but grin.

"But let me at least call Morgan and tell him what we're about." He paused in the act of doing up his shirt, and Jake saw a small tremble in his hands. He cleared his throat and continued. "And let him know about Isabelle."

Jake looked over at the limp form across the room. He felt the corners of his mouth turn even further downward. "Whatever you say, Mac."

Warren's phone was another throwback to the 1950's, a large rotary device fixed to the wall beside the sink, and appeared to be one of the few things that hadn't been destroyed in the fight. Mac dialed a series of number and stood waiting. Jake could hear the phone ringing through the receiver, and then saw the grey-haired man frown. After the phone had rung more than twenty times Mac hung up the receiver.

"He's not answering," he said. "This should not be. Morgan should be waiting for us."

For the first time since Jake had known him, Mac sounded worried, and it scared the fuck out of him. "Okay, so what does that mean?" Fear made his voice climb a little higher than he'd intended.

"It means we're on our own, Jake." Worry made the creases on Mac's face even deeper. "There is no help coming, even if we were to go and look for it. There is no one left but us."

Surprisingly, this revelation didn't make Jake feel any worse. On his own was where he'd been his whole life, since his old man died when he was twenty. He'd never had help coming to him before, so he really shouldn't expect any now.

Warren stood, unsteadily, and picked up his shovel handle from where it lay on the floor. "I'm coming too," the portly man said.

"You think that's a good idea, Warren?" Jake asked, raising one eyebrow.

"Fuck no!" Warren said. "But those fuckers broke into my place, attacked my guests, and busted up all my furniture. What kind of guy would I be if I let that stand?"

Jake reached out one finger and gave Warren a poke. The chubby man staggered and sat heavily on the chair behind him.

Mac put a hand on Warren's shoulder. "Your courage out-does your strength today, friend."

"Yeah, Warren," Jake said. "You're going no place in an awfully big hurry."

Warren grunted, but didn't argue. "So, what do you want me to do?"

Mac looked over at Isabelle and his face took on a strained quality. "We must leave our fallen until we can come back for her." He looked at Warren, his face serious. "Watch over her. Don't leave her alone."

Warren nodded. He didn't look excited about the idea of staying with Isabelle's body, but he didn't protest either.

Mac looked at Jake, his eyes hard. "We must answer the bell."

Nodding, Jake stooped down at picked up Satan's drywall hammer from where he'd leaned it against the couch. "Do you have any idea of where we should go?"

Mac picked up his sword from where it rested against the chair he'd been sitting in. "I might have a feeling."

*   *   *   *   *

They got into the old Mercedes, once they made sure Warren was able to get to the phone to call the police if anyone should come back to the gym. Jake thought about calling the chubby man an ambulance, but medics would surely holler for the cops once they showed up at the gym and discovered Isabelle's body with stab wounds in it.

Jake didn't know how much use Mac was going to be. The man was torn up something awful and did not walk to the car with his usual quick, efficient stride. Instead, he shuffled, taking short careful steps, moving like a man his actual age. When Mac sat down in the car, he opened the glove box and pulled out a small whet stone and began running it up and down the blade of his sword with hands that were smooth and steady.

"Where do you think they are?" Jake sat down in the driver's seat.

"The black building, where you saw the two men who killed you talking with Kast."

Jake nodded, he'd been thinking much the same thing.

The stone rang along the blade. "You don't need the gift of sight to see that place, do you, Jake?"

The boxer shook his head. "What do we do when we get there?" This kind of thing, a two man rescue mission straight out of an old western movie, was so far beyond Jake's realm of experience that it might as well have been brain surgery. "I mean, they're not just gonna invite us in, give us Emily and Gareth, and apologize for the inconvenience, right?"

Snicking the stone along the edge of the sword, Mac did not look up. "Do you want the truth, or is it all right for me to lie to you?"

"Tell me the lie first."

Mac peered at the sword in the dim light from the street lamp outside the gym. "They will see us coming and shit in fear. We won't lay our eyes upon them because they'll flee before us, running like their asses are on fire, leaving the girl and her son unguarded. In an hour, we'll be feeding them cheeseburgers and laughing about this."

Jake huffed and ran a hand over his short hair. "Okay, and what about the truth?"

"The truth, Jake, is I don't think we will live to see this

through. I think we'll go to that building and find our deaths. Our lives will be sold dearly, no mistake, but they will be sold just the same. Without Morgan and Isabelle, without help, Emily and Gareth are lost to us. I don't believe we can get them back."

"Thanks for sugar coating it so well."

Mac shrugged and sharpened his sword. "You asked for the truth so you got it."

Jake looked out the window, staring at the dirt and random growth of the alley. He'd never before given a shit about anything in his life, and the first time he does, it's a death sentence. Why was he doing this? Why was he killing himself for two people he hardly knew?

He thought about it for only a moment and had his answer. He remembered the face of a small boy, looking up at him with trust in his eyes, and a promise made. Jake was not a man who gave his word lightly, in fact he never gave it at all. He hated being relied on by other people almost as much as he hated having to rely on them. But, his word being given, he found the idea of breaking it made him ill. The idea of walking away from Gareth and Emily broke his heart.

He did not have it in him to walk now. It could not be done.

He stuck the key in the ignition of the Mercedes, and the car started with a growl. "Fuck that, man," he said as he put the car in reverse and backed out of the alley. "Those fuckers won't be the end of me, and they won't be the end of that kid. They're the ones who ought to be afraid. They're gonna be a sorry bunch of pricks when I get there." Jake realised the sound of the whetstone had stopped. He looked over at Mac. "What?"

"Brave words, Jake." A grin bending his creases. "Do you mean them?"

"Fucking rights I do."

"Good. Let's see them through to truth."

Jake drove through the dark, still city. It was getting close to dawn, and a mist had formed in the streets and between the houses. Its ghostly hands swirled around the Mercedes, as they passed through the silent streets.

"What do you know about the Fates, Mac?"

The grey haired man put the stone in the cup-holder beside him and ran his hand along the blade of the sword. "Why do you ask such questions now, Jake?"

"'Cause you seem to be convinced we're about to be killed. If you're right, there won't be another opportunity to ask."

"Very well." Mac laid his sword against the seat, point down in the carpeting. "I don't know what I'll be able to tell you, but I'll answer as best I can. What do you want to know?"

Jake looked over the steering wheel, his shoulders hunched forward and his brow knitted together. What was it he wanted to know? Why was he looking at this so hard? He'd never been much for questions at any point in his life except, 'when is my next fight?' Why did he need these answers so badly now? He didn't know, but he hoped the right questions would lead to the right answers. "I know you said not to believe the Preacher—Will—, but he said some stuff that leaves me wondering."

Mac smiled. "I never said not to believe him. I said to be careful. He would not flat out lie to you, but much of what he says will be nonsense. What did he say that troubles you?"

"He said that 'not everything is as it should be', and something about the Fates not making their own choice when they chose me." He glanced over at the older man. "Am I supposed to be doing this?"

"I hate to sound cryptic, Jake, but only the Fates know for sure."

Jake let out long, frustrated breath. "What are these fucking Fates, man? Is there any way I can ask them what happened? Isabelle said they were a consciousness, but is there any way I can talk to them?"

"The Fates are hard to explain, Jake," Mac said and rubbed his creased face. "To tell you true, I don't even know why we call them 'The Fates'." His gaze fell to his feet, as he blew a breath out through his nose and turned in the passenger seat, wincing, to look at Jake.

"Our gifts, our second chances, come from somewhere," Mac said. "It's not a genetic accident, and it's not some random happenstance, of that much I'm sure. Where these gifts come from, I don't know that we can really explain, but we've been calling the source 'The Fates' for hundreds of years, as far back as the recorded history of the clans. Isabelle was right; they, or it, are a consciousness. They are some kind of higher power that touches our lives. What their goals or agendas are, I have no idea, but I can tell you they support us in our struggle. They give us our gifts, like my sight or your strength, to use in the battle against the dark. Do the Fates work the same for the dark clans? I don't know. But I have seen their influence in this war, and know them to exist."

"So I can't talk to them? Send 'em a letter? Call 'em collect? Nothing?"

"Nothing," Mac agreed. "You have more questions?"

Jake thought for a moment. "The thing with the kids."

"What of the children, Jake?"

"What were those freaks doing with that kid we rescued and the kid we… " a memory of the tiny, rotten body in the bath tub flashed into his mind, "… the kid we didn't get to? I know you said something about rituals that were old and shit, but really, man, what could they be doing murdering little kids?"

Crossing his arms, Mac looked at the road. "I have thought many times about that since our first battle together, Jake. I have even looked at Morgan's chronicles to see what purpose such a sacrifice might have held. Always, it was for power. Raw energy. The goal might have been different each time, but always the life they took was a source of fuel for the ritual they were undertaking, like coal for a steam engine. The life of a child is even more valuable because their innocence gives their life strength, a strength that hasn't yet been blunted and worn down by the course of their lives.

"Morgan believes the dark clans don't get their strengths as gifts from the Fates. He believes they use such rituals to bend the Fates into giving them their gifts, almost like they're stealing them. But usually rituals like that call for blood from the suppliant, or perhaps the life of an animal, but only very rarely the life of a human, or more specifically a child."

Jake drove on in silence for several moments, letting Mac's words bounce around in his head, as the glare from the street lamps shone through the windshield of the Mercedes. Then, something in his head clicked.

"Okay," he said, and glanced over at Mac. "You said they use those rituals to bend the Fates to get their strengths, right?"

"Or, at least that is one possibility, and a theory of

Morgan's."

"Well, is that right or isn't it?"

Mac shrugged. "It's certainly possible. It would explain how men who are focused on committing such evil could receive the same gifts that we use to stop them."

"Okay, so they're using these rituals to get the Fates to do what the dark clan wants them to do, right?"

Mac grunted, and nodded.

"And the life of a kid is extra powerful when doing this freaky voodoo shit, right?"

"Well, it's not voodoo, Jake, but the life of a child is more powerful, yes."

Jake hitched himself up in his seat, gripping the steering wheel with both hands. "So, if they killed enough kids, with all that power coming from them, what could these assholes accomplish?"

Mac's brow lowered as he studied Jake's face. "I'm not sure exactly what you mean, Jake, but if they sacrificed several children, there would be much power at their disposal, indeed."

"With so much power, how far could they bend the Fates?"

"I don't know, Jake," Mac said.

"Could they have made the Fates choose me over someone else? Could they have tricked the Fates into giving a second chance to a worn out prick like me, instead of someone who really deserved it?"

Mac said nothing and looked at his feet, rubbing at his creased face with calloused fingers.

"What if I was supposed to die in the parkade?" Jake continued. "What if I was meant to help Emily just once, and then be done, but the bad guys tricked the Fates into giving me another chance and made me her guardian, protector, whatever?

"Or, what if I wasn't meant to see her at all? What if she was supposed to take a different route, where someone else would see her and help her, but someone fucked with the Fates and steered her in front of me? What if this is all a scam, fueled by the lives of little kids, and I'm the punch line at the end of some cosmic joke?"

"If that were the case," Mac said slowly, "it would mean they took many children other than the ones we found." The older man looked out the passenger side window, staring into the misty night. "So many small lives that I didn't see…"

Jake beat the heel of his hand against the steering wheel. "What if they used some of their power to cloud your vision and keep you from seeing what you normally would? What if they picked me to get the second chance 'cause they knew I would fuck it up, just like I've fucked everything else up in my useless fucking life?"

"Do you believe that, Jake?" Mac turned from the window and looked at him. "Do you believe that you've fucked up this chance?"

"Look where they are now!" Jake shouted. "I did fuck it up cause Drake's got them. I didn't stay and protect them like I was supposed to. This is my fault." He looked away from Mac and back at the road. "They wanted a fuck up and they got one."

Mac shook his head. "No, Jake. I see no fault here. I see a man who has been thrown into a horrid circumstance and is going to do what he thinks is right. I see a man willing to give up his life to help two people who are nearly strangers to him."

Jake said nothing, instead he sat stewing over the steering wheel. Mac reached out and gripped his shoulder. Jake, reluctantly, looked over at the older man.

"Right now, it doesn't matter if the gift was intended for you or not. What matters is what you do with it now that it is yours."

"What if I don't do enough?"

Mac shrugged. "Only the Fates know, Jake."

They crested a small rise in the street, and the corner of the huge, black building came into view. Jake pulled over, switched off the lights of the Mercedes, and killed the engine.

"Well," Jake said, looking through the windshield of the car. "Here we are."

"Here we are, indeed."

Doubts clouded him as Jake thought about the conversation with Mac. What if Drake and his people really did use the lives of children to bend the Fates and gave Jake the gift instead of someone else that actually deserved it and would do something useful with it? If that was the case, and he was never meant to watch over Emily and Gareth, would barging into this building only lead to their deaths? Should he wait and see if he and Mac could get help, or would that be worse than what he was doing now? He wished he had more time, and wished he knew more about what was going on. As he sat there in the Mercedes, making silent wishes while Mac sat beside him, something his old man used to say flashed in his mind.

'Wish into one hand, and shit in the other. See which one fills up first.' Duncan Ross, ever the optimistic philosopher.

Truer words were never spoken, Jake thought.

"Okay," he said, reaching into the back of the seat to grab Satan's drywall hammer. "There is a door in the back, where I saw the two douche bags who stabbed me talking to Kast. I think we should start there."

"Very well, Jake."

The boxer opened his door and put one leg out. "After that, I don't have a fucking clue."

The two men climbed out of the Mercedes and moved to the sidewalk. Jake frowned at Mac, as the older man moved stiffly away from the car, his sword held down by his leg.

"Are you sure you can do this?" Jake asked.

"No," Mac said through gritted teeth. "Are you sure you can survive without me?"

"I'm not sure I can survive with you here."

"Good." Mac straightened. "Then quit your prattling and lead the way."

With another frown, Jake started towards the building, keeping to the edge of the sidewalk and out of the street lights as much as he could. It was still dark, and there wasn't anything moving on the street besides the two men. Even the ubiquitous street people were absent at such a grey hour.

As they reached the corner of the building, Jake slowed and then came to a stop beside a fence, separating a vacant lot being prepped for construction from the black building. The boxer looked behind him to see Mac, sweat beading on his creased face, shuffling up behind him.

"How you holding up?" Jake asked.

"I'm fine," Mac said, out of breath, wiping a hand across his forehead. "Which way now?"

Jake hefted his hammer and peered around the fence. There

was a narrow alley, just wide enough to drive a car down, directly on the other side of the fence. It appeared as though it led to the back of the building. He tilted his chin towards the alley.

"I think we can get to the back down here." Jake gave Mac another worried glance.

"I'm right behind you," the other man said.

Jake started down the alley, and then swore quietly as he looked up. A small black camera, mounted on the wall of the building, was pointed straight at them. "What do you figure the odds are they're watching us stumble around like fucking morons?"

"Better than average."

"That's what I thought." Jake hurried down the alley as fast as he thought Mac could manage.

As they reached the far corner of the building, Jake glanced up to see another camera, this one pointed away from them, down the alley towards the back door. Jake moved to stand directly beneath it, crouched slightly, then jumped and gave the camera a swat with Satan's drywall hammer. The camera shattered with a small pop of electricity.

"Why did you do that?" Mac asked, as he caught up.

"So they couldn't see us," Jake said, the answer so obvious to him he thought the other man was going faint from loss of blood.

"Do you not think, Jake, the people inside might notice a camera that's gone off, more so than a camera with two shapes moving through the dark?"

Jake closed his teeth with a click. "Fuck."

"Fuck, indeed," Mac said, leaning to peer around the corner. "I see no one. Is that the door you spoke of?"

Jake looked around Mac and nodded. "Yeah, that's the one."

Mac moved away from the corner and leaned back against the black stone of the building, as he wiped the sleeve of his shirt across his face. "All right, Jake," he said running a hand over his short, grey hair. "Once we get inside, we cannot slow. We must move without hesitation. We have to go forward and put down anything that comes against us. The girl and her boy, they will be wherever Drake is, and if I know Drake's kind— arrogant and powerful—he will be as high as he can manage.

That is where we go."

"Do you think they'll have a lot of people with them?" Jake asked. He didn't want to sound worried, but he did anyway.

"They will not be unguarded." Mac lifted his sword with a pained grimace.

Jake clenched his jaw and pulled in a deep, whistling breath through his nose, held it and let it out slowly. More than one hundred times he'd stepped in the ring in his career as a boxer, but none of those fights meant near as much as the one he was walking to now. This time, he wasn't fighting for a purse, or a title, or even beer money. He was fighting for the lives of people he'd only just met, but cared deeply for. The realization, that he cared more about Emily and Gareth than he did about himself, slapped him in the face. He didn't remember ever feeling like that, and it made his chest feel both icy and hot at the same time.

He shook his head and did his best to push the feeling away. He needed all his focus before he walked into whatever waited for him. Unlike a boxing ring, this fight didn't have any rules and there was no referee to save him when he got knocked on his ass. If he went down, he wasn't coming back up.

"Are you ready, Jake?" Mac asked, his creased face ashen in the shadows.

Jake pulled in another breath and nodded.

"Then lead and I will follow."

Without hesitation, Jake rolled around the corner of the black building and made for the door he'd seen Kast use. He had his hammer above his shoulder and tried to mimic the quick, little conservative steps he'd seen Mac use when they rescued the child from the shit hole house. When he reached the door, he glanced behind him to find Mac had kept up, but was sweating all the harder and growing paler by the minute. Jake reached out and tried to twist the big steel knob of the door, but it didn't budge.

Stepping in front of the door, Jake tried to wedge the tip of the hammer's spike between the door and its steel frame, and then put a little pressure on the haft to pry the door open. He glanced over at Mac and the older man shook his head.

"If they don't know we're here already, Jake, they expect our coming. Now is not the time to be silent."

Jake nodded, somewhat relieved. Subtlety was not his strong suit.

Lifting the hammer high above his head, he smashed it down on the steel knob with a crack that sounded like a gunshot in the silence of the alley. He then jammed the hammer's spike into the knobs hole and wrenched on the door with all his considerable strength. The door came open with a squeal of twisting metal.

Jake lunged through the open portal, hammer held ready. He found himself in a broad hallway, with branches going to each side and ahead of him. In the middle of the central hallway stood a portly man in a yellow jacket that said 'Security' on the breast.

The man, who must have been hurrying towards the door when he heard Jake breaking it open, skidded to a halt, his eyes and mouth wide. He fumbled at his belt, and Jake saw he was trying to pull free a hand-held radio

Before the guard got the radio free, Jake transferred the hammer to his left hand, took two long steps and punched the guard under the nose with his right. The guard's head snapped back and he tumbled backwards to the carpeted floor.

"Not exactly what I expected," Jake said as Mac moved into the hallway behind him.

"What do you mean, Jake?"

Jake checked the three hallways that branched from where he stood and saw no sign of any other security guards. "When you said Drake would be guarded, I figured it'd be those crazy homeless fuckers we dealt with before. Not some guy who's showered recently, wearing a bad shirt and a yellow jacket."

Mac leaned over the guard and felt his neck. "If Drake is operating from this building, he'll have to keep the appearance of legitimacy. He's likely running some kind of an actual business from here to cover up his dark work and won't want to call attention to himself. Having a reeking homeless man guarding your door would certainly draw a few eyes."

"Good point. Now what?"

Mac pointed above Jake's head. Jake turned and saw a blue sign with an arrow pointing down the main hallway and the word 'elevator'. "Up, Jake. We go up."

Mac started walking down the hallway. Jake bent over the limp guard and started searching his pockets. Mac turned and gave a creased frown. "What are you doing, Jake? We do not rob people. We're supposed to be the good guys, remember?"

"I'm not robbing him." Jake patted around the man's waist and found a ring of keys clipped to his belt. He tossed the keys into the air and snatched them back with a clink. "These might come in handy."

Mac nodded. "Well thought."

Together, the two men continued down the hallway, Jake one step ahead, hammer raised. Mac closely followed, his sword held up, but the point unsteady and wavering. The hallway was deserted, devoid of movement or sound, save the faint whir of the ventilation system. The lack of people, of opposition, began to make Jake nervous and edgy. The raw violence and frantic movement of a confrontation was easy, something Jake was used to, but this slow searching, the anticipation of the coming fight, made him twitch.

"Where is everyone? Shouldn't someone have come out of a closet, made a grand speech about how we're nothing but shit on the bottom of their boot, then tried to kill us?" Jake looked back at Mac.

"I certainly expected to be challenged more than this," Mac said, giving a small nod, his ashen face was stony. "This is not what I expected at all."

Jake looked at him, one hand raised in question. "So what does it mean?"

"It means either they're not here, or they don't care we've come."

"Which one is worse?"

"Both are equally troubling." Mac tried, without success, to hide a grimace.

They passed an intersecting hallway and checked both directions before continuing. Jake saw nothing down the hall except more harsh florescent lights and a closed doorway. He began to relax his grip on the hammer while his heart felt like it tumbled into his guts. If no one cared they were in the building, besides the now-unconscious security guard, then Emily and Gareth must have been taken elsewhere.

He suddenly had horrific visions of Gareth tied down and lying in the middle of a strange symbol on a dirty floor, while filthy vagrants stood over him, chanting, as the boy cried. Or, worse, used up and lying in a grimy bathtub.

A feeling of stark hopelessness gripped him, robbing him of his breath and his will, as the thought of Gareth's death embedded itself in his mind. He closed his eyes tight, shaking his head to rid himself of the images, but they were all the clearer in the darkness behind his eyelids. He'd been too slow, he'd not done enough, had not been strong enough, and a child now paid the price for Jake's inability.

"What if we're too late?" Jake asked, as he and Mac stalked down the hallway.

Mac's lips were pressed in a thin line, and he took in a deep, rattling breath. "You're defeating yourself before the battle is fought, Jake." The older man huffed as he walked, as though he were running down the hallway instead of moving at a slow walk.

"What's that supposed to mean?" Jake's voice sounded a little petulant, even to him.

"Not an hour gone you spoke of the fear your enemies should feel. Now, when we are close to those enemies your heart starts to give out and you've already decided we're beaten. Remember your anger and hold on to it. If we are too late, then we are too late, but we won't leave this building with our heads hung and our thumbs in our mouths. We will leave with blood on our hands and vengeance in our hearts. There have been many wrongs done here tonight and I am not a man to let them stand unanswered." Mac took in another ragged breath. "Neither are you."

Cold fear still lurked in Jake, but a hot bloom in the centre of his chest swept the chill aside. Mac was right, they may very well be too late, but Jake couldn't let himself believe it while there was still a chance to reach Gareth and Emily before they were killed, or worse. He owed it to them to at least try. If he reached the top of this tower and found they were gone, he would turn the city upside down until he found them.

If he was late arriving, he'd find the people who'd taken them and a heavy bill would be settled.

They reached the elevator. A single button stating 'car call' sat in a steel frame next to a set of broad double doors. Jake pushed the button.

Almost instantly an electronic, fake-sounding, bell rung and the doors slid open. The inside of the elevator was a stark contrast to the plain white walls and carpeted floor of the ground floor hallway. The back wall of the car glittered with a full-length gold mirror, the floor and sides stood contrast in black marble flecked with speckles of shining red, a highly polished brass pole ringed the walls at hip level.

The stylish elevator, with its dim lighting, looked like the dark maw of a hungry beast compared to the harsh brightness of the hallway. Jake felt like he was being consumed, as he stepped through the doors.

Bright steel buttons, numbered one through twenty-six, glowed with faint blue lights. A black panel set at eye level in the wall displayed a bright number '1'. At the bottom of the rows of numbers was a slightly larger button, surrounded by a blue ring, marked with a four pointed star. Jake looked at the button and thought if he were a rich douche bag, who kidnaped little kids, he'd probably have something near as ridiculous marking his location.

"You think this is the one?" he asked Mac, a hint of sarcasm in his voice.

"As I said before, if I know Drake's kind, he will be as high as he can get."

Jake nodded and pushed the button. Nothing happened. He pushed it several times, but the doors of the elevator remained open, and nothing on the black display changed. Beside the button was a raised plastic pad, with a small red light on it. Remembering the security guard's key ring, Jake pulled it out of his pocket and found a round fob, matching the charcoal colour of the plastic pad.

Jake pressed the fob to the pad. There was a digital beep and the light on the pad turned green. He looked over at Mac, who nodded once, and Jake pressed the button with the star on it. The blue ring around the button flashed brighter, the fake sounding bell chimed again, and the doors closed.

Mac glanced down at the keys in Jake's hand. "Well thought, indeed."

The elevator started moving upward, rapid but smooth, and the sequential numbers flashed by on the black display. Jake gripped his hammer and wrung the haft with sweat slicked hands, as his heart picked up momentum, climbing at the same rapid pace as the elevator.

"Be ready, Jake." Mac lifted his sword with a shaking hand. "Move out of the elevator and away from the door, as quickly as you can. If there is someone waiting for us at the top, we don't want to try and fight in this little box."

Jake nodded and pulled in a long, deep breath through his nose.

The elevator slowed, and then came to a stop. The black display showed the same four pointed star as the button Jake had pressed. The elevator chimed again, like the ring-side bell at the start of a fight. The door slid open and Jake stepped from his corner.

Hammer raised and jaw clenched, Jake lunged out of the elevator and to his right. Mac right behind him, moved quickly for a man so broken, stepping opposite Jake as he came out of the elevator.

They were in a broad hallway. Black marble tiles bordered a deep, plush red carpet, and expensive looking art hung on the dark walls.

Besides the two sweating men, and the paintings, the corridor was empty.

"What the fuck, man," Jake said, exasperated, as he lowered his hammer. "Isn't there anyone in this goddamned building?"

Mac didn't answer, but grimly studied the room.

"Isn't this one of those times you should be getting a 'feeling'?" Jake asked. The words came out harsher than he'd intended. The false starts and constant surges of adrenaline, along with the rank exhaustion in his bones made him agitated and cranky.

"It doesn't work like that, Jake," Mac ignored the bite in the boxer's comment. "But I don't need my gift to know where we should go next."

Jake looked over at Mac, whose eyes were focused down the

hallway. Jake followed the older man's gaze and saw a broad set of double doors, made of some kind of hard wood, with elaborate brass handles.

"Jesus Christ," Jake said. "I feel like we're in a James Bond movie. Isn't this where some guy comes out of a secret panel and throws his hat at us?"

"Be careful what you wish for." Mac moved forward cautiously.

Jake, his sarcasm forgotten, moved with him, raising the hammer once more, as he eyed the paintings suspiciously, waiting for a set of eyes to start moving to watched them.

When they reached the doors, Jake looked at the handles. There was no lock on the door, but the handles themselves would keep people away well enough, Jake thought as he looked down at them.

The top of the handles were shaped like naked, arching women, whose faces were filled with what might have looked like ecstasy. When Jake looked down at the bottom of the brass carvings and saw there were horned demons ripping at the legs of the women, he knew the artist didn't intend them to look happy.

He wondered what kind of hell he was stepping into, and what kind of misery Gareth and Emily might be enduring.

Mac tilted his chin at Jake, to get the boxer's attention, and then looked at the handles. Jake nodded and reached out to grip one of the carvings in his left hand. The images on the handles bit into his palm, and he felt distinctly filthy. Mac nodded to Jake, and the younger man yanked open the door and stepped through.

A strange sense of relief flooded Jake, as he was finally confronted with other people, but that relief turned to sick fear as he realised what he saw.

The room was huge and open, with high ceilings made of industrial-looking steel beams. The wall behind Jake was solid, but in front of him was a curving wall of floor to ceiling windows giving a dramatic view of the slowly waking city. Against the windows, to Jake's left, was a black leather couch, and on the couch were Emily and Gareth. They were not alone.

On the arm of the couch, next to Emily, sat Naeven. He had

one of his long-fingered hands wrapped in her silky hair and his pointed nose touched her face, as he nuzzled her in a deeply disturbing manner. He looked over at Jake, sneering, and the boxer wanted to grin, seeing the other man's chin swollen and bloody from where Jake had ripped off part of his beard.

At the other end of the couch sat Gareth, still in his pajamas, his small hands folded in his lap, as he shook with fear. Standing next to the boy, bare chested and huge, a monstrous hand set gently on his shoulder, was Kast.

The giant gave a dark grin, the tattoos on his bloody face bending. "Hello, clansman." He had a slanting bandage covering the right side of his face, but his remaining eye was bright and clear, and murderously glared at Jake.

"So this, finally, is Jake Ross, the man who adamantly refuses to go away."

Jake's eyes swung to his right, to see a man in a high backed office chair swivel away from the windows. The boxer thought, for just a moment, that the scene would be almost comical if the man had a long-haired Persian cat in his lap. He did not, however, and he stood up, tugging at the sleeves of his dark suit. Jake knew, instantly, that he must be looking at Ethan Drake. He remembered what Emily had said about him; he was the best looking man she'd ever seen, but he was deeply ugly.

Drake had the ageless quality you see in certain celebrities. His face was smooth and youthful, but somehow experienced. His dark eyes displayed in a friendly smile, but it had a falseness about it, like he was a used car salesman trying to sell you a junker that would kill you. Tall and athletic, with the perfectly proportioned body of a male model, Jake got the distinct impression he was very dangerous.

Even Jake had to admit he was remarkably handsome, but as Drake walked forward, the light shifted across his face and there was something awful in the shadowed planes.

"Kast said you would come," Drake said, slipping one hand into the pocket of his sharply pressed pants. "Something about the honour of warriors, or some such. He was so sure you would come, in fact, he insisted the way be left open for your arrival. I didn't believe him, but here you stand."

"Yeah, here I am," Jake said. "Now what?"

179

"Now what, he asks me, Kast." Drake shook his head. "You are the one who came to me, Mr. Ross. You tell me why you came."

Jake looked over at Mac. This was getting bizarre. He'd come looking for Emily and Gareth, and expected a fight, not a rousing game of twenty fucking questions. Drake watched him, his dark eyes still playing at a smile.

Jake pointed Satan's drywall hammer towards the couch. "I came for them."

"Ah, the truth of it," Drake said happily. He turned towards the windows, opening his arms towards the lights of the city. "A hero on a glorious quest to save his lady love and her son." Drake put his hands on his hips and pivoted his head from one end of the visible horizon to the other. "Well, they are not for the taking." He turned back towards them, and Jake took a step back despite himself. The darkness that lurked beneath Drake's face crawled a little closer to the surface, causing a ripple in his handsome facade, and it was terrifying.

Jake didn't know what to say. He looked from the smiling Drake to the trembling Emily and back again. He was in a stand-off in the middle of a wide open room, and he had no idea what to do about it.

Mac spared him the sick feeling of doing nothing. "They are not yours to take either, Ethan. Release them now and we can part ways amicably."

"Amicably?" Drake asked, turning his eyes to Mac. "Who says we want to be amicable? Kast, despite that outmoded notion of honour he carries around with him, has no intention on being amicable. In fact, I think his intention is to take both of Mr. Ross' eyes in payment for the one that was taken." Drake took a few sauntering steps towards Emily and Gareth. "Of course, if it were up to me, I'd let you have them. I don't have any interest in this silly little girl and her bastard son anyway."

Growing ever more puzzled, Jake had the distinct impression he was about to be tricked. "If you don't have any interest in them, why did you take them?"

Giving another bright smile with his even teeth, Drake turned dramatically towards Kast. "Why did we take them, Kast?"

"Because we gave our word we would," the giant rumbled,

his remaining eye fixed on Jake in a bloodshot glare.

"Right," Drake said, tapping the heel of his hand against his forehead in mock amazement. "That thing about our word again. Right you are, Kast." He turned back towards Jake, slipping his right hand back into his pocket and gesturing with his left. "We were, I guess you could say, sub-contracted to obtain the boy. We started off trying to keep it friendly, keep it low profile, under the radar, but the girl," he gestured towards Emily, "is almost as stubborn as you are, and refused to cooperate. I was sure the two idiots we sent to talk to her a week ago would be able to convince her to see things reasonably, but then you had to stick that crooked nose of yours into our business, and sour the mash, so to speak."

As he was explaining himself, Drake seemed almost giddy, and it made the hairs on the back of Jake's neck tingle.

"Since then, you've refused to go away, Mr. Ross." Drake's face darkened; the mask of cordiality slipping. "You've assaulted my employees, positively ruined Naeven's beard, and taken Kast's eye. Even after we shut up that insufferable bitch, Isabelle, you insist on coming back for more." Drake crossed his arms and stood with one foot pointed out. "I am quickly losing my enthusiasm for this business, and I am glad it will soon be over."

The mention of Isabelle made another hot spike of adrenaline shoot into Jake's chest. He knew that Mac, Emily, Gareth and he were all in great peril. A light touch was needed for dealing with the dramatic man in front of him. Unfortunately for them all, Jake never considered himself to be much for subtlety.

"Enough of your fucking bullshit," he said, dropping Satan's drywall hammer to hang next to his leg, and lowering his chin as though to protect it from a punch in the ring. "I've come to take Emily and her son home, so shut up and give them to me, or shut up and get busy swinging, cause the only one here who enjoys the sound of your fucking voice is you."

Drake smiled all the wider. "That's what I like about you, Mr. Ross, not a man to play at civility. No mincing of words. Not very gentlemanly, though, is he Kast?"

"Not at all," the giant agreed.

His already limited patience slipped even further, Jake's eyes shifted from Drake to Kast and back again, waiting to see what they would do. "So, what's it gonna be?"

Drake looked at his watch. "As amusing as this banter with you is, Mr. Ross, time passes quickly and I have much to do today. So, what will be, my angry friend, is a conclusion to this ridiculous business, and a ridding of the pains in my ass. Namely, you and that silly little bint over there. Naeven, show in our guest."

The half-bearded man stood and yanked on Emily's hair hard enough to make her cry out., then released her with a little shove. He walked to a door in the wall to Jake's left, sneering as he went, and opened it.

Morgan stepped into the room.

Jake felt his heart lift. Help had arrived. The odds had evened a little. He and Mac were no longer outnumbered. Jake wanted to cheer and gloat in the face of Drake's arrogant prattling.

The boxer's elation was short lived however, and he felt an icy stab of fear and fury as he looked over at Mac. The gray haired man was not smiling. He stared at Morgan, a frown bending his creased face.

The cold hand of realization slapped Jake squarely in the ear, as he watched Morgan step softly into the room, wearing his easy, friendly smile. They had not called Morgan. Mac hadn't been able to reach him. The red haired man had not come here at their summons, but had come on his own, and could not have known they would be here.

Mac raised his sword and took a step towards the clan leader. "Morgan?" So many questions asked with a single word.

Naeven pulled one of his long knives and moved to stand between Mac and Morgan.

Drake clapped his hands together and shook them. "Oh, how I love to see such strife among family," the dark man said happily. "It just rings of honesty."

"Morgan?" Mac asked again, his voice little more than a croak.

The clan leader raised his hands, placating. "It's all right, Mac, Jake. It's all right. I can explain everything." His voice was calm, reasonable and warm, and Jake felt himself wanting to listen.

"Oh, this should be delightful." Drake rocked back and forth on his toes like a child in line at a carnival.

"You were never meant to get involved in this, Mac," Morgan said. "And I'm sorry, but you have to let me explain."

"What are you doing here?" Fury and misery warred on Mac's face.

Morgan held out one hand towards Gareth. "I've come for my son."

CHAPTER THIRTEEN

s the words left Morgan's mouth, Jake looked over at the boy and could see the resemblance, something he'd never realised until he saw father and son together in the same room. The handsome, round features, the colour of his eyes, every feature gave evidence of Gareth's parentage.

Emily raised herself from the couch where she'd been lying, and looked over at Morgan. "Your son? What?" She sat up fully, brushed the silky hair away from her face and studied Morgan with tear reddened eyes. "What do you mean, your son?"

"He is mine, Emily," Morgan said, his voice smooth and soothing. "He is mine, just as you were mine for one night a little more than seven years ago. He is our son, and I have been waiting these years to come and claim him."

Recognition and wonder dawned on her pretty face, and she slowly stood. "I remember you, now. I met you at a movie theater and somehow you talked me into taking you home."

Morgan nodded and smiled gently.

The wonder shifted off her face, as her eyes went wide and furious. "What do you mean, you've been waiting to claim him? I was eighteen, you piece of shit. You knew I had a kid and

you've been waiting to claim him? You can't fucking have him!"
She stalked towards Morgan, her slender hands clenched into
trembling fists. Morgan's smile faltered a little in the face of her
fury.

When she was only a couple steps from the red haired man,
Naeven spun, his long coat billowing around him. His hand
snaked out, latched onto her silky hair, and pulled her backwards. She fell on her rear, giving a small yelp of shock and
pain, as she landed.

"Down, bitch," Naeven said as he slid back to his place
between Mac and Morgan.

"How can this be, Morgan?" Mac asked, disbelief thick in
his voice. "The Fates do not allow us children after we die."

A change came over Morgan, and Jake found it almost as
terrifying as the darkness that boiled beneath the surface of
Drake's skin. The smile left the clan leader's face and his eyes
grew hard, narrowing beneath his red brows. His posture
changed, his shoulders rounding forward and his knees flexing.

"The Fates?" Morgan asked, and snorted, his mouth quirked
with wry amusement. "I make my own fate, Mac. Too long have
I stood at the whim of those elusive powers. No more. Now,
they do as I tell them, and I do as I please."

"What are you talking about?" Mac took another step towards Morgan. The gray haired man's creased face was pinched,
as he glared at the clan leader. "What do you mean, the Fates do
as you tell them?"

"For one with such sight, Mac, you are blind." Morgan's
voice was venomous now, the friendly tones completely
vanished. "Look at your brutish friend here." He pointed at
Jake. "You really think such a low born, selfish, ignorant goon
would be chosen to be a guardian of my son? Of a child of such
magnificent power? No, they chose another, better suited to
guard the boy, but I turned Them to my will and, instead, they
chose a played out fighter with hardly a dollar to his name."

Mac stood open mouthed and staring. "The children," he
said, so softly Jake could barely hear it. "At the cost of the
children."

The vision of the child in the bath tub flooded into Jake's
sight, unbidden and violent. It shocked the boxer all the way

down to his toes, as he remembered the rotting, mutilated form that had once been a small life. He thought, also, of all the children that Morgan might have used that Mac had never known about. He wondered how many of the missing posters tacked up on telephone poles and wrinkled in the rain were because of him, and Morgan's plan.

The Preacher was right, the Fates had been bent, and it had been done by Morgan at the cost of innocent lives.

"Why me?" Jake asked, the memory of the broken child making his voice furious and gravelly. "Why did you pick me for this?"

"Because I knew you would fail." A small, not at all friendly smile grew at the corner of Morgan's mouth. "You made it much farther than I expected you would. But this is over, just the same."

"Isabelle," Mac said, his voice weak. "You killed Isabelle."

Morgan shook his head. "Actually, I think it was Naeven," the slender man nodded with a smirk, "who killed Isabelle. When she phoned me to tell me where my son was, it was an opportunity I could not ignore, and I passed the information along. I had hoped to keep this from her, and you, Mac, until it was done and the benefits of it reaped. But this idiot," he pointed at Jake, "couldn't let it alone, even after we told him the girl was unimportant."

"Benefits?" Mac shouted, his voice thunderous and echoing. "What damned benefits? You murdered children, Morgan. You conspired with our enemies and murdered children. How could there possibly be any benefit?"

Morgan crossed his arms and shook his head, his expression sad, disappointed. "I knew this would happen if you found out what I was doing before it was finished, which is why I kept it from you." He grinned. "If it makes you feel any better, it was difficult, Mac. That sight of yours is a problem all its own and screening you away was almost as much work as giving Ross a second chance."

Mac shook his head, his shoulders slumped forward, chin on his chest.

"It really is a shame, Mac," Morgan said. "A shame you won't be able to stand with me when this is finished. All the years of work and planning that have gone into this day. Do you have any idea how hard it is to bend the Fates? No, of course you don't. And you don't care, either. That's always been one of your limitations, Mac. Your view is so narrow. You can only see what is directly in front of you. You've never been able to see the grand design."

"What design?" Jake asked, Morgan's words frustrating him even more than the Preacher's rambling.

Morgan clucked his tongue and walked towards Gareth. The red haired man stopped at the arm of the couch, and smiled down at the top of a head that was just a shade lighter than his own. Gareth, his small hands clutched together in his lap, stared at the floor and trembled slightly.

"This child," Morgan said, laying his hand on Gareth's head, "is special beyond imagining. It took me years of searching to find a girl with the right qualities to ensure I'd be able to plant seed in her, to create this life." He ran his hand down Gareth's face to cup his chin and tilt his face upwards. "This child possesses a power this city has never seen, and I will use that power to lift our clan above all others and cleanse this city of its filth."

"There is no clan," Mac said, his voice low and dangerous, the desperate sorrow gone, replaced with a chord of iron. "You killed it."

Morgan glanced up and shrugged. "A tragic, but necessary loss. There will be other soldiers chosen. There always are. And when they come, our clan will be mighty. The blood of this child will give us such power that none will stand against us."

"Very well, Morgan," Drake said, looking at his watch again, apparently getting tired of Morgan's preaching. "You've had your say. Is our business done?"

Morgan reached down and scooped up Gareth. The boy was rigid with fear, but the red haired man cradled him as though he didn't intend to murder the child. "Almost. You'll see these two," he looked at Mac and Jake, "are taken care of?"

"We will. Anything else?"

Morgan shook his head. "That will do."

Drake gave an exaggerated roll of his eyes. "Finally. You really are an insufferable bastard, Morgan. Why do I keep dealing with you?"

"Because I am so persuasive."

Jake had been watching Emily, who had gotten back to her feet and was, in turn, glaring murderously at Morgan. But at Morgan's words the boxer's eyes snapped to the red haired man's face. He was persuasive, Jake thought. Too persuasive.

Then, Jake thought of the gifts he and the others had received; his strength and ability to heal, Mac's sight, Isabelle's speed. Morgan's gift was Charm, the power to persuade and seem reasonable even under the most infuriating circumstance. Even now, when Jake knew Morgan to be a liar and murderer, he still felt himself sympathizing with the man's reasoning and wanting to believe him. He understood, now, why Gareth possessed such a magnetic personality. With two parents so powerfully alluring to those around them, how could he not?

"What of the girl?" Drake asked Morgan, gesturing to Emily.

Morgan shrugged. "She is nothing, a vessel only. Do what you want with her."

"Ah, Naeven will be pleased. He's had his eye, and other parts of his body, turned towards her since this business began."

Morgan turned from the couch and carried Gareth towards the door he'd come through.

"Oh, Morgan," Drake called. The red haired man turned. "Your persuasiveness, and the large sum of money you gave me, are losing their appeal. If Kast's honour wouldn't be so bruised, I'd have killed you already. This is the last time we make a deal. If I were you, I'd not come before me again."

"The next time I come before you, Drake, it will be the end of you."

Drake grinned wide, the awful darkness boiling beneath his face. "So be it."

Morgan stepped through the open door and was gone.

Naeven stretched his arms out wide, a long dagger in each hand. "At last. I've had more than my fill of that yapping bastard. Now, we can get on with the more enjoyable points of this dismal evening." He eyed Emily lasciviously.

Kast stepped away from the couch and placed himself in the centre of the room, directly in front of Jake. The giant man smiled at him, as though they were friends, about to enjoy a good talk. Jake knew they would be communicating, but it wouldn't be with words.

He looked from Naeven, to Kast, to Drake, and back to Kast, thinking feverishly of what he should be doing. Neaven stood between him and the door, and Kast stood between him and Emily. Mac stood still, his head hanging, slim trails of tears on his creased face. Jake couldn't say he begrudged the older man his sorrow, his entire world had just been crumpled up and tossed in the shitter like a handful of toilet paper, but now was an extremely bad time to be having a breakdown.

Naeven spun again, one arm looping around Emily's neck, as he slid up behind her and pressed his face against hers. "You know what I'm gonna do to this bitch, Ross? Anything I want, that's what." He touched the tip of one dagger to her face, bringing forth a small bloom of blood. Then he turned and shoved her back towards the leather couch, spinning again to step past the weeping Mac while he pointed a dagger towards Jake. "After I kill you, I'm gonna fuck her six ways—"

The slender man's bragging was abruptly ended when Mac lashed out with his sword, quick as thought. The last three inches of the blade sliced smoothly through the side of Naeven's neck. Blood sprayed through the air. Naeven's face took on a look of profound surprise, as he dropped his two daggers and reached for his ruined throat. He fumbled for a moment, trying to stem the gushing blood, then his knees sagged and he pitched forward onto the marble floor.

"That man," Drake said, looking down emotionlessly at Naeven's body, "talked entirely too much."

"Morgan!" Mac hobbled towards the door the other had left through.

Kast moved to intercept him, but Drake held up a hand and the giant stopped. "Our contract with Morgan is done, Kast," Drake said. "His safety is his own concern."

Kast stopped and nodded, then turned his bloodshot eye towards Jake. "Our time has come at last, Clansman."

"Indeed it has," Drake said, looking again at his watch. "This little enterprise has long since started to bore me. I will leave you with Kast, Mr. Ross, to settle your accounts, and bid you farewell." Drake gave a little bow and, careful to keep Kast between Jake and himself, walked out the doors.

Several things occurred to Jake, all at once. First, he thought about going after Drake, but he'd be turning his back on Kast, and he didn't think he could take both of them. Then he thought about running like his ass was on fire, but that would leave Emily alone to fend for herself, with Kast for company. Quickly, he came to the conclusion his only option was to take Emily out of that building with him, or die trying.

He could only assume Kast would insist upon the latter.

The giant took several steps forward and rolled his shoulders forwards and back, then leaned his head side to side, producing loud cracks.

"This is the way the Fates intend things to be decided, Ross." A smile cracked through the dried blood on Kast's tattooed face. "Two warriors, men of honour no matter what banner they carry, meeting in single combat. The victor, the last man standing." Kast flexed his huge hands, the muscles on his bare arms and shoulders standing out in stark relief beneath the black patterns of his tattoos. "This is what men like us are for, Ross. It is not for us to plan and scheme, but to shed honest blood, to do the heavy work. Do you agree?"

Jake wanted to make a scathing, sarcastic retort to decry Kast's apparent insanity and obsession with notions of honour, but he found he couldn't. This was where he belonged, this was something he understood: meeting your opponent, in the ring or on the street, and finding out what you're made of. There was no planning here, no mysteries or plotting, there was only the man in front of you and his desire to put you down.

It was what he'd known since he was old enough to wear a pair of boxing gloves, and it was the only thing he was good at. He was about to find out just how good.

Jake dropped Satan's drywall hammer on the floor with a dull clang and peeled off his stained jacket.

As Kast had been talking, Emily had been edging away from the couch and towards the door Morgan had taken her son through. When Jake dropped his jacket on top of the hammer, she bolted, running for the exit.

Without looking at her, Kast lunged and grabbed the back of

her neck, and pulled her off her feet. Emily cried out in pain and kicked her legs while her long nails dug at Kast's fingers. The giant's eyes never left Jake's as he pulled the stripper towards him so his lips were close to her ear, heedless of her struggling.

"No, no, my love. You cannot go. You are the prize we strive for." He tenderly kissed the side of her face. "Worry not for the girl, Ross. When you are dead, I will give her an honoured place at my side and she will be treated like a queen." He gave her an effortless shove, and she sprawled onto the marble floor. "She might be taken like a brood mare, but she will be treated like a queen. You have my word."

"I've had enough of your fucking words." Jake raised his fists. "You people do way too much yapping. No more."

Kast laughed, a great bellowing bark. "Well said, Ross. Spoken as a true warrior. You are right. No more words." With a snarl Kast attacked.

Jake was forced to give ground, towards the doors they came in. Kast was incredibly fast for a man so big, and his heavy fists flew towards Jake with alarming speed. The boxer back-pedaled, his head weaving to avoid the punches and his hands trying to knock away the rest. One of Kast's chunky black boots lashed out against Jake's foot, and the boxer lost his balance, missing a step. As Jake tried to right himself Kast's right fist collided with his face and sent him sprawling.

A white flash burst in Jake's vision, as pain exploded in his face and neck. He flew across the room, crashed into the stone floor, and slid into the wall. He shook his head to clear the lights dancing in his vision and tried to get up. He didn't think he'd ever been hit so hard in his entire life, and he didn't know how he was still breathing, let alone conscious.

His attempts to get up became more urgent, as he heard Kast's heavy boots slap the marble floor. Jake looked up in time for Kast's huge hand to clamp under his chin and haul him to his feet. Kast lifted his other hand to pummel Jake's face. With a desperate surge, Jake wrenched from Kast's grip, twisting to his right, and the giant's hand crashed through the drywall where his head had been.

Jake threw a kick, with his own steel-toed boot, into the back of Kast's knee. The giant's knee buckled forward, only fractionally, but it kept him from turning, and Jake threw a hard right that crashed into the giant's jaw. Kast grunted, but did not even come close to going down. He backhanded Jake with an almost dismissive gesture. Lights exploded in the boxer's head again, as he staggered backwards, but managed to keep his feet.

Kast turned to face him, his massive hand rubbing at his jaw, then turned his head and spit. Jake heard a tooth clatter off the floor.

"You fight well, Ross. First my eye, now a tooth. Well done."

Jake wanted to make a witty reply, but his ears rang and he couldn't think of anything except the words 'ow' and 'fuck'.

Kast lunged forwards again, throwing heavy punches. Jake slid beneath the giant's whistling hands and pounded into Kast's body with a desperate speed that surprised Jake himself. The blows collided with Kast's ribs and solar-plexus, but the man was so hard Jake felt like he was hitting a dump-truck. The giant dropped his arms and grabbed Jake around the upper body, then latched one big hand under his chin and lifted the boxer from the ground. White spots appeared, again, in Jake's vision, as Kast's massive fingers started closing off his wind pipe.

Kast lifted Jake higher and shook him like he was made of paper. "Is this not a better way to die, Ross?" Kast's his breath foul on Jake's face. "No scheming or deals in the dark. Only the thrill of honourable combat. Now, you can be welcomed into the halls of the honoured dead as a soldier to your cause."

Jake felt the strength draining from his limbs, as he gripped Kast's wrist, trying to pull himself away. He looked over Kast's cannon-ball shoulder at Emily. She sat on the couch, her balled fists pressed to her mouth as she watched Jake die. He thought, as consciousness began to desert him, that he would miss her when he was dead.

"Do not be ashamed of defeat, Ross. There is honour in your effort."

Jake's eyes snapped open and focused again on Emily's tear-puffed face. If he let himself die, she would be alone, and he promised her son he wouldn't leave them. For once in his life, he needed to be a man of his word.

Jake looked down into Kast's bloody face. "Don't you ever

get tired of the sound of your own fucking voice?" he croaked, with what little air he had left, and rammed his finger into the gauze-packed space where the giant's eye used to be.

Kast roared in pain, throwing his head back and dropping Jake. The boxer sagged to his knees, sucking air through his battered throat. Kast clapped a hand to his ruined eye, and fresh blood splashed through his fingers and onto Jake's face.

Jake struggled to his feet. He pushed his way through the haze of pain and exhaustion threatening to make him pass out, and raised his hands again. Kast lashed out with his bloody fists, flailing blindly, as he sought Jake.

"Ross!" the giant bellowed. "Ross, I'm going to pull your head from your body and drink that bitch's blood from your empty skull. Do you hear me, Ross?"

"I hear you just fine, fuck face." Jake surged forward, reaching into the dregs of his strength, and lashed out with his fists. He threw punches on instinct and habit, rather than in conscious thought. Kast tried in vain to defend himself, but Jake's hands crashed through his defenses and smashed into Kast's bloody face.

Kast made a vain attempt at attack, throwing a sluggish punch at Jake's head. The boxer slipped inside Kast's arm and delivered a vicious upper-cut to the giant's chin. Kast's head flew back, flecks of blood flying into the air, and the huge man sagged to one knee, his fist planted on the floor.

Jake stood above him, looking down. Kast glared up at him with his remaining eye, then spit blood on Jake's work boots.

"Well fought, Ross." Kast wiped a tattooed hand across his mouth.

Panting heavily, Jake nodded. "Is it over, Kast? Are we done here?"

Kast laughed, softly, a gravelly chuckle that came from deep in his chest. Then he hawked and spat another gob of blood. "What do you think, Jake Ross? When do you think this will be over?"

Jake wanted to turn and walk away, to step through the ropes and go back to the dressing room, but he knew this was no a civilized ring, and there was no bell to end the round. Kast wasn't a prize fighter, he was a soldier, and he didn't expect a referee to come and save him, nor would he help raise his opponent's hand in victory.

Jake shook his head, and sighed. "We'll be done when one of us is dead."

Kast nodded, his face grim. "You speak truth, Jake Ross. When one of us is dead. Honour demands it."

With a roar Kast launched himself off the floor and towards Jake. The boxer was ready for it, knew it was coming, and lunged forward on his left foot, throwing his hard right hand. The punch, the same Jake had finished countless fights with, crashed into Kast's chin when he was halfway from the floor. The giant's head snapped back and his massive body followed. He tried to regain his footing, his arms flailing, but he stumbled backwards and crashed through the window behind him.

Kast did not scream, as he flew into the open air amid of shower of shattered glass. He twisted his huge body and glared at Jake, snarling his final defiance, then plummeted from sight.

Jake stood, his heart pounding and his breath hissing raggedly through his savaged throat. He slid one foot tentatively forward and peered past the floor and towards the ground below. Kast lay on the sidewalk, a dim and twisted shape marring the circle of light from a street lamp. Jake watched the shape for three breaths, waiting for it to get up and walk back towards the building, but it remained still, and the boxer breathed a sigh of relief.

He turned away from the window and walked towards the couch and Emily, stepping over the still form of Naeven as he went.

Emily's silken hair was disheveled and matted, sticking to her tear streaked face. She looked up at him as he came, then stood and threw her arms around his neck.

"I thought he was going to kill you," she said, her voice unsteady.

"Me, too," Jake said, letting her cling to him. "Come on," he said after several moments. "We have to get out of here. The cops might be slow, but they'll never miss a three-hundred pound man splattered on the sidewalk."

He pulled away, slowly, looking down into her face. "Do you have any idea where Morgan would take Gareth?"

She pulled back, her eyes bright and wide as they met Jake's, and shook her head. "I didn't remember him, Jake, until I saw him tonight." She rubbed a shaking hand over her face. "I spent all this time thinking that I just didn't know who Gareth's father was."

"It wasn't you," Jake said, doing his best to sound reassuring. "It was that smiling bastard."

"We have to get him back, Jake," Emily said. "We have to get Gareth."

"We will." Jake looked at the door both Morgan and Mac left from. He grabbed one of Emily's hands, pulling her behind him, as he started towards it, stopping to pick up Satan's drywall hammer and his coat. "Maybe Mac caught up to him. Maybe Mac's got Gareth."

The doorway emptied into a small lounge, vacant except for a bar in one corner, and three leather couches around a low table. At the opposite end of the room, next to another bank of windows, another door stood ajar.

They hurried through the room, and out the other door, into a dim hallway. Jake was looking up at a red exit sign when the toe of his boot struck something that clattered across the floor with a metallic clank. When he looked down to see what he had hit, he saw Mac's sword. Just beyond the sword, at the end of the hall, he saw a crumpled shape.

As he neared the shape, it gave a soft moan.

"Mac!" Jake knelt next to the moaning form. He pulled the older man into a sitting position and a hiss of pain escaped Mac's lips. Jake looked down and saw a knife, similar to the ones Isabelle had carried, buried to the hilt in Mac's right shoulder, right below the collar bone.

"Oh, by the ever-fucking Fates, that hurts," Mac said, his eyes shut tight with pain.

"Jesus Christ." Jake looked down at the knife. "What should I do? Should I pull it out?"

Emily knelt on Mac's other side and put a hand out to stop Jake's reaching mitt. "No, you have to leave it. If it hit an artery, it'll start to bleed when you pull it out."

"You have to go after Morgan," Mac hissed. "I tried to stop him, but he took the boy." Mac opened his eyes and pointed towards the floor with his left hand. "I cut him, follow the blood."

Jake followed his hand and saw a narrow trail of blood leading away from Mac, the splattered drops standing dark on the white tile floor of the hallway. They led a short distance past the exit sign and stopped at what looked like a narrow service elevator.

"What about you?" Jake frantically glanced from Mac to the blood trail. "I can't just leave you here. Kast went out the window, so the cops are gonna come for sure?"

"Kast is dead?" Mac winced at the effort of speaking.

"He is."

"Then there is far more to you than anyone thought, Jake Ross. Whether Morgan interfered or not, the Fates chose well in you."

Jake shook his head. "Never mind that shit now, man. We've gotta get you out of here."

Mac nodded. "True enough. Help me stand and I will be able to walk."

Jake scooped his hands under Mac's armpits. "You ready?"

"As I am likely to get," Mac said.

Jake lifted him to his feet, wincing as the man let out a short cry. Emily ducked under Mac's uninjured arm and slipped one slender arm around his waist. She took the wounded man's weight with a purse of her lips, and nodded at Jake. His admiration growing, Jake nodded back.

Beside them, was an unassuming elevator, and Jake punched the button with a scarred finger, then stopped to pick up Mac's sword and Satan's drywall hammer. As he heard the elevator car whirring into place, Jake cocked the hammer over his shoulder and placed himself in front of the door. The whirring stopped, a pleasant chime sounded and the door slid open.

The floor of the small elevator was covered in a smeared coating of blood, small footprints visible on the white tile.

"Oh my God," Emily said, when she saw the blood and the footprints in it. "Is that Gareth's?"

Mac, still wincing, shook his head. "No. The blood is Morgan's, and your boy is fighting him. He is strong for a child so small."

Jake, even though Gareth was not his, felt a swell of pride knowing the boy was putting up a fight. He stepped into the elevator and looked on with some trepidation, as Mac and Emily shuffled in. Once they were inside, Jake looked to the panel of buttons and found one, marked 'P1', with a bloody thumb print on it.

"We had to get a break eventually," he said, as he pressed it. He gave Mac a worried look, as the elevator descended. Mac's face was even grayer than it was before, moving towards a shade of stark white. "Mac, are you gonna make it?"

"I've survived worse. I won't heal quite like you, but I'm still hard to kill."

Jake nodded, not satisfied, but somewhat reassured. "Where is Morgan taking Gareth?"

Mac pressed his bloodless lips together. "He will have to know you'll be coming for him, so he won't return to his house. Drake will be furious once he finds out Kast is dead and their clan's part in Morgan's schemes cost Drake his most powerful lieutenant. Morgan is alone and friendless, so he knows he cannot hide for long." Mac stopped, apparently thinking, glanced down at Emily, then back at Jake. "He will likely try to kill the boy and harvest his power."

Emily sucked in a sharp breath and clapped her free hand over her mouth. "No." Fresh tears sprang up in her eyes.

Struggling to tamp down his panic, Jake swallowed a thick lump newly formed in his throat. "Okay, where is he going to do this?"

"He will seek a place of power. Somewhere where the land is special, most likely near moving water."

"What?" Jake asked. "Why? Isn't that some kind of vampire shit?"

Mac shook his head. "No. Water is a source of life. People need it, live near it, travel on it, eat from its depths. You find the right place along a river and you can feel the energy. Morgan will seek a place near moving water."

"Great," Jake said, looking up at the display above the elevator doors. "The city is only built on a gigantic fucking river. This oughta be a piece of cake."

"I don't know what else to say, Jake. But you must find

them quickly to save the boy."

The elevator shuddered to a stop, dragging a fresh moan from Mac, and the door chimed open. The blood trail continued out the doors and along the pebbled surface of the floor of the parking garage.

Jake stepped out and looked around. There were very few cars in the stalls, and the blood trail led deeper into the garage, not towards the door, as Jake would have suspected. The blood trail was smeared and, sporadically, Jake could see a small, ragged footprint. Gareth still fought, Jake realised and smiled.

He opened his mouth to ask Mac a question, but left it hanging open as a thin, echoing sound reached his ears.

The scream of a child.

Shortly following the scream, Jake heard the high-pitched whine of an engine revving hard. Headlights appeared several aisles over from where they stood. The small import Jake had seen parked outside Morgan's house on their first meeting, screamed into view.

Jake dropped Mac's sword to the ground with a clang, and gripped Satan's drywall hammer in both hands. He charged forward, racing to intercept the car. Morgan must have seen him coming and increased his speed, the engine of the small car screeching ever higher.

Jake burst from between two support pillars, almost even with the speeding car, but still several paces away. He looked into the driver's side window and saw Morgan, smiling at him smugly, as he pinned Gareth to the passenger seat with one hand.

With desperate fury, Jake hurled the hammer. The smug expression on Morgan's face shifted to alarm, as he turned his head and tried to duck. The hammer smashed into the driver's side window, flying into the interior. The car swerved to the right, sending the front passenger side tire into a high curb surrounding a support pillar. The tire popped with a loud bang and Morgan had to work quickly, his hands spinning the steering wheel, to correct the car. He was able to bring the vehicle under control and rounded a corner to the right, heading for the exit ramp, pieces of the shredded tire flying behind him.

Jake thought about running after the car, but decided it

would be futile. He turned and ran back to Mac and Emily.

"Can you get him to Warren's?" Jake dug in the pocket of his jeans for the key to the Mercedez, then held it out.

"Yeah, I can get him there." She had tears in her eyes, but a determined look fixed on her face, as she took the key.

"If you give us the car, how will you follow Morgan?" Mac leaned heavily on Emily.

"Fuck," Jake said aloud, as he looked about. "I'll have to try and boost a car. You guys need to get out of… "

His words trailed off, as he looked to the right of the entrance, at a parking spot with the words 'security only' painted in red on the floor in front of it. He dug in his other pocket, and found the security guard's keys.

Jake held the keys up, pointed at the small, white Ford SUV parked in front of him, and hit the little unlocked symbol on the fob attached to the ring. He prayed silently as he did it, and almost screamed in joy as the headlights flashed.

Mac nodded his head. "Well thought, again, Jake."

"Take care of him," Jake said, touching Emily's face. A gesture of tenderness that surprised him; something he wasn't accustomed to giving or receiving. "I'm going after your boy."

Emily nodded. "We'll meet you when you have him." There was no doubt in her voice, and her belief gave the boxer strength. He nodded and turned for the security vehicle.

"Jake," Mac called, and the younger man stopped to face him. "You'll need this." Mac pulled his arm from Emily's shoulders, bent with a groan to pick up his sword, and held it out to Jake, hilt first.

He didn't have the foggiest notion how to use the bloody thing, but Jake took it anyway. "Thanks."

"Now, go," Mac said. "And bring my sword back to me when you're done with it."

Nodding, Jake turned and ran towards the Ford.

CHAPTER FOURTEEN

The engine of the small Ford started immediately with a faint growl. Jake grabbed the gear shift in the centre console, dropped it into drive, and pulled out of the parking spot. He raised a hand to Emily and Mac, as the girl supported the older man and guided him towards the exit and hopefully on to the waiting Mercedes.

Jake pulled the small SUV up the ramp of the parking lot and onto the same street he'd stood on when he first met the Preacher. He'd waited too long after Morgan drove out and the small import was long gone and lost to sight. Finding the Ford had been a stroke of luck, but it was spoiled and Jake pounded his fist on the steering wheel. "Fuck!"

Out of the corner of his right eye, he saw a black object on the road. He pulled off the ramp and into the street and stopped beside the thing he'd seen. He rolled down the driver's side window and peered down at it, realizing it was a piece of rubber; a part of Morgan's blown tire. Jake looked ahead of him and saw another piece of rubber and idled slowly towards it.

Like following a trail of bread crumbs, Jake looked for more pieces of rubber and followed them south along the street until he grew close to the major artery of 104th Avenue. There, the pieces of rubber stopped, but a gray mark on the pavement, like a fresh scar, appeared, and headed west, away from the city centre. The rim, Jake thought, as he looked at the mark, still peering out the window, the rim of Morgan's blow tire was marking the pavement.

Jake drove faster now, the long gray mark plain and clear in the headlights of the Ford. Straight west it led, through the residential areas, past schools and fire-halls. Jake followed the mark until he came to the crest of a huge hill that led down into the Flats. He could see the roadway clearly almost to the river, and slowed for a moment, checking for any signs of his quarry.

"Where are you taking that kid, you prick?" he asked the steering wheel, as he gripped it and peered over the hood of the Ford.

The red glow of brake lights, and a flash of something else, appeared at the bottom of the hill, almost out of sight. Jake looked closely, squinting hard, and saw the flash again. It looked like sparks, sparks from the rim of Morgan's wheel.

Jake grinned and pinned the accelerator of the small Ford. The engine screeched and the vehicle surged down the hill, rocking over a set of railway tracks. Jake kept the gas pedal pushed down as hard as he could, gaining enormous speed down the hill, more than once he creating sparks of his own, as the howling Ford bottomed out over the bigger humps in the roadway.

The farther Morgan drove on the damaged rim, the easier he was to follow. Twin scars now appeared, as the rim was worn down and both sides touched the asphalt. Through the Flats the trail led, past dilapidated houses and into the heavily industrial-ized area. There were other vehicles on the road, the early risers on their way to work. One, or several, of them must have seen Morgan's car, and a speeding import driving on a sparking rim would surely draw the attention of the police.

The trail turned south, following South Fraser Way, a road that ran parallel to the Fraser River. As Jake turned and followed it, Mac's prediction about Morgan finding a body of water replayed in the boxer's head. If the red-haired man wanted to be near a body of water, he wasn't going to do much better than this.

Jake rounded a curve in the road and the headlights of the Ford hit the rear of a vehicle, the licence plate flashing briefly in the light. Jake hammered his foot on the brake, skidding to a stop on the gravel shoulder of the road. Morgan's little import, the rim of the front tire bare and smoldering, was nosed down into the ditch next to a chain link fence. Grabbing Mac's sword, Jake threw himself from the driver's seat of the Ford and ran up to the import, yanking the driver's door open.

He growled in frustration. Empty.

The sky grew brighter in the east, but the light was still sparse and the day was likely going to be cloudy. The rim of the import still glowed a dull red from the friction with the road, and Jake knew he couldn't be far behind. He could see nothing from where he stood, and he turned about in frustration, growling through clenched teeth.

He jumped across the ditch and peered through the chain link fence. On the other side was an open field, the grass grown knee high, with nothing to hide behind and no sign of Morgan.

Jake reached out his left hand and gripped the links of the fence, then leaned his head on his arm. He'd been so close behind them, but now they were gone. Despair welled in him, and Jake slumped forward, pressing into the fence.

As he leaned, the fence gave way and he almost lost his balance. He looked up, annoyance tickling the edges of despair. Could he not even grieve without something being a pain in his ass? He examined the fence and saw it was split to his left. The cut was barely perceptible in the faint, gray light, and was unnoticeable until Jake leaned on the fence. He examined the cut more closely. It reached up to his sternum. Not very big, but big enough for a man to squeeze through. As he crouched to look at the fence, he saw the long, yellowed grass on the other side was freshly matted by footsteps.

There was something else; a dark stain on the grass.

Hope bloomed in his chest, the warmth of it sending fresh strength to his tired limbs. Scrabbling on his hands and knees, trying not to stab himself with Mac's sword, Jake squeezed through the narrow opening.

Crouched low, moving as quickly as he could, Jake studied the trampled grass and the drops of blood. They led straight west, towards the river, and Jake followed them.

The grassy field banked sharply downward, and Jake found himself sliding on his ass the last few feet to a paved roadway. He cursed again, loudly, as he looked around for any sign of the way Morgan had gone. Dirt from the embankment littered the surface of the narrow road. Jake found a set of booted foot-prints heading south, parallel to the river again. He took a chance and started running, hoping he'd be lucky and Morgan would stay on the narrow road and not deviate into the bushes on either side. The red haired man carried, or dragged, a child, and even Gareth's small, struggling weight would slow him down. Despite his fatigue, Jake thought he'd be able to make up some ground.

He hurried, sweating freely from both exertion and fear, and nearly sprinted down the roadway. The bushes on both side ended abruptly, and Jake found himself looking into a massive open space, the surface of it all paved. He was at the very edge of the Surrey river port, in one of the overflow areas for containers and cargo. Several hundred yards ahead of him, he could see the massive structure of the yard's crane, used to haul the big metal shipping containers off the barges as they came in. Also ahead and to his left were several open, apparently unused, warehouses. To his right was the slow moving mass of the Fraser River.

Nowhere could he see Morgan or Gareth.

Despair threatened to overwhelm him again. It choked off his reason and soured his will. He turned his head, searching frantically, but tears stung his eyes and blurred his vision.

Unable to bear the frustration, desperate, he clenched his fists and screamed, "Gareth!"

In a matter of heartbeats, he heard an answer. "Jake!"

The boxer's head snapped to the right, following the sound. It was faint, but he was sure he heard it, not just a trick of his exhausted mind.

He turned and sprinted, running on the asphalt, next to the wooded area that marked the edge of the docks. Soon, he reached the edge of the river.

The asphalt ended at a concrete abutment, and sat a dozen feet above the water. Jake turned his head side to side. To his right, the end of it obscured by bushes and overhanging trees, sat an old wooden pier, its mass a darker shape against the black water. The pier was so old there were weeds growing out of its surface, and it smelled of old tar and rotting wood.

"Gareth?" Jake yelled again when he saw no sign of movement. There was no reply this time, but the boxer saw a dark shape move against the lights of a warehouse across the river. The shape was near the end of the dock, and it froze when Jake yelled, but started moving again almost immediately. Jake threw himself onto the pier's surface, and pounded down its length, the old boards spongy beneath his work boots.

The surface of the pier was relatively narrow compared to the huge concrete docks used for modern ships, but after a hundred yards, opened up into a bigger square—an unloading area for goods or passengers.

Jake slowed, as he reached the end, and saw Morgan's dark shape hunched forward over Gareth's supine, wriggling form.

"Morgan!" Jake shouted in challenge. "Morgan, get away from that boy!"

The red-haired man casually stood up and turned toward Jake with his friendly grin fixed on his face. Jake stepped back in spite of himself. The grin was fixed and familiar, but the eyes above it were wide and shining in the dark. Jake could see insanity dancing behind them.

"You're too late, Jake." Morgan smiled. "It's too late to turn back now." The clan leader sidled away, a movement so subtle the boxer didn't know it was happening until it was done, and placed Gareth between himself and Jake.

Jake looked down at the child lying on the filthy surface of the pier. He was bound, hand and foot with thin cords, and there was a white rag tied around his mouth. Around him, drawn in chalk on the rotting timbers, was a thin circle in turn ringed with strange symbols Jake didn't recognise.

The sight of Gareth, bound and weeping, brought a wave of fury up from Jake's gut, and he stepped forward, raising Mac's sword and focusing his eyes on Morgan's forehead. The spot looked like it needed a little steel in it.

As Jake moved, so did the red haired man, another subtle movement, and placed his foot on Gareth's neck. The boy whimpered in fear and pain, and Jake stopped short, dropping into a boxer's crouch.

"It does not have to be like this, Jake," Morgan said. Jake didn't see him move, but suddenly a long, broad bladed dagger appeared in his hand, as though by magic. "We do not have to be enemies, you and I. When this is done, I will be powerful beyond reason, and you could share in that power. Together, you and I would wipe this city clean, scour away the grime and the filth and leave it a shining haven for the light."

The words were softly spoken, Morgan's face still calm, but Jake could hear a feverish, fanatic tone beneath them, and it made his scalp tingle.

"A haven for the light?" Jake asked. "You really are fucking crazy. How can you say anything is for the light when it's dipped in the blood of a child? What's the matter with you?"

"Nothing is the matter with me," Morgan said. "I'm better than I've ever been. After almost two hundred years of fighting this war, I've finally found the courage to do what needs to be done. We cannot hope to beat the dark unless we are willing to walk in it a little ourselves."

Jake shook his head. "Murdering a child is more than a little dark, Morgan. It's fucking black. Right down to the bone."

Morgan continued, as though Jake hadn't spoken. "Our enemies have no rules, Jake. They don't care about anything, and it gives them an advantage over us. They always prevail because they are willing to do anything to win, and we keep holding back, playing by rules no one ever said we have to use. My hands might get a little bloody in the process, but think of the good I can do once this is done."

"There is no good here," Jake said. "Not when it costs Gareth's life."

The reasonable mask on Morgan's face cracked, and he leaned forward. "What is one life in the course of a never-ending war?" he shouted, spit flying from is lips, the mist of it catching the light from the distant warehouse. He seemed to realise he'd slipped and straightened, running a hand through his hair. "It is a cost I am willing to bear when I consider the advantage it will bring to us, and the clan we will form, Jake."

"There is no fucking 'we' here."

"But there could be." Morgan's eyes brightened, his hand moving in a placating gesture, drawing Jake's gaze.

With an effort, Jake pulled his attention from Morgan's hand and focused it back on the bearded man's face.

"Our clan is decimated." Morgan's dulcet tones caressed Jake's mind. "But the weak, those without vision and understanding, have been left behind." His hand moved again, once again drawing Jake's attention. "It is a time for us to rebuild, Jake. You and I. With your strength and my vision we will build a clan that will make the forces of the dark shudder."

The weight of Morgan's words settled on Jake. The need to trust the man flowed over the boxer's fury like cool water. The clan leader's words seemed so reasonable. His judgment so sound. He was a man who could be trusted in a life where Jake had never trusted anyone, ever. Perhaps he, they, could change this city. Change it for the better.

Morgan, his movements subtle, stepped around Gareth. The constantly moving, placating hand lifted and settled on Jake's shoulder. He had never longed for the comfort of another   human, as much as he needed Morgan's. Jake glanced down and longed to rest his face on that steady hand.

"The age of the dark is over, Jake. You will stand at my right hand and be the force to pummel our enemies. You will be the face of the light."

Jake nodded his head in agreement, the sword in his hand drooped towards the ground, as Morgan's words resonated in his brain.

"As Champion of our clan," Morgan continued, his bearded face close to Jake's ear. The voice, even though Morgan stood close enough to embrace, felt like it came from a long way off. Like Jake stood at the mouth of a long tunnel and Morgan whispered from the other end.

"You will receive many rewards," Morgan's voice, honey coated and sibilant, echoed in Jake's mind. He closed his eyes and strained to hear. "Anything you want, you will have. The girl, Emily, she will be yours. You can have her."

Jake opened his eyes. Something about what Morgan said pricked at his brain. He wanted to push it away, to allow his mind to rest, but something scratched across his mind. He tried to speak, but nothing came. He licked his lips, reaching desperately in his head for the thing that itched at him.

Finally, with a great effort, he uttered a single word. "Emily?"

"Yes, I will give her to you for your service."

A vision of Emily's face drifted through the darkness, a memory of her looking at him, trust in her eyes. She trusted him. She trusted him to bring her boy back. He could not betray that trust. He felt as though he was at the bottom of a deep pool, but the weights that held him fell away and he drifted towards the surface.

"She is not yours to give," Jake said, barely a whisper, but the words resonated in his own ears with the ring of truth.

The smile on Morgan's face faltered. "But, Jake, if you would only listen to me, and see the truth in what I'm saying, you would realise I am a man of my word, and what you want can be yours."

The image of Emily's face firmed behind Jake's eyes, blocking out the seductive hum of Morgan's voice. The darkness that surrounded Jake faded, and the world came back into focus. He looked up, meeting Morgan's eyes, and felt hot fury crash through the last tendrils of Morgan's hold on him.

Filling his lungs with the cold air of the morning, he screamed in Morgan's face, "SHE IS NOT YOURS TO GIVE!"

Morgan's smile turned to a sudden snarl and the knife in his right hand streaked towards Jake's neck. The boxer shifted forward and snapped up his left arm to intercept Morgan's blow. Wrapping Morgan's arm with his, Jake yanked the red haired man close and rammed Mac's sword into his chest.

The snarl on Morgan's face turned to a worried frown. He looked at Jake, tilting his head to one side, and then tried to smile and speak. No sound came, but a sputtering, bloody cough. He sagged forward, his bearded face pressed against Jake's cheek.

"I," Morgan said, his voice choked and wheezing, "was only..." He tried to pull in a breath, "trying to do..." he coughed again, "what's right."

Jake pushed Morgan back far enough to look into his eyes.

"This is what's right."

With a grunt, Jake shoved Morgan away. The red haired man slid off the sword with a sickly popping sound, and tumbled into the river. Morgan's body bobbed once, then settled, face down, and turned lazily as the current caught it and carried it slowly from the pilings of the old dock.

For the space of several breaths, Jake watched Morgan's body float away, the tension draining from him, as the distance between them increased.

A whimpering behind him made Jake turn, and he crouched down beside the wriggling form of Gareth. He untied the gag around the boy's mouth, and then used it to wipe the majority of the blood off Mac's sword. Jake tossed the rag into the river and used the tip of the sword to slice through the cords binding Gareth's wrists and ankles. As soon as he was free, Gareth threw his arms around Jake's neck and clung there, shaking. Jake didn't bother trying to dislodge him, but patted him with his calloused hands, checking for blood or injuries.

Once satisfied the boy was whole, the boxer scooped his arm beneath Gareth's rump and stood. He took a moment to rub one scuffed boot back and forth, several times, across the symbols Morgan had chalked on the surface of the dock, then walked slowly towards the road.

CHAPTER FIFTEEN

fter stopping to retrieve Satan's drywall hammer from the interior of Morgan's small car, Jake drove the 'borrowed' security SUV calmly towards Tartan Boxing. He'd just killed a man, and the second less than an hour ago. He even had the bloody sword in the back seat of the stolen car he drove. He was relatively certain he didn't want any police attention.

As he drove, Jake examined Gareth, who had not said a word since he'd been freed.

"You okay, pal?" Jake asked.

Gareth nodded.

"All right," Jake said. "So, you wanna talk to me?"

"You kept your promise," Gareth said, his small face serious.

Jake's mind flashed back to the conversation with the boy in Warren's kitchen. Technically, he'd told Gareth he wouldn't let anyone take him, which had turned out to be untrue, but the boxer didn't feel it necessary to point out that fact.

"You sound surprised, little man," Jake said.

The boy had his hands folded in his lap, as he'd done on numerous occasions, and his lips were pressed into a thin line.

"A lot of people," Gareth said, speaking slowly and appearing to be considering his words carefully, "always tell you they're gonna do stuff, and then never do it. My mom's boyfriends do that all the time. They say they're gonna show me this, or take there, or whatever. But they're only saying it to make my mom happy right then, and don't really mean it. They say things like that so often you stop even trying to believe them." He looked up at Jake, his blue eyes narrow. "But you didn't do that. You did what you said you were gonna do." He turned his eyes forward again. "That's important, isn't it?"

Despite the misery and violence he'd seen in the last two days, and the horrid exhaustion weighing him down, Jake couldn't help but smile. The resilience Gareth had shown in the face of the horrors he'd experienced over the course of the night, and the insight he'd drawn from the things he'd seen, gave testament to how special the boy was. If a child could learn something from these trials, then, perhaps, Jake could, too.

Gareth looked up at him, waiting for an answer to his question.

"I never thought about it much before, Gareth, but yeah, doing what you say you're gonna do is important." Jake thought of Emily, the first person who had ever put their faith in him. "It lets people know they can trust you. That maybe you could be a good man."

"I wanna be a good man."

Jake smiled wide. "You will be, Gareth."

The boy nodded agreeably and sat quietly, as the reflections from several street lights danced their way across the hood of the security vehicle.

"Jake?" Gareth asked.

"Yeah, pal?"

"Are you my mom's boyfriend?"

Jake smiled again. "No, Gareth. I'm just her friend." He turned his head towards the boy. "I'm your friend, too."

Gareth nodded again. "Good. Friends are important."

"Yes," Jake agreed. "They are."

*　　　*　　　*　　　*　　　*

210

Jake parked the security SUV in slanting rays of orange morning sunlight several blocks away from Tartan boxing, behind an old warehouse, away from the street. He left the keys in the ignition in hopes that someone else would steal it, and drive it around for a while so it couldn't be traced back to him. He found a first aid kit in the back hatch with several rolled bandages and a bottle of hydrogen peroxide. Jake wet a roll of bandages with the peroxide, then rubbed down all the surfaces in the car he could think of that he'd touched, including the smear of Morgan's blood left of the back seat from the blade of Mac's sword. Once he was done wiping the car down, he found a storm drain, lifted the grate, and dropped the bandage in.

He would have to assume the police would come looking for him anyway, once they'd located Kast's body on the sidewalk of the street, and saw him and Mac on the building's security video. But that was no reason not to try and be careful.

Gareth was still barefoot and exhausted, so Jake carried him, the boy's face pressed into his sweaty, blood-stained neck. Light enough, Gareth was hardly a burden, but Jake quickly wished he'd hidden Mac's sword and Satan's drywall hammer somewhere, as they were cumbersome things to carry while trying to manage the boy and not cut a finger off at the same time.

Jake breathed a huge sigh of relief when he passed between two buildings and came in sight of Tartan boxing's back door and saw it was not surrounded by police cars.

The back door was still damaged and standing ajar. Jake nudged it with his foot and cautiously stepped through as it creaked open. He stood to the side of the door, Gareth sleeping on his shoulder, and let his eyes adjust to the dim light after the brightness of the early morning sun outside. Once he could see clearly, and was sure there was no one else waiting for him on the bottom floor of the gym, he walked to the stairs.

"Warren?" he called, wanting to be sure it was safe before he walked into the small apartment and trapped himself.

"We're here, Ross," came Warren's immediate reply. "You can come up."

Jake mounted the creaking stairs, the boy, exhausted beyond measure, still asleep with his small arms around the boxer's neck.

He was halfway up the stairs when Emily appeared at the top, fresh tears in her eyes. She gasped when she saw her dozing son, her hands covering her mouth. Jake dropped the sword and hammer at the top of the stairs and tried to hand Gareth to his mother, but Emily wrapped her arms around both Jake and her son, squeezing them fiercely. She stood on her tip-toes and kissed Jake's face, several times, crying all the harder while she did it.

"Oh, my God, Jake," she said between kisses. "Thank you. Thank you for getting him."

Jake cleared his throat and felt his face burn, as Emily kissed him. Even now he still felt embarrassed in the face of the young woman's gratitude. He stood still and wrapped one arm around her slender waist and hugged her in return, as she put one hand on the back of his neck and pressed her cheek against his.

Gareth stirred and lifted his head. "Mom," he said, smiling and rubbing his face.

"Hey, baby," Emily said, taking Gareth from Jake. "You okay?"

The child leaned back slightly, perched on his mother's hip and gave a small shrug as he yawned. "I'm okay. Jake came and got me."

Emily looked at the boxer, her smile wide and bright beneath exhaustion-bruised eyes. "He sure did, baby."

Looking at the boy in wonder, Jake shook his head. He didn't have much experience with children—before last night, none, in fact—but had it in mind most kids would be blubbering wrecks if they'd endured what Gareth had. Yet the boy, except for being obviously tired, was bright eyed and smiling at the sight of his mother. He'd even taken a measure of insight from his experiences, evidenced by his conversation with Jake on the way back from the river. If he could come through such a traumatic night with such ease, what could he do if he was safe and nurtured? The boy's potential was endless.

"How about you, Jake?" Emily asked, concern on her face. "Are you all right?"

Jake shook himself from his reverie. "Yeah, I'm all good."

She nodded. "So is Gareth, thanks to you. I owe you, Jake. Big time." She reached out and gripped his bloodied hand. He smiled and squeezed back.

Jake looked past Emily and into the small apartment. In their absence, it appeared Warren and straightened out the room as best he could, righting the furniture that wasn't broken and trying to restore some semblance of order to his home. The chubby man sat on one of his kitchen chairs beside Mac, who lay on the, now lopsided, couch. Warren had his curved needle is his hand, and there was a row of small, even stitches in Mac's shoulder where Morgan's knife had been.

"How is he?" Jake asked, as he gently pulled his hand from Emily's grip and stepped closer to the couch.

"I'm awake," Mac said. "You don't have to talk about me like I'm not here."

"He's a smart ass," Warren said, without looking up as he squinted through his glasses at Mac's wound. "But he'll live." Warren took a pair of scissors off the lid of the first aid kit next to him and snipped off the thread he had pulled. "That knife didn't hit anything vital, so it'll heal so long as it doesn't get infected. That, plus everything else that's busted on him." He turned and looked up at Jake. "Are you two assholes done yet? I'm running out of thread."

"I hope so," Jake said.

"Not quite," Mac said, struggling to sit up from his reclined position on the couch. "We have to take care of our fallen."

In the elation Jake found at bringing Gareth back to his mother, he'd forgotten about Isabelle, and the memory of the dead woman hit him like a blow to the head. "Right," he said, looking at the ground. "Where is she, Warren?"

The chubby man didn't speak for several seconds, instead busying himself tying a sling around Mac's neck to support his wounded arm, then putting items back in the first aid kit. Eventually, he looked at the closed door to the spare bedroom. "She's in there. I cleaned her up as best I could, but it wasn't much." He looked up at Jake again. "I didn't know her, Ross, but she deserved better than what I could give her."

"If you treated her with care," Mac said, pushing himself slowly off the couch with a grimace, "then it is all that she would have hoped for, and more." He looked at Jake. "She is of our clan. We will see to the rest."

"Now?" Jake asked.

"Now," Mac said.

"What about them?" Jake asked, tilting his head toward Emily and Gareth.

"They will be safe, I think. Kast is gone, and without his chief lieutenant, Drake will be slow to show his face. Besides, without Morgan's influence Drake has no interest in the boy. When he comes now, he'll be coming for you."

"Great," Jake said. "Just what I need. More new friends." He turned to Emily. "Will you be okay while we finish this?"

She nodded, and shifted Gareth higher on her hip. "We'll be fine, Jake. We'll stay here with Warren until you're done. I think we have a few things to talk about later." She smiled at the boxer and touched his arm.

"Warren?" Jake looked to the chubby man from the corner of his eye, as he returned Emily's smile.

"Are you sure there isn't anyone else who's going to come fuck up my house while you're gone?"

"Yeah, Warren, I'm sure."

"Okay, then. You do what you gotta do."

Jake walked slowly to the spare bedroom and pushed open the broken door. Isabelle lay on her back on one of the cots, orange sunlight punching through the curtains and painting a slash of colour across her chest. Her face remained in shadow, ghostly pale in the sparse light.

Warren had done a good job, Jake thought, as he walked to the edge of the narrow bed. Most of the blood had been washed from her face, her knives had been pulled from her body and placed in a pile next to her, and her blood stained clothes had been straightened as much as they could be.

"What do we do now, Mac?" Jake asked, his voice growing thick in his throat. The woman before him had not been kind or tender, and had not treated him with much compassion. But, in the end, she'd looked upon him with respect. They'd shared a moment that gave them a little comfort, removed them from the horror around them, and allowed them both to forget they were in the middle of an unremembered war, for a while. The last, Jake thought, is what was most important.

"We will take her to an honoured place," Mac said, his voice flat, all the emotion squeezed out, as though he were afraid it would cause him to break . "A place where I have laid comrades before."

Jake nodded and wrapped Isabelle in one of the white sheets on the bed, then hoisted her in his arms like a bloodied groom carrying his ghost bride. Mac gathered up Isabelle's knives and fell into step behind Jake. Together they walked down the stairs like a broken funeral procession.

Once outside, Jake carefully slid Isabelle into the trunk of the Mercedes, folding her into the fetal position to make her fit. It was then that he broke.

Exhaustion, regret, and heartbreaking sorrow flooded upon him all at once. The sight of Isabelle in the trunk of the car was the crack in the dam. He let out a choked sob and tears streamed down his face.

"Jesus-fucking-Christ, Mac, we can't do this to her. We can't stuff her in here like luggage."

The older man slid his un-bound arm around Jake's shoulders and squeezed. "This is the best we can do right now, Jake. She was a soldier. She would understand."

Nodding in mute agreement, Jake closed the trunk, very softly, afraid to slam it in case he'd disturbed her. He then fell into the driver's seat and started the car, as Mac climbed in beside him.

As they drove they spoke very little, only enough for Mac to point Jake in the right direction. They traveled south-east through the city, blinking into the sun and headed towards South Surrey. A couple of the landmarks were, familiar to Jake from the night Mac had brought him to meet Morgan, and the boxer slowed as he recognised the driveway to Morgan's house.

"No, Jake," Mac said, "not here. Keep going."

They carried on east, past several farms and acreages, then south, until Jake thought they must soon reach 0 Avenue and the US - Canada border, in an area where the properties were big enough you could not see your neighbour's house from your kitchen window. Mac pointed Jake onto a gravel road leading into a thick stand of trees.

The road they were on was barely more than two strips of tire-worn gravel winding through the trees. Fifty yards off the main road, they came to a gate, closed with a thick chain and a broad, brass padlock. Mac opened the glove box and produced a brass key, and held it out to Jake.

Taking the key, Jake got out of the car, unlocked the chain, dragged the gate open, then got back into the car and drove on.

The road continued, winding into the trees, slanting upwards slightly, for a little more than a kilometer, until it finally emptied into a narrow clearing. On Jake's left sat an ancient-looking log cabin, the door and windows gaping empty and the moss-covered roof sagging inwards. To his right sat a row of four large, white stones.

Jake brought the Mercedes to a stop in front of the cabin and put it into park. He leaned forward and examined the old structure with a frown. "Where are we?"

Mac opened the door and swung his legs out. "An honoured place, Jake. A place we come to remember." He heaved himself out, walked slowly towards the old cabin, and ducked through the open doorway. Jake still hadn't moved a few moments later when Mac returned with a long handled shovel in his good hand, then walked past the front of the car and towards the row of white stones.

Sighing wearily, Jake opened his door and got out.

Mac stopped beside the stones and jammed the shovel into the soft ground. Jake came up beside him and examined the stones, each of which reached roughly the height of his knee. They were unmarked, but the boxer had an idea what they were for.

"This land has been part of our clan for as long as I've been a member of it, and far longer if Morgan is to be believed." Mac paused and rubbed at his creased face with his one hand. Jake wanted to reach out to him, to try and provide some comfort. In the matter of hours, everything Mac believed about the world had come unraveled. Jake could feel the pain of it radiating off him.

Mac stopped rubbing his red eyes and looked back at the stones. "Each of these stones marks the resting place of one of our own, each a soldier fallen for our cause. We come here when one of us is lost, or when we need to remember our dead."

Having no idea what he should say, Jake stood and nodded,

looking down at the markers.

"I knew two of them," Mac said. "They were trusted friends, and one day I will tell you their stories, and that of the others who lie here. For now, we have to lay another friend to join them." He stepped to the left of the last stone and started dragging his heel through the carpet of leaves, marking a rough rectangle in the ground beneath. With the grave marked, Jake took the shovel and started to dig.

He worked without speaking for a time, the soft ground giving way easily, while Mac watched his work, stony and silent.

He was over a foot into the ground, when Jake stopped and looked up at Mac. "What are we going to do now?"

The older man didn't respond for several breaths, staring into the raw dirt near Jake's feet. Eventually, he turned his pale blue eyes to meet Jake's. "We will carry on, Jake."

A spike of bitterness stabbed at the boxer, and he rammed the shovel into the ground to lean on it. "Carry on doing what, exactly? Morgan fucked you, man. He lied to you, killed Isabelle, and tried killed his own son. He murdered little kids so that he could make the Fates do what he wanted, brought me into this life when it wasn't meant for me, and lied through his fucking teeth the whole time. How do you carry on after that?"

Mac didn't answer for a while, staring at Jake as the boxer stared back. Then, the older man blinked slowly and rubbed a grubby hand across his face. "How do we not, Jake?"

The boxer opened his mouth to ask if Mac had lost his fucking mind, but stopped when the other held up his hand.

"Morgan lost his way," Mac said. "He'd convinced himself what he was doing was right. Somehow, he justified acts of treachery and murder, all the while turning away from the light and walking deep into the dark. When I think of that, of how few there are of us left to do what's right, I cannot imagine doing anything else.

"The girl, Emily, and her son are special. I've barely been near them and I can see it without looking. I don't know what that means for them, or what they will do in the future, but I know they need to be protected. The boy needs to be nurtured, and sheltered, and taught to walk in the light, because if the likes of Drake and his ilk realise his value and get their hands on him and turn him to the dark, the world will suffer for it.

"Who is going to guide him if not us?"

"Look at me, man," Jake said. "Just take a look at me. I'm a fighter, not a teacher. I don't know how to look after a child. I promised that poor kid I wouldn't let anyone take him and ten seconds later Kast had him. And you heard Morgan. He bent the Fates to pick me because he thought I would fail. He knew I was a fuck up. What am I gonna do for that kid?"

Mac shook his head, as Jake spoke. "But you did not fail, Jake. You defeated Kast, one of the oldest and most powerful members of any dark clan. You stopped Morgan and resisted his power, which few men have ever done. And you brought the boy back safe. If you are not suited for the task, then no one is."

"But it wasn't supposed to be me," Jake protested. "I'm not the man for this."

"Perhaps Morgan was honest at the end, when he said he bent the Fates into choosing you for this second life. But, perhaps he himself was fooled and the Fates intended it to be you all along. It's a riddle we will never have the answer to. No matter if you were intended for this life or not, you did not fail. You've made great use of the gifts you were given, and I believe you will continue to do so."

"I don't know, Mac," Jake said, looking down at his bloody, fighter's hands. "I don't know if I can do it."

"I do, Jake. You and I are what's left of our clan, and it is up to us to rebuild it. We must guard the boy and his mother. We can do it, you and I, but we must finish this first."

Jake looked up and found the other man grinning, a slight twist to his creased face. He could not help but grin back.

Fighting through his exhaustion, letting the shovel work away his worry, Jake dug Isabelle's grave. When he was finished, he took her body from the trunk of the old Mercedes, and laid her gently in ground.

As he filled in the grave, weeping again, as he pushed the fragrant earth onto Isabelle's still form, Mac walked into the trees above the grave markers.

Jake worked slowly, carefully smoothing the dirt over the hasty grave, letting the sorrow he felt flow over him, embracing it. He never wanted to forget this moment, or the cost of Mac's war.

The older man returned several minutes later, levering a large white stone, moss-covered and jagged, down the hill with a broken branch. Jake reached out with his work boot and stopped the stone, as it rolled towards him.

"There is a spot up the hill," Mac explained, "where these stones sit in a dry creek bed. I thought this one would suit Isabelle."

Jake crouched down and rubbed at the moss with his hand, revealing a pale white stone, shot through with streaks of some kind of darker crystal. He didn't know Isabelle well, but from what he did know, he thought Mac was right.

Straining against its weight, Jake shifted the stone to the centre of the grave, so it was even with the other markers, and stepped back to stand beside Mac.

"Should we say something?" Jake asked.

Mac shook his grey head. "No words are needed, Jake. Isabelle knows we care for her, and this is not the last time we will visit her." He bent awkwardly, kissed his fingertips, and then touched the stone. He turned without another glance at the grave and walked towards the Mercedes. "Come, Jake. We have much to do."

Standing alone, Jake looked down at the grave he'd dug. He thought of the person in it, and what she meant. The last few days had taken Jake's narrow world, opened it wide, and then smashed it with a sledge hammer to leave the pieces lay where they would. As he looked down at the grave, Jake realised he'd never buried a friend before. In truth, he'd never really had a friend.

As he stood there, he knew his life was forever changed. He couldn't just go back to his mundane life, drifting between a shitty job and a failing fight career, once he'd seen what lurked just off the corner of your eye.

He glanced at Mac's back, as the other man shuffled towards the car. Jake had a choice now, as he saw it, to try and put his self-imposed blinders back on and go back to sitting on a fork lift. Or he could throw his lot in with Mac, see if he could take these gifts the Fates had given him, and try to do some good.

Tyner Gillies

He crouched down and put his hand on Isabelle's stone, and found it strangely warm in the cold morning. An image flashed into his mind: Emily and Gareth, honest friends who were trying to take nothing from him. Friends who only wanted to give him their warmth. He had to think on the image for only a moment, and then he turned and followed Mac to the car.

About the Author

Award Winning Author, Tyner Gillies, is a storyteller, lawman, Scotch drinker, and a bit of a meat head. He lives and works in the Fraser Valley, BC with his wife and a cat who is mostly a pain in the ass.

http://www.tynergillies.com

Manufactured by Amazon.ca
Bolton, ON

34342627R00127